PARADISE ROAD

CJ DUGGAN

Published in Australia and New Zealand in 2015
by Hachette Australia
(an imprint of Hachette Australia Pty Limited)
Level 17, 207 Kent Street, Sydney NSW 2000
www.hachette.com.au

10 9 8 7 6 5 4 3 2 1

Copyright © C.J. Duggan 2015

This book is copyright. Apart from any fair dealing for the purposes of private study, research, criticism or review permitted under the *Copyright Act 1968*, no part may be stored or reproduced by any process without prior written permission. Enquiries should be made to the publisher.

National Library of Australia
Cataloguing-in-Publication data:

Duggan, C. J.
Paradise road/C. J. Duggan.

ISBN 978 0 7336 3389 8 (pbk)

Teenagers – Australia – Fiction.
Man–woman relationships – Fiction.

A823.4

Cover design by XOU Creative
Cover photographs courtesy of Corbis
Author photograph by Craig Peihopa
Text design by Bookhouse, Sydney
Typeset in 11/14 pt Minion Pro by Bookhouse, Sydney

For my mum, for sharing her love of black and white movies and the beauty of the written word.

Prologue

'You're not going back to Paradise.'

I remember it all so clearly. The words tumbled out of my mum's mouth as if in slow motion. It was the equivalent of someone pulling the rug from underneath me. The violent, unexpected jolt of that one sentence had my head reeling with panicked thoughts: memories of sneaking out windows, driving in cars with hot surfer boys . . . of Ballantine's head between my thighs on his couch.

Oh, my God, had they found out about all this? I wondered. Had my grades slipped so badly that this was the drastic solution? I quickly blinked and laughed nervously.

'W– what?'

It had occurred to me that maybe my parents were just having a laugh. They did, on the odd occasion, try to be funny, but as I took in their serious stares I felt my world slipping away from me.

They were deadly serious.

The words that followed were nothing but white noise to me as I stood there gaping. From what I could gather, Uncle Peter had scored his dream job up north and was relocating his family from Paradise. They would rent out their home to another family, effectively leaving me homeless and unable to finish my Year Twelve at Paradise High. There was really no delicate, non-diva-like way to put it – I was devastated.

The weeks that followed weren't pretty; in fact, there is a significant amount of cringing I do merely thinking about it. The festive season came and went in a blur. Awake all night, asleep all day: in many ways I was your typical teenager. I lay in bed, curtains drawn, buried in a cocoon of despair – pretty standard stuff. I was like one of those tragic heroines from a Jane Austen novel, staring across the field, sobbing in the rain.

Ballantine, Ballantine.

It was rock bottom. And what was worse, I couldn't even call him to make it right. Trust me, I'd tried. I lasted all of two weeks in Red Hole before I dialled his digits, but there was no answer. And when I tried again a few days later it said his phone was unavailable. I'd obviously been dumped.

Welcome to Pity Town! Population: me.

I spent far too much time sitting in my darkened room wearing elastic-waisted tracksuit pants, a sloppy t-shirt, no makeup and my hair swept up on top of my head like a bird's nest. My desk was littered with fun-sized Snickers wrappers and countless packets of Starbursts. Any time there was a knock on my door, and a slither of light peeped through, I avoided the instinct to scurry into the furthest corner of my room and hiss at the intruder, which was usually my mum bringing in a tray of something not saturated in sugar for me to eat.

Dad just kept out of my way – like, literally. He would see me storming down the hall and do a complete about-face like a frightened villager escaping a natural disaster. There were days when it was his duty to make sure I was kept alive, so on one occasion he knocked on my door and opened it a crack. I quickly reduced the window on my computer and snapped my head around. My hooded eyes glowered at a tray sliding into my room, shifting its way across the floor with the aid of a broomstick handle.

A small smile curved the corner of my mouth at my dad's not-too-subtle joke. 'Very funny,' I called out.

The broom simply retreated and the door closed. It was at that point that I started toying with the idea of getting my shit together.

The next day there was a knock on my bedroom door. I didn't answer, hoping that whoever it was would take it as a signal to leave. But the door opened and the aroma of mouth-watering roast chicken with rosemary and garlicky goodness hit me hard. I recognised it for exactly what it was: Mum cooking my favourite meal as a bid to lure me out of my cave. My stomach rumbled. Someone switched on the light, causing me to flinch. I had been staring at the computer screen so intently and for so long I hadn't even realised that the sun had gone down. I was still mad, mad as hell, and I swivelled in my chair like a villain, arching my brow with an air of 'Yes, can I help you?'

'G'day, Smudge!'

Oh sweet Jesus.

My Uncle Eddie stood in the doorway dressed in his Sunday best (even though it wasn't Sunday). He wore a powder blue '70s-style safari suit, acquired, no doubt, from one of his op shop sprees. He nodded his head out to the hallway. 'Carn, Smudge, your mum says grub's up.'

I cringed at every mention of my childhood nickname, which Uncle Eddie had come up with after a messy Vegemite-sandwich-eating incident when I was about three years old.

I dragged my feet to the table, took a seat next to Dad's brother, and began to eat. Damn, it tasted good.

'So, Smudge, how did you like the big smoke?' Uncle Eddie finally broke the uncomfortable silence, speaking with his mouth full and a dribble of gravy running down his chin.

I grinned past the pain of watching him eat like a caveman. Flicking a knowing look to my parents, I straightened in my seat, cutting into my chicken. 'It was amazing: made lots of friends, learned *so* much in school, everyone was *really* nice.'

Uncle Eddie nodded. For all of my uncle's mortifying public displays, he was at least interested in what I had to say.

'So when does school start up?' he asked, wiping up the excess gravy off his plate with a piece of bread.

'As in, when am I going back?'

I could feel my parents' eyes boring into me, although I made a point of not looking at them.

I sighed, stabbing my piece of pumpkin. 'Apparently I'm not.'

'What? Not go back?' Uncle Eddie yelled, outraged. You had to hand it to Uncle Eddie. He knew how to create a scene. What a legend.

'I know, right?' I gave him my best look of despair.

Eddie turned to my dad. 'What's the go, Rick? You heard the girl, she loved it.'

'Stay out of it, Eddie,' Dad warned wearily.

'Pfft, I'm the head of the table, ol' mate, and I demand to know why my niece is on the verge of tears.'

Mum took this as a cue to start clearing the table, even though I wasn't finished. 'Blame my brother-in-law, Eddie,' she said. 'He's moving the family up north for a new job.'

Uncle Eddie looked lost in thought as he dug a toothpick between his teeth, foraging around for leftovers. Ew. His eyes darted from my dad to me and back again. He shrugged casually. 'What's that got to do with anything?'

Dad rolled his eyes. 'Lexie was supposed to be staying with Jen's sister.'

It took a moment for that to sink in. He looked resigned to the fact that my situation was impossible. 'Well, Jen, that was an absolute triumph, what's for dessert?'

Mum smiled, relieved the subject of conversation had changed. She brought over a piece of mango cheesecake to a very appreciative Uncle Eddie. 'Lexie, did you want some, luv?'

I moved to stand. 'No, thanks, I think I might just call it a night.'

I made it halfway across the room when Uncle Eddie's voice rang out. 'Hey, Smudge, how old are you?'

I paused in the doorway, turning to see him shovel a fork of creamy mush into his face.

'You're, like, nineteen?'

'Seventeen,' I corrected him. 'Well, eighteen on the eighteenth, actually.'

'This month?'

I shrugged. 'Yeah.'

My dad's head shifted from me to Uncle Eddie, uncertain where this was going.

'Well,' Uncle Eddie said, licking each of his fingers clean of cream, popping one at a time from his mouth with satisfaction, 'I don't want to state the obvious, but why do you need Jen's sister? Surely you're old enough to get your own place; I mean, you're of age, and from what I can tell, you take after your mother in the brains department, so what's the problem?' Uncle Eddie lifted his hands, palms up, as if it was an obvious no-brainer.

My eyes widened, looking at my uncle, who, most of the time, embarrassed the hell out of me and seriously grossed me out, but who, right now, left me in complete awe of his genius.

Of course. Why hadn't I thought of that?

Trying to contain my excitement, I glanced hopefully at Dad, who had closed his eyes, and then at Mum, who stood frozen in the kitchen wielding a spatula, as if battering Uncle Eddie to death was a real temptation.

'Well, no need to thank me. Great dinner, Jen, as always.' Uncle Eddie belched as he stood from the table. 'Best call it a night. Good luck with your new venture, kiddo,' he said, rubbing my head on the way past. He paused at the screen door, looking back and shaking his head. 'Oh, to be eighteen again.'

Silence loomed in the wake of Uncle Eddie's departure and genius suggestion: awkward, hear-a-pin-drop silence. It took everything in my power not to look happy or smug. I remained calm and cool and innocently shifted my gaze towards my dad, who, before I could even utter a word, shook his head and said, 'No! Absolutely not.'

And that's when the silence ended and all hell broke loose.

'What do you mean, no? You didn't even give me a chance to speak.'

'I know what you're thinking,' he scoffed.

'Oh, right, I forgot you have become really adept at reading my mind lately.'

'Lexie, don't go running wild with any ideas that Eddie has. They're not exactly based in reality most of the time,' added Mum, certain I would laugh, roll my eyes and agree. And, yes, under any other circumstance I would have, but not this time.

'On the contrary; I have never heard anything simpler, or more perfect.' I replied.

'Oh, right, and where are you going to stay, and how are you going to afford to live? I suppose that's where we come into this grand scheme of yours.'

'I don't know. I'll get a job, find a cheap place to stay. I can figure it out.'

My mind was reeling, and the excitement in me built. This could happen, this could really happen. On January eighteenth I would be an adult and I could do what I liked, and if that meant taking a bus and two trains back to Paradise, then so be it.

A small smile broke across my face, and it was the worst thing I could have possibly done. Dad got up from the table and stalked out of the room towards his man cave.

Mum came to stand next to me. There was no rage, only sadness. 'You really want this?'

Hope grew inside me. 'More than anything.'

Mum's lips pressed together in a thin line, as her eyes darted across my face, taking in the pleading depths of my eyes.

'Mum, please. I have to grow up some time.'

She glanced at the closed door of Dad's man cave, before looking back at me. 'I'll talk to him.'

My lungs filled with air. I was ready to explode in jubilant squeals.

'There will be rules.'

'Yes, yes,' I said, trying to control my excitement.

'You'll have to find a job.'

'Done.'

'A place to stay.'

'Absolutely.'

'And you will have to behave.'

I swallowed, smiling sweetly, trying my best not to flinch. 'Of course I will.'

Well, two out of three ain't bad.

Chapter One

My bag dropped to the floor, along with my jaw.

I stepped back out of the doorway, wondering if I had entered the wrong room. No, this was definitely the right room, although I would never have guessed it. Gone were the Blink 182 posters, gone was the dressing table crammed with nail polishes, Impulse cans and Lip Smackers. And instead there was a queen-size bed (the one bed – seriously, where was my bed?) with a *tasteful* cream-coloured cover and *tasteful* scatter cushions, and two new matching bedside tables with matching lamps. Where was I supposed to fit in with all this?

'What do you think?'

Aunty Karen's voice near my ear caused me to jump. How had I not heard her shoes, I thought, glancing down at her bare feet and polished ruby red manicured toes?

'It's different,' I said, my eyes roaming and settling on the big aluminium window with sliding glass, the very one that I used to sneak out of, the very one I had followed Ballantine out. A pang of nostalgia hit me, but then looking around at the unrecognisable space only cemented how things had changed; even in such a short space of time, life had gone from familiar to the unknown.

Aunty Karen walked in, swiping her hand across an invisible wrinkle on the bedspread before fluffing up the already perfect cushions.

'We thought we'd make the bedrooms more comfortable, more user-friendly, for the new tenants. They're Dutch, you know?' Aunty Karen looked at me as if their nationality should mean something to me.

'Oh, right.' I nodded, feigning interest.

I wonder what Amanda had to say about this.

'So am I not sleeping in here, or –'

'Oh, you girls will have to sleep together; we haven't painted Gus's room yet.'

Whaaaaat? Me and Amanda sleeping in the same bed? We could barely stand being in the same room as each other.

'It's just until you sort out your accommodation arrangements.' Aunty Karen smiled, patting my cheek as she left the room.

The way Aunty Karen had said 'until *you* sort out your accommodation' suddenly had me feeling very alone. Mum said Aunty Karen would help me find a job and a room, but I started to feel like I was in the way here, that I was just an additional complication they didn't need right now.

•

I was afraid to unpack. Even having my new mobile on charge in this crisp white room looked unseemly and out of place. There was nowhere to go and nothing to do without getting in the way or making a mess. Aunty Karen didn't say as much, but her thin smile said it all when I pulled out a stool at the kitchen island and placed my elbows on the marble top.

'Um, I think I might go for a walk,' I said.

'Good idea! Go stretch your legs,' Aunty Karen said with enthusiasm, as she scrubbed at an invisible mark on the countertop.

I slid off my chair, making sure to place it back in perfect alignment with the others, even though I was certain that Aunty Karen would wipe any evidence of me having sat there away with her cloth.

'Okay, back soon,' I said, making my way out of the kitchen, half expecting a 'Don't be long' or 'Be back before dark' but there was nothing except the distant sound of a Dustbuster whizzing to life as I closed the door behind me.

•

I walked into a darkened room; the loud animated beeps and pangs rang out from the television screen, followed by a smattering of gunfire as James Bond successfully warded off a series of would-be assassins.

My eyes shifted from the screen to a figure slumped in a beanbag, stubble lining his jaw, dark circles under his bloodshot eyes and empty bowls by his side of what looked like day-old Weeties.

I turned to Laura, raising my eyebrows in a question.

'Amanda and Boon broke up,' she whispered so low I almost missed her words. I blinked as what she said slowly registered in my mind.

Holy crap! Amanda and Boon were no longer?

I wanted to press her for more information but my rampant thoughts were cut off by Laura's voice.

'Boon, look who's here; Lexie's back!' Laura yelled over another burst of gunfire.

'Hey,' he managed, unblinking, eyes fixed firmly on the television.

He looked awful, soulless, like a heartbroken zombie. Just like I did when I returned to Red Hill.

This is what heartbreak looks like.

'Come on, I think you've seen enough,' sighed Laura, leading the way to her bedroom.

'Poor Boon,' I said. I understood what he was going through. If this is what he looked like I really didn't want to see Amanda.

'Oh, fuck Boon, he's being ridiculous.'

My head snapped around. I'd never heard Laura swear. Coming from the little pint-size slip of a creature, it didn't seem right. She opened the door to her bedroom, which was in stark contrast to the darkness we left in the lounge. Flooded by natural light, and painted a cheery light yellow, her bedroom had a really cool series of white floor-to-ceiling bookshelves her dad had built her. Her room really represented her: bright and sunny – well, except for right now.

'Ugh, he is driving me nuts,' she said, flinging herself onto her bed. 'It's just so, so –'

Awful, sad, heart wrenching . . .

'Pathetic,' she said, shaking her head.

I laughed, trying to lighten the mood a little. 'Oh, I don't know. I really feel for him, it must be hard.'

'Seriously, though, he needs to just get over it, it's just becoming tragic.'

I could feel the hair rise on the back of my neck at the mention of that word. It was how Amanda had once described me.

'He needs to just man up. I mean, look at you. Ballantine didn't even come and say goodbye and I don't see you moping about, you've got over it.'

Okay, now I was getting mad.

I wasn't over it. I took a deep, calming breath. With the mood Laura was in and her stance on the subject I really didn't feel like arguing the point with her.

I had come here for answers; Lord knows I had a million questions, even more so since hearing about Amanda and Boon. It felt like everything had changed. I took a steadying breath, preparing to launch into them, to ask about Ballantine, and Amanda and Boon, when her words interrupted my thoughts.

'So, have you found somewhere to stay?' she asked. 'I did ask Mum about you staying here.'

My eyes snapped up; I straightened in my chair. 'Oh?'

'Yeah, she said no,' she said matter-of-factly – typical blunt Laura. 'But she wondered if you'd tried any of the teachers? Sometimes they put up foreign exchange students. Principal Fitzgibbons and his family put up Fabrizio from Italy last year.'

I burst out laughing until I caught the confused look on Laura's face. 'Oh God, you were serious?'

'Beggars can't be choosers, Lexie. Dad said boarding anywhere in Paradise is really expensive and all the good places are taken.'

This was something that I had feared, but as far as shacking up with Mr Fitzgibbons, the balding, bowtie wearing principal of Paradise High and his family, was concerned, that was not going to happen. I would sooner go back to Red Hole and die from a broken heart.

Chapter Two

'Are you sure you don't want to come over tonight?' I dragged my feet down the hall.

'What, and spoon with you and Amanda? No, thanks,' laughed Laura.

'We could crash in the lounge or something.'

'Considering the circumstances,' Laura nodded her head towards Boon, who still hadn't moved from his beanbag, 'it's probably not a good idea.'

What? Oh, *now* she was thinking of her brother? Puh-lease.

I shrugged. 'Whatever; you're a terrible friend.'

Laura laughed. 'Piss off.'

'I don't approve of your language, Laura. You've changed.'

We made our way through the dim lounge room. 'Boon, Lexie's leaving now.' Laura yelled it out as though she was talking to a deaf, senile old lady.

Boon raised his hand in acknowledgment.

And then I remembered the day Mum had charged into my room when I was in the depths of despair, ripped the blankets off me and demanded I move, waking me out of my self-indulgent stupor. It didn't solve all my problems, but at least it had gotten me out of the house and doing something:

mani, pedi and shopping. I looked at Boon, thinking, okay, I wouldn't exactly recommend taking him to get a makeover, but I could surely try Mum's method.

Laura hovered in the doorway waiting to walk me out but instead of joining her I marched straight towards Boon, ripped the game controller from his hands and moved to turn the TV off.

'Hey, what the fuck?' he spat out.

'Up!' I said in my best motherly, take-no-shit voice.

'What?'

'Shut up! You are giving me a lift,' I said, as if it wasn't up for negotiation.

Boon blinked, his face full of thunder as if seeing me for the first time. He scoffed. 'I'm not taking you anywhere.'

'Yes, you are and you're even going to have a shower before you do, so hurry the fuck up,' I said loudly.

Okay, so Mum would never have said that to me in a million years. Still, this was a stubborn, heartbroken boy. I needed to be ruthless.

Boon sat there, glowering at me for so long I thought we were in a staring competition, and for pride's sake I really didn't want to lose. Just when I thought he wasn't going to budge and I would have to leave him wallowing in self-pity, he moved. The beanbag rustled and he slowly pulled himself to stand as elegantly as you possibly could out of a beanbag. He stood before me, intimidatingly close, his eyes burning into mine.

'Who are you? And what have you done with that mousey farm girl Lexie Atkinson?' he asked, his serious eyes ticking over my face as if I were a stranger.

A small smile kinked the corner of my mouth. 'You know what, Boon, you just gave me the compliment of my life.'

Boon's hardness melted, only a little, but I saw it. 'I think I liked the old Lexie better,' he mumbled, running his hands through his dishevelled hair and looking at the scattered rubbish around his beanbag as if seeing it for the first time. He shuffled out of the lounge to (I hoped) have a shower before giving me a lift back to Aunty Karen's.

'And have a shave,' I yelled out after him.

He scoffed. 'Don't push your bloody luck,' he said before slamming the bathroom door behind him.

I smiled.

Laura moved to stand beside me. 'What did you just do?' She looked at me in amazement. 'Seriously, how?'

'Sometimes people just need a bit of tough love,' I said.

'Oh, don't worry, I've been giving him plenty of tough love.'

'Sometimes, though, there is a difference between giving tough love and –'

'I know, I know, being compassionate.' Laura cut me off, rolling her eyes.

'Actually, I was going to say "being an arsehole".'

Laura did a double-take. 'Are you calling me an arsehole, Lexie?'

Without acknowledging the question, I just grinned. 'Tell Boon I'll be out by the car.'

•

Not wanting to rub salt into the wound I had Boon drop me off at the Black Cat Café, only a few blocks from the house. The last thing he needed was a potential run-in with Amanda.

I sat in a booth opposite him, wincing at the rate he was scoffing his triple-chocolate sundae.

'You're going to get a brain freeze at that rate,' I warned.

'Isn't this the point where you joke about me not having a brain?' He looked up with a cheeky chocolatey grin. It was a good thing to see a hint of the old Boon.

'Don't tempt me.' I laughed, sipping on my iced coffee.

We had driven there in silence, ordered and sat down with the awkwardness of a blind date. But all that had melted away the second the ice-cream arrived. There was something truly magical about ice-cream.

Much to Boon's credit he hadn't mentioned Amanda once, didn't ask me awkward questions even though he knew that I was living under the same roof as her and would be privy to inside information. I was glad he hadn't but then I desperately wanted to ask about Ballantine. Oh screw it, I thought, I couldn't keep tiptoeing around the subject. Better to go straight to the source: Ballantine's best friend?

I stirred the cream through my drink, psyching myself up. Had he mentioned me? Missed me? Partied hard without a care and bedded some random girl for the rebound? I felt sick. I pushed away my drink, ready to ask the question, the question I had been too afraid to ask Laura.

'Hey, Boon, can I ask you something?'

Boon scooped up the last of the chocolate syrup from his glass sundae boat. 'I guess,' he shrugged.

I cleared my throat, rubbing away the condensation from my glass. 'How's Ballantine?'

It was such a simple yet intense question for me; I wanted so desperately for the answer to be 'devastated, incomplete, a shell of a man since you left', but I was terrified the answer would very much be the opposite. So I quickly filled in the silence. 'Is he still working at the Wipe Out Bar?' Yes, that was smart, Lexie, find out when he's working next, that was the best bet.

Boon pushed aside his sundae bowl, snaring a serviette from the dispenser and wiping the excess chocolate off his face, all the while a line creasing his brow as though he was rolling my questions over in his mind.

'Laura didn't tell you?' he asked.

'Tell me what?'

Boon scrunched up his serviette and placed it in the dish, his eyes locking with mine in confusion. 'He left.'

'The Wipe Out Bar? When?'

Boon shook his head. 'He hasn't just left the Wipe Out Bar, Lex.'

'W– what?'

'He's gone . . . from Paradise.'

Chapter Three

'Gone?' I said, a little too loudly.

Boon looked uncomfortable now. 'Yeah, gone. He and Boppo and a few others upped boards and went to Bali.'

My shoulders melted in relief. 'Oh, he's gone on a holiday,' I said.

'Well, not exactly. Bali was the first stop; they've been called up for a potential sponsorship, but that bit's a secret – that's not to leave this table.'

'Really? Oh my God, Boon, that's amazing.'

Admittedly I knew jack about surfing but I knew enough to know that if you were good enough to get a sponsorship then you were kind of a big deal. I'd heard them talk about it often enough and the general consensus was Ballantine was definitely good enough, I just never knew he wanted it. Obviously there was a lot I didn't know.

'Yeah, I guess.' Boon shrugged, picking at a knot in the timber of the tabletop. It suddenly dawned on me that this was probably not great news for Boon at all.

'W– why didn't you go with them?' I knew I shouldn't have asked, I knew it the second Boon's expression darkened, as if almost pained by the words as he turned his head to stare out the window of the café.

'What, Laura didn't tell you that either?' he scoffed.

I sighed. 'Obviously there's a lot Laura didn't tell me.'

Boon's eyes flashed darkly, meeting mine with a flare of deep anger. 'I'm repeating Year Twelve,' he said.

I didn't know what to say. I simply stared at Boon, helpless and wordless, which probably just made things worse.

Broken up with Amanda, repeating Year Twelve and missing out on a surf tour was pretty much the trifecta of despair right there.

'Do you want to talk about . . .'

'No!' he said adamantly. I didn't need to be told twice.

I cleared my throat, trying to think of something to say, a change of subject perhaps, but try as I might my mind kept coming back to one selfish question at the forefront of my thoughts.

'So how long does the tour last for?'

A week, a month? Deep breath. I could wait; I mean, I wasn't going anywhere and it wouldn't be easy but I could wait, I had to see him, to explain, to set it right . . .

'A year, maybe more.'

'WHAT?!' I shouted, drawing the attention of the staff and other customers.

Boon grimaced, motioning for me to take it down a peg or two. 'Jesus, Lexie, people are looking at us.'

My mouth gaped, as the full-fledged feeling of disbelief slammed into me. 'A year?' I repeated, almost afraid to say the words because it seemed to make them real.

Ballantine knew I'd be coming back, he knew I had to finish Year Twelve, but he hadn't stuck around. And why *would* he when, to him, there was nothing to hold on to? In his mind I had lied about Dean, indicating there was more going on than I had admitted to. That stupid bloody incriminating note in all its innocence had looked really bad.

But the more I thought about it, the more angry I got. If he had just come and said goodbye, confronted me instead of being a coward, all this would have been so very different.

'Like you said, Lexie, it's an amazing opportunity, one that was too good to refuse.' Boon was trying to be reasonable.

But I was not in a reasonable mood, far from it. I simply nodded. 'Look, I'm going to go, thanks for the ride,' I said, shouldering my bag and sliding out of the booth. I'd almost made it out when Boon grabbed my arm.

'Forget him, Lexie, you're better off just moving on,' he said, his lips pressing together in a grim line.

'What choice has he given me but to move on?' I said to Boon before walking away.

•

It felt like my heart was breaking all over again, but I knew there was one place that would make me feel better.

I had forgotten about the searing heat of the sun in Paradise. I could feel it burning into my skin. I really wished I had changed out of my jeans first. This was a journey that saw me stepping over the wooden barrier at the end of the street, breaking the line from melting bitumen to grassy embankment down to sand, stepping awkwardly down the steep concrete steps crudely chiselled in the landscape. It was no easy feat to watch your steps and gaze out at the horizon at the same time. I took a moment to stop, to look out and admire the view before me. The ocean was choppy and murky, the wind was blowing my hair into my eyes, momentarily robbing me of the sight of the waves breaking on the sand.

The scene wasn't as peaceful and calming as I'd hoped it would be, but much like everything about today, nothing was as I'd expected. I walked down the last of the steps, pausing to take off my shoes and roll up my jeans before stepping onto the beach. I felt the soft sand under my feet as I walked to the water's edge, the cool powerful surge of the waves washing over my feet.

I inhaled a deep, salty breath, closing my eyes and lifting my face to the sky. I exhaled, long and slow. I had to fight against the wind and the power of the waves, which seemed as if they wanted to devour me. They weren't how I'd remembered them. Today they didn't seem friendly or inviting. I could definitely see a pattern here.

Maybe I was just being a Debbie Downer but I felt lost. I believed, naively as it'd turned out, that I'd return to Paradise and all my cares would melt away – I would track down Ballantine, explain the note, rekindle what once was, get a job and a place to stay before school started and, hello, amazing new life. It had all seemed so simple, but the reality was not working out the way I'd imagined.

What am I going to do? Where to start?

One thing was for sure, I was going to learn from my mistakes. I wasn't going to get myself into the same mess as before. I would start 'Operation get your shit together Lexie' first thing tomorrow. But first I had to shake this feeling of hopelessness, of thinking that what lay before me was impossible. I needed to wipe the slate clean, and just as the thought came to me I smiled, raking my hands through my hair and catching it at the nape of my neck.

Could I? Should I?

But before I could over-analyse like I tended to do, I started to slowly step into the water, going beyond the point of fear as the cold, frothy waves lapped at my shins, then my knees, thighs, waist until I dived in just before the next wave hit and before I had a chance to remember my fear of sharks. I broke through the surface, gasping in shock as I tried to scrabble and find purchase with my feet on the sand. My heart pounded in my chest. As soon as I got my bearings something unusual happened: I started to laugh, laugh like a lunatic as I revelled in the thrill of doing something that I would never have done before. The ocean terrified me and I wanted no part of it, and yet here I was, feeling the thrill of facing what scared me. The cold water cooled my skin and, as if by some cleansing miracle, washed away that hopeless feeling. All of a sudden I knew with utmost certainty that by stepping into something head on and facing my fears, I could do anything. I felt the water wash over me and my outlook was never clearer.

Tomorrow I would take the first step towards changing my life forever.

Chapter Four

Okay, so it had seemed like a good idea at the time.

I now stood on the nature strip in front of Aunty Karen's house with a pool of seawater dripping around me, looking and feeling like a giant drowned rat. I had to have a think about how I was going to do this, because going inside soaking wet was not an option. Even with Aunty Karen's car noticeably absent, I really didn't want to risk it. I wouldn't put it past Aunty Karen to employ infrared technology to track my dirty footprints. I padded my way up the path. Unlatching the side gate that led around to the back of the house, I just needed to get back to the pool area, to the garden hose, to wash off the sand that was everywhere.

After hosing all the sand away and shuddering at the cold feeling on my sun-kissed skin, I wrung my hair out and glanced through the window, making sure no-one was home. Before anything else could happen, I had to get these jeans off. With each squeaky, soppy step I had taken on the way home, one thing I was painfully aware of was how much tighter my jeans felt, and before my circulation was cut off permanently, I had to get them off me. Slowly and rather painfully, I edged them over my hips, awkwardly peeling off the soaking wet denim that had almost become an unwanted second skin.

Breathing a sigh of relief, I flipped them over the back of the sun lounge before throwing myself onto the cushions, flaking out in my knickers and t-shirt – so ladylike. I shielded my eyes against the blistering yellow disc in the sky – at least I would dry quickly.

After what had been the longest day ever, I closed my eyes, enjoying the sensation of the sun on my salty skin . . .

Until, inevitably, I was broken from my peaceful slumber. 'What are you doing?'

I jolted awake, squinting up, disorientated. The shadow that loomed over me with a look of disgust was Amanda.

'Why are you lying around in my backyard in your undies?'

I sat bolt upright, stretching the fabric of my t-shirt down in mortification.

Amanda simply shook her head. 'Jesus, Lexie, you're not in Red Hill anymore. Put your clothes on,' she said, moving to the back door.

•

After showering and making myself decent again, I wiped the steam away from the mirror, and paused in horror. 'Oh crap!'

What was reflected back at me was not a girl, but a rock lobster; gasping, I pulled my top aside to see the stark contrast of white against red. I was such an idiot. I could already feel a sun-smart lecture coming from my aunty and uncle: a great step in the right direction of being responsible.

I groaned, pulling the door to the bathroom open and walking down the hall to face the music – the music being the animated voices in the kitchen.

Pausing in the doorway, I took in the scene before me: Amanda leaning on the island bench snaring grapes from the fruit basket one after the other, barely drawing breath as she laughed and talked over her day with Aunty Karen, who was busy fussing over dinner. It occurred to me that Amanda didn't exactly seem heartbroken. This hardly looked like a girl who had just broken up with her boyfriend. When I had left Paradise I couldn't eat, couldn't function; I had locked myself away for weeks, and Amanda was looking like she didn't have a care in the world.

Amanda glanced over in my direction. 'Oh my God!'

Aunty Karen gasped. 'Oh, honey, you got a bit of sun today.'

You could say that again, my body was on fire! How long had I been dozing in the sun for?

'You look like a bit of toast – white underneath with jam on top,' laughed Amanda.

'Oh, hon. That's going to peel for sure,' winced Aunty Karen.

Great! Just what I needed. I had planned to return to Paradise looking like I had just stepped out of a salon, all windswept and gorgeous, not like a rock lobster with flaking skin. Not hot.

'Here, slather yourself in this.' Aunty Karen produced a pump action bottle of coconut moisturiser. 'This will cool you down and nourish your skin.'

'Thanks,' I said, squinting at the label before pumping a white blob into my palm. I wondered if I could bathe in the stuff.

'Hey, Mum, Lucy is coming over tonight. Can I get the stereo out of storage?'

My head snapped up. 'Lucy?' I said, a bit too loudly.

Surely she wasn't talking about Lucy Fell, arch nemesis, and super-mega bitch to all.

Amanda's eyes narrowed.

'Lucy Fell? The one you hate?' I reiterated.

Amanda shrugged. 'We hung out at schoolies. She's so funny. Now there's a girl who knows how to party.'

I could feel my blood boiling; oh, wait, maybe that was the sunburn? No, it was definitely rage. 'The same Lucy who deliberately spilt a drink all over me at the Wipe Out Bar?' I flicked my gaze to Aunty Karen, imploring her to remember exactly who this girl was, but she was too busy inwardly debating between French or Italian dressing for the salad.

I turned my gaze to Amanda. 'Lucy-fucking-fell-on-her-face?' I said quietly.

'Don't call her that,' yelled Amanda. 'You don't even know her.'

Ha! I didn't need to know her. Lucy Fell had been part of the trouble between Ballantine and me. I knew they had dated; I wasn't completely clear on the details but I really didn't want to know. And now, her and Amanda were BFFs?

'You really need to get over it,' sighed Amanda, who slid off her stool, grabbing a salad bowl and heading towards the dinner table 'She tripped. It was an honest mistake.'

I glared at her back, before turning to Aunty Karen. 'Really? Lucy Fell?'

'Oh, honey, maybe you could mend a bridge with Lucy. With Amanda being away maybe the two of you could hang out? It might be really good for you to have someone to do stuff with.'

Was she serious? Never in a million years would I ever be so desperate. Even if I had to bed down in a flea-ridden backpackers with no friends and no money, I would never be friends with Lucy, ever. Had aliens taken over the whole family?

I smiled thinly, rubbing the cool lotion into my heated skin. 'I'll be right, I have plenty of friends.'

Aunty Karen smiled at me sadly. 'Of course you do.'

She turned to the oven to inspect the contents, leaving me to my pump bottle and hateful thoughts.

•

You know the situation is pretty dire when Uncle Peter is the most enthusiastic over your return to Paradise. He raised his eyebrows in surprise to see me sitting at the kitchen table. 'I forgot you were coming back,' he said.

Gee, thanks.

'Your dinner's in the microwave,' called out Aunty Karen from Gus's room.

I watched as Uncle Peter walked over and pressed the microwave, flinging the door open to find a steamed piece of lemon pepper fish and salad. He looked confused, trying to fathom how he was going to microwave salad. He grabbed the plate and simply walked out of the kitchen. 'I'll be in my study,' he called out, and that was my grand reunion with Uncle Peter.

Aunty Karen was continuing her obsessive-compulsive efforts to make the house a show home, and Amanda was lounging on the couch watching TV like a zombie until the doorbell rang and she leapt up and stepped over the coffee table. 'I'll get it.'

In she walked like a nightmare, all blonde, perky and sun-kissed. Lucy was laughing about something and suddenly stopped when her eyes landed on me. Yes, I was burnt and shiny with lotion: I wanted to die.

'Oh, hey, Lexie, isn't it?' she asked, as if she wasn't quite sure if she remembered my name. Bitch.

I gave a small salute and a pained smile.

'So is *she* going away with you?' Lucy directed her words solely to Amanda.

'No,' Amanda scoffed.

Lucy's big saucer eyes flicked back to me. 'So what are you doing here?' she asked with interest.

'I'm finishing Year Twelve.'

'Where are you going to stay then?'

'I'm working it out.'

'What, so you have no place to go?' she asked, mock shocked.

'It's only my first day back.'

'Still, what if you can't find somewhere to stay?'

Each question only added to my anxiety.

'Don't worry, I will.'

'Oh, I'm not worried,' she laughed, 'but I sure would be if I were you.'

I scowled at her.

'You really should have worked it out months ago. My cousin rents and she says the rental prices in Paradise City are astronomical and all the share houses are snapped up in the peak season; you're not going to find anywhere on such short notice, like, no way.'

'Come on, let's go to my room,' Amanda said.

Lucy shrugged, giving me a smug smile. 'Good luck.'

I watched them leave, hating her more than ever, hating her for pointing out the painful obvious facts about my ill-planned return. I had a little over two weeks before my eighteenth, and that was all the time my parents were giving me to find a job and a place to stay before I got shipped straight back home with an express stamp on my forehead.

Peak season in Paradise City. What had I been thinking?

Chapter Five

I was on fire.

My breath shallow, rapid, my teeth indenting my bottom lip as soft, barely contained whimpers pierced through the dimly lit room. My hands grabbed at the sheets, hanging on for dear life as I rode the waves of crippling pleasure – a familiar, heart-pounding pleasure I had almost forgotten was possible.

Ballantine.

His clever mouth trailed a maddening path over my heated skin; attempting to soothe the burn with gentle kisses that only made me burn all the more.

Daring to unanchor myself, I let go of the sheets and gently touched Ballantine's cheek, my fingers moving to divide the folds of his thick, dark hair as he hovered over me, blocking out what little light there was. Looking into his beautiful face, a boyish grin curving the corner of his mouth, I smiled. I was home or was it heaven or Paradise? Whatever this place was called, I was there.

I cupped his face. I knew that one kiss would bring him back to me, bring it all back like he was never gone. His hot mouth crushed against mine, needy and hungry, his tongue delving to taste me, his hands sliding to feel me, all of me, lower, lower, lower.

More. I wanted more.

And he gave it to me. My head fell back, my eyes closed as my body lifted, begging for more and yet knowing it wouldn't be enough; would it ever be enough? I blinked away the insanity, focusing on the here and now as Ballantine's strong grip scooped around the back of my neck, and brought me closer.

No, this isn't a dream, I won't let it be.

I pushed him back so I could take control. I felt his hot skin burn against mine, the hardness pressing against my thigh as he ground against me, liking this sudden change – me over him now. He urged me on with whispered words of encouragement and deepened kisses that were bringing me to the edge of madness. I grabbed his hand, slowly guiding it to set his hot palm against my chest, wanting him to feel the erratic pounding of my heart. He held it there as I lovingly trailed my fingers from the back of his hand down his arm. I traced my nails over his tanned skin, over the light dusting of hair on his forearm, bleached by the sun. The tip of my finger followed the intricate swirl of ink curving all the way up along his bicep, up and up towards his shoulder. I blinked, confused, following the trail with my finger, sliding over the smooth, hot skin I couldn't bring myself to tear my eyes away from.

Ballantine doesn't have tattoos . . .

I froze, lifting my hand away quickly as if in response to an electric shock, but I was too slow. My wrist was snaked by an iron grip and my widened gaze flicked down to lock with a pair of green-brown eyes, unmistakeable green-brown eyes.

Dean.

My mind reeled; my rampant thoughts fought against the reality of straddling him, a dream that turned into a nightmare within the blink of an eye. My insides twisted and anger bubbled underneath my skin and yet I did nothing. Nothing when he smiled that infuriating smile, nothing when he oh so slowly sat up, nothing when his eyes, mere inches from mine, ticked over my face with great amusement. Nothing. It was like I had no voice, no will of my own, and then to add to this impossible moment of madness . . . he kissed me.

Dean fucking Saville kissed me.

And oh how he kissed.

Slow and deep. My spine, rigid a moment before, melted into his touch and what was the brink of a nightmare seemed to morph into something very different, something wrong, very wrong and yet so bloody good. I gasped as he playfully nipped at my earlobe, his hot tongue teasing the sensitive spot as he whispered, 'I knew you'd be back.'

And before I could answer . . . he kicked me.

Ooomph.

Wait. What?

'Ouch.' I stirred, feeling the pain near my shin pulse and then subside as I rubbed and blinked the sleep from my eyes. What the . . . ugh.

I peeled myself to sit upright, taking in the sleeping – make that drooling – form of my cousin Amanda next to me. Smacking her lips together and rubbing her nose with the back of her hand, she twisted around, scrunching the covers around her shoulders in a giant cocoon. I dodged her flailing limbs and glared down at her. Only when she made those deep, nasally breaths of sleep did I settle back down again, ripping my half of the blanket from her and clutching the covers to my chin. I was wide awake, a permanent frown etched on my brow as I inhaled deeply.

It was just a dream, Lexie, it was just a dream. A sexy, sexy dream.

I glanced sideways at my snoring cousin and cringed.
Awkward.

•

After a sleepless night enduring a kicking cousin, sexy yet disturbing nightmares, and the continuous burn of my skin, not to mention the worries of the world churning around and around in my head, I woke with a headache but also a steely determination to make things work. I slammed a stack of résumés on the kitchen table; they were the first things I'd printed off and packed. I had thought myself so smart and prepared but, yeah, it was now clear it was going to take a little more than that.

I scoured the local paper for rental properties, mainly in the rooms-to-let section, and my heart sank; even for a one-bedroom or house share, the prices were ridiculous. I bet my parents already knew this and wouldn't they be delighted? Everyone seemed to be rather in the know about the realities of the world except me. I'd had such tunnel vision in wanting to get back here to Ballantine I hadn't really thought about the logistics of it all. A shift or two at Macca's was not going to cover the rent, that was for sure.

I was seriously screwed. I thudded my head to the table. With my forehead pressed against the cool glass, a thought struck me. I straightened. 'Aunty Karen,' I called out, scooping my résumés together.

The clicking of her heels announced her arrival. 'What is it?'

'Can I please get dropped off down Arcadia Lane?'

'I suppose. Why?'

I grabbed for my satchel, wincing as I looped the strap over my head to sit on my sunburnt shoulder. 'Dad always said the best way to get your foot in the door is to pound the pavement. You never know who's going to quit a job from one day to the next,' I said excitedly.

'Oh, okay, then. Do you have any ideas what you might like to do?'

I shrugged. 'I have no idea, but if I have to work three jobs, I will.'

Aunty Karen smiled. 'Look at you, so determined. I wish Amanda would get herself a job, her life seems to be one giant party; needless to say, getting her out of Paradise might calm her down a bit.'

I paused. 'I haven't asked because I didn't want to bring it up, but how is Amanda going since, you know, her and Boon broke up?'

'Oh, she's fine,' Aunty Karen answered. 'Amanda broke up with him, she said she didn't want to be heavily committed to someone, which I think is a very grown-up decision to make.'

Amanda broke up with Boon? What the hell?

'Oh, good. I just thought, you know, that she would have been a little bit upset by it, I mean she really liked Boon.'

'Oh, you know Amanda, out with the old and in with the new.' Aunty Karen laughed it off.

I'd only been here twenty-four hours and I was already over these people!

Aunty Karen grabbed her keys. 'You ready?'

I straightened my spine, leading the way out the open door. 'Ready,' I said with a nod of finality. Let's do this. The sooner I could sleep in my own bed without Amanda and get away from snarky passive-aggressive Lucy, the better.

•

I placed my résumé on shop counter after shop counter, smiling and generally just being my usual charming self. Some staff seemed interested; others gave you the feeling that as soon as you were out of sight your résumé was going straight in the bin. I had started the day enthusiastically but by the time I was down to my very last résumés, I wasn't feeling so great. I hadn't been picky either. From surf shops to ice-cream parlours, alternative tie-dye hippy shops with nose-piercing accessories and collectable bongs to McDonald's and cafés: I really couldn't afford to be choosy. I'd clean toilets if I had to. My parents had said they'd provide some cash to help with my expenses, but I still needed a job to cover my rent.

I collapsed onto a bench in the shade, rubbing the damp skin at the base of my neck, fanning myself with my last five résumés. My eyes shifted lazily across the swarm of people walking along the arcade, spending up in tacky tourist merchandise shops and fending off kids who were begging to go into Timezone to pump all the last of their parents' change into video games. Even though all of these things were more familiar to me than the first time I'd arrived in Paradise, I still felt like an alien entity. I glanced along the boardwalk, where my eyes rested on an ever-familiar landmark.

The Wipe Out Bar.

It was a place I swore I would never step back into. Bad things happened there; well, to me, anyway. Owned and run by Ballantine's ogre-ish but hot older brother, it was a place I didn't need to be. But my traitorous heart started to pound against my chest with the very memory of the last time I was there with Ballantine, a time when we promised to be together. I had to push away the thought, thinking of Ballantine would do me no good, it seemed to lead to me envisioning him laughing and hooking up with some beach babe in Bali.

Ugh, I felt sick.

I squinted against the sun. Maybe I should pop in for a cold drink, I was dying of dehydration.

Before I could talk myself out of it, I got up, carefully weaving through the crowd, my heart drumming faster with every step I took closer to the imposing, double-storey building on the corner of Arcadia Lane. I came to a stop, loitering near the front. The place was looking as tacky and shabby as ever.

A girl with a sweet smile, holding a menu out front, turned to me. 'Will you be looking for some lunch then?' she asked with a strong Irish lilt to her voice.

Ha! Dean was no fool. Stick the exotic eye candy with the charming accent out front to lure the customers in. Exploitation, much?

'Ah, no, thanks, I might just go in and see the drinks menu.'

'Sure thing. The drinks menu is above and on the bar,' she added helpfully as if this was my first time.

I smiled. 'Thanks.' I walked in and thought, she really did have a lovely accent. It was by far the warmest welcome I had ever had at the Wipe Out Bar. Perhaps it would feel like a different place now?

But as I walked into the main bar I caught sight of the same inflatable shark 'Hank', wedged in the nets hanging from the ceiling in the bistro area. So, yep, nothing had changed. Although the usual bar wench, Sherry, was nowhere to be seen. Instead, a young peroxide-haired chick dressed in the customary black uniform was behind the bar looking all biker-mole attractive. Seriously, did Dean hire anyone ugly?

I slid onto a bar stool, grateful that the dull lighting would make me look less like a sundried tomato.

'You 'right?' nodded the bleached blonde.

'Just a Coke, thanks,' I said, digging into my satchel and finding my Roxy purse, casually glimpsing up at the second storey, wondering if Dean was lingering anywhere, maybe in his Bond villain chair looking over the monitors watching my every move. Nearly two months had passed, two whole months without a word, and still my thoughts immediately returned to the very place Ballantine and I had sat together, on that first night. We had gone from secret liaisons in the middle of the night, stolen thrilling moments by day, to nothing. Absolutely nothing. And I knew what people were thinking when they gave me their sympathetic looks: 'Maybe it was just a summer fling.'

But I knew it was more than that; I was the one who had spent those nights with Ballantine, I knew the time we had together was more than that, but as I sat at the Wipe Out Bar I started to feel overwhelmed. I had to get out of here, it was too soon. I took a last sip of my drink and left it on the bar barely touched, getting up to leave with Peroxide Girl's eyes flicking quizzically to my drink and then to me.

'Sorry, I have some place I have to be, thanks,' I stuttered, juggling my purse and papers as I exited the dim bar into the blinding brightness of the sun so quickly that I didn't see the person I slammed into – hard, really hard.

Reeling back, stammering apologies, I tried to gather my scattered papers from the floor. On my hands and knees, retrieving a piece of paper from beside a jean-clad leg, I stilled. 'Oh God.'

I slowly looked up, as it dawned on me whose leg this was. Lifting my eyes, the sun was blocked by the silhouette of a notorious Paradise figure.

Dean Saville peeled off his shades, a wolfish grin lining his face. 'Lexie Atkinson.'

Chapter Six

I stood slowly, straightening my spine and lifting my chin, trying to look calm and unflappable, desperately trying not to think about this morning's sexy dream he happened to make a cameo appearance in.

Dean was a good foot taller than me and a crooked little grin curved across his infuriatingly handsome face. 'When did you get back?' he asked.

'Yesterday.'

'And here you are, darkening my doorstep,' he said, all smug.

'I didn't come to see you,' I snapped, readjusting my bag.

Dean's green-brown eyes flicked from my face to my shoulders; I knew he was looking at my sunburn, judging me.

Time to go, I thought, before he said something that would just piss me off more. 'See ya,' I announced, pushing past him and storming away.

'Hey, you dropped something,' Dean called after me.

Oh crap.

There in Dean's hand was one of my résumés, and he was reading it with much interest. 'Excellent communication skills, with the ability to work as part of a team or unsuper–'

I snatched the paper from his hands.

'Looking for a job?'

'No, I mean, yes, but not here,' I said quickly.

Dean plunged his hands into his pockets. 'That's okay, I wouldn't hire you anyway.'

Wait, what?

'Why not?' I glowered. Against my better judgment I was offended.

'Looks like it's going to be a beautiful day, what's left of it,' he said, turning and walking towards the Wipe Out Bar.

'Why wouldn't you hire me?' I called after him.

'Might want to be careful, the sun's got a real bite in it,' he yelled without so much as a backwards glance as he disappeared inside.

Jerk.

•

The days melted into each other and instead of looking forward to my impending eighteenth, I was actually dreading it. With each day that passed with no success on the job or accommodation front, my mood darkened. Even with Aunty Karen and Uncle Peter chipping in to help me find a place, there was nothing. There wasn't even an opportunity to indulge in the 'roll up into a ball and hide away in the dark' kind of despair, as Aunty Karen was continually vacuuming under my feet, or wiping fingerprints off every glossy surface (and there were a lot of glossy surfaces).

After a week and a half of fruitless searching, I was sitting at the kitchen table glaring at the newspaper when Amanda walked in.

'What is your problem?' she asked, padding her way through the sliding glass door in her skimpy little shorts and bikini top.

I gave her my best deadpan expression, which was just my normal look these days. 'Do not ask me questions,' I said, thinking I much preferred it when she ignored me.

'Jesus, you're bloody scary these days, Lexie. You need to lighten up a bit,' Amanda laughed, snatching an apple from the fruit bowl. I swear to God she was becoming more and more like Lucy every day. All she needed was to dye her hair blonde and she would be her twin, but not necessarily the evil one.

'You need to turn that frown upside down,' Amanda singsonged.

'And how about you fuck off?' I muttered, turning the page of my *Paradise City Sun*.

Amanda almost choked on her mouthful of apple, giving me a wide-eyed watery look. 'Excuse me?'

I didn't tear my eyes from the classifieds. 'You heard me,' I said, with little enthusiasm.

Amanda scoffed. 'Lucy was right, you're a bloody psycho,' she said, padding her way out of the kitchen.

Maybe I had lost it? The Lexie of old would have been freaking out at the fact that after ten days of looking, and several unsuccessful interviews for shit-kicker positions, I was still jobless and soon-to-be homeless. That was until my parents arrived to whisk me back to Red Hill.

Even though I was failing in every aspect of my life there were some things I had to hold onto, my pride being one of them. I couldn't give up yet. I tugged the cap of my red marker off with my teeth and began to circle some possibilities.

Dog walker.
Babysitter.
Receptionist.

Everything I circled seemed to be a bit far-fetched, but desperation does funny things to one's mind. I knew this the second my pen hovered over the next ad.

    Bar Staff Needed – Phone Dean.

Blunt and matter-of-fact, like the man himself, I thought, shaking my head.

'No. Way,' I said to myself. Desperate, perhaps, but not that desperate . . . although I had to wonder as I sat back in my chair, biting my lip and frowning at the paper. Why did I circle the ad?

I glanced at the calendar on the wall. There was less than a week until my parents arrived, seven days to be precise. I sighed, looking from the calendar to the ad and back again.

Fuck my life.

Chapter Seven

I had been interviewed enough over the last ten days to know what to do and what not to do. The practice had given me more experience and confidence each time. And yet I could have had a hundred interviews, but none of them would have prepared me for this one.

Sure, I may have been a little misleading when I rang up and spoke to someone called Cassie. I assumed she was the peroxided bar girl. She'd wanted to organise a time for me to come in and meet with Dean, which was kind of obvious. I wasn't that big an idiot to think I could avoid that one, but for some reason when she asked me for my name I blurted out Alex instead. Oops.

Maybe I was providing a bit of a buffer to at least get my foot in the door. If Dean had seen the name Lexie there was no way he would make time to hear me out. He had already said he wouldn't hire me.

I dressed as I would for any interview: respectable, neat and smart with my black fitted pedal pushers and slim-fit black t-shirt. If nothing else it proved I had the black uniform nailed. I braided my long blonde hair in the style of *Lara Croft Tomb Raider*, ready for action to sling some drinks and gun down some enemies if needed. The braid fell over my shoulder, making the blonde stand out in stark contrast to the black. Mercifully my skin had gone from beetroot red to a deep golden brown. I'd moisturised it to within an inch of its life. Amanda complained it was like sleeping next to a giant coconut.

I sat at the bar, willing myself not to fidget, to not look nervous, knowing that this place had eyes everywhere. Cassie, the girl behind the bar, smiled at me. She seemed friendlier than Sherry had ever been. It had me wondering what had happened to Sherry. Was hers the position I was applying for?

My thoughts were interrupted by the ringing of the bar phone, shrill enough to be heard over the music blaring from the speakers. It made me jump out of my skin – guess I was more on edge than I realised.

'Wipe Out Bar, Cassie speaking.' Cassie's eyes shifted to me. 'Only one,' she said, giving me a knowing smirk. 'Well, I told you to make it bigger. All right, all right, I'll pass it on . . . See ya.' Cassie hung up the phone.

'Dean's running a bit late but he said that you could wait in his office; there's tea and coffee up there if you want some.'

I scoffed. 'How hospitable,' I said, glancing up the staircase. My eyes shifted to where Cassie was staring at me, a look of surprise on her face.

Oh shit, Lexie, tone down the sarcasm.

I smiled brightly. 'Thanks, that'll be great. Um, where do I go?'

'Follow me,' she said, stepping away from behind the bar. I acted innocently, as if this was my first time being led up those steps, as if what lay behind that door was a complete mystery to me. Cassie opened the door and gestured to me to head inside. 'Take a seat, tea and coffee's over there.'

She pointed to the corner near the sink, the same one I had washed my clothes in the night Lucy dumped a drink on me. Yep, I was pretty well acquainted with this room, it was the room in which Ballantine had come to see me, the night I'd reassured him that nothing was going on between Dean and me. I had seen the doubt etched on his face that night. I learned that they were more than work colleagues with bad blood. They were half-brothers and, even to this day, I couldn't believe it. They were just so different.

Ballantine was no angel, that was a certainty, but he was sweet. Dean, on the other hand, he was just a giant smart-arse who seemed to bring out the worst in everyone. Again, I had to ask myself: why was I here?

I moved into the office, looking out through the one-way glass, peering over the bar.

'He won't be long, Alex,' Cassie said before stepping out and closing the door behind her.

I almost looked behind me wondering who she was talking to, until I remembered that I was Alex.

Smiling to myself, I wondered if Dean would come walking up those steps thinking he was about to interview some bloke called Alex. Well, he was in for a bit of a shock, I thought as I walked around his desk, my hand skimming the glossed surface. I sat down in his huge chair, swivelling it from side to side before pushing myself back with a sigh, linking my hands behind my head and crossing my ankles on top of the desk like the boss man himself.

Okay, I thought, I was seriously tempting fate here. I took down my legs and moved from his chair. Glancing at the kettle, I couldn't think of anything worse than having a hot drink on a summer's day.

I sat in the chair on the other side of the desk, taking in my surrounds. A mounted Beatles picture, filing cabinet, lounge: everything was the same and yet something was different. I shifted around in my chair until I finally worked out what it was.

The long line of monitors, just under the one-way glass – they were all turned off. Maybe he turned them off when he wasn't here? Or maybe he turned them off when interviewing potential staff so as not to freak them out. Now that made sense. I couldn't help but think maybe I should have just waited for the call back from Video Ezy to give me an interview time. Working for them, rewinding videos and calling up people with overdues seemed a lot less complicated than working here. Although I was getting ahead of myself. I didn't have the job yet, nor was I likely to get it.

•

The waiting was intense.

Maybe this was a test, to make anyone who had walked in relaxed start to fidget and second-guess themselves. Plant them up in a box with no chance of escape. Smart, real smart.

Bloody hell, where the hell was he? I had been stuck in here for twenty minutes; there was running late and then there was bordering on being rude.

I started pacing, making my way towards the one-way glass, thinking that at least I would be able to see him when he was coming up the stairs, not that I was sure what kind of benefit that would provide. There was no way of preparing for this, I thought, none whatsoever.

Like a real Lara Croft badass I watched all the action of people coming and going below. I was just about calmed into a trance-like state when my phone rang, causing me to leap in surprise. 'Bloody phone,' I complained, walking across the room, unzipping my bag and delving into the abyss.

It didn't ring often but when it did it scared the crap out of me every time. I located it, taking a calming breath as MUM flashed up on the screen. I pressed the button. 'Hello?'

'Lexie, hello, can you hear me?'

The reception was terrible, with us yelling back and forth at each other like a scene out of *The Three Stooges*. I went to stand next to the sink where the reception seemed to clear.

'How's that? Can you hear me now?' I yelled, covering my other ear with my hand.

'Oh, that's better, I can hear you now.'

Awesome. Glad that had been established.

'Did I call at a bad time? I just wanted to wish you luck on your job interview,' she said.

It was something Mum did for each and every job I'd gone for over the past ten days. She'd rung to wish me luck even though she didn't really mean it. Much to her credit, though, I did think she legitimately felt bad after I received the 'better luck next time' rejection letters. My parents weren't completely heartless, they could sense the disappointment in my voice no matter how upbeat I tried to be.

'Now remember, just be yourself.'

I almost laughed.

Yeah, don't be Alex.

'If you don't get this one, well, there are plenty more fish in the sea,' Mum said with great optimism. The thing was, she was wrong. If I didn't land this job there really was nothing else. I wasn't here for career advancement or pleasure, this was me hitting rock bottom. Forget homelessness; no job meant no money and no means to find somewhere to stay in a week's time when Aunty Karen, Uncle Peter and Amanda handed over the keys to another family and I was on the street or, worse, buckled into the back seat of Mum and Dad's Pajero. I desperately needed this job.

'So the job you're interviewing for, are the people nice? That's just as important.'

I winced. 'Nice? No, this one's more an act of desperation. Believe me, this is not my first choice,' I said with a laugh, trying to keep it light and less depressing than the reality.

'Oh, Lexie, that's not funny.'

'Believe me, I'm not joking,' I scoffed, looking up to check my makeup, only to freeze. There, in the reflection of the mirror, stood Dean, casually leaning in the doorway, his eyes narrowed like a lion honing in on its prey.

'Mum, I– I've gotta go,' I said, pressing the end button before she had a chance to reply. It was then I felt how dry my mouth was, how my stomach twisted and my heart raced as I slowly turned.

Dean peeled his arms from their crossed position over his chest; he stepped into the room, slamming the door closed behind him so loud I blinked, jumping a little, watching on as he pressed his back against the door, taking his time to speak. 'Hello, Alex.'

Chapter Eight

I swallowed hard.

Had he overheard the conversation with my mum? Oh God. My foggy mind tried to retrace my conversation. What had I even said? Whatever it was, I was sure it wasn't flattering – something about desperation. Bloody hell. Rather than running out of the room with my tail between my legs, I decided on another angle, one that might have me dragged out by security and barred for life, but the way I saw it, I had nothing to lose.

Straightening my back, trying for an air of confidence, I said, 'You're late.'

Dean raised an eyebrow in surprise. 'You're kidding,' he snorted, as if I had some gall to pull him up on his punctuality.

'I'm deadly serious,' I said, moving towards my bag, trying to disguise the tremble in my hands as I unclipped it, quickly dumping my phone inside and pulling out my résumé. I handed it to him without missing a beat. 'I have volunteered at the Rotary Club's Eastern Christmas picnic every year since I was fourteen; I served sandwiches to the firefighters in the last two summers; I have cooked a barbecue for around two hundred locals at the Moorwall Rodeo. I have never worked in a bar before but I am a fast learner. I am punctual, smart and enjoy a challenge. I have excellent communication skills and I work well as part of a team –'

'Or unsupervised,' Dean finished my sentence.

I nodded my head. 'Yes.'

'Now why does the thought of you being unsupervised seem like such a bad idea?'

'I have references,' I said, ignoring him, still holding out the paper to him, giving it a bit of a wave to punctuate my point.

Dean strode over to his desk, taking a seat. I dropped my arm, refusing to let the sinking feeling inside take over from my mission as I turned to face him. He wasn't looking at me, he was shifting paperwork to the side of what was a relatively clean desk for a male.

I was getting a bit jack of having to sell myself in such a way that made me want to cringe, but I really needed to get this job. I could continue pitching myself as the employee of the freakin' year, or I could beg – pffft, no way. Maybe tears would work? No, that would almost be like begging and I still had my pride; pride that was slowly sinking as Dean looked set to torture me.

'Do you think you're a trustworthy person, Lexie?' he asked.

Oh crap, my past history didn't exactly paint me as Mother Teresa and he knew it.

'Yes.'

'Then why are there scuff marks on top of my desk?' he asked, his green-brown eyes eventually flicking up to me questioningly.

What? Oh fuck.

'Scuff marks?' I echoed, tilting my head to see what he was talking about, as if I was genuinely curious about what he was saying. 'Look, I don't know what you do in your personal time, but don't look at me.' I held up my hands.

A devious glint flashed in his eyes. 'This desk cost $4000; the only feet that will be on here are mine and the only part of a woman that will ever be on here is her palms.'

I swallowed. I could feel the heat creep up my neck and I blushed profusely, as an image flashed in my mind of exactly what he meant, a very hot image that made me shift uncomfortably. I really hoped Dean couldn't sense how awkward I had become, as my eyes dipped to the shiny gloss of the mahogany top.

'Been many palms on your desk then?'

Dean, who was looking cocky, suddenly froze, as if shocked by my question. Hell, I was shocked it had come out of my mouth too.

He tried to hide his surprised grin by rubbing the stubble on his chin, wicked thoughts no doubt running through his mind like a sordid slideshow. He looked at me with a spark in his eyes. 'A few,' he said.

Oh God, don't think about it, Lexie, don't react.

I cleared my throat, choosing to reel this away from such murky waters. On the plus side at least it had diverted attention away from the scuff marks I had put on his ridiculously overpriced desk.

'Well, this is a very unorthodox job interview,' I said.

It appeared to have worked as all humour slipped away from Dean's face, his expression darkening into his usual steely resolve. 'This is not a job interview,' he said, pushing up from his desk and heading for the door. He twisted the handle and pulled the door open, then stood to the side and looked at me pointedly.

Was I being dismissed? Really?

Looking up at him incredulously, I said, 'Look, I don't know what happened to your overpriced table but –'

'How old are you, Lexie?'

'W– what?'

'How. Old. Are. You?'

'I'll be eighteen in five days.'

'So you're seventeen.'

Wow, he was a real mathematician.

'For the next five days, yes.'

Dean sighed, shaking his head. 'Well, that's a shame; you can't work behind the bar unless you're eighteen.'

'I will be. In five days.'

'Ah, yes, but that's no good to me now, is it?' He held the door open wider.

I glanced out to the landing and then back up at him. 'Oh right, such a staff shortage that you can't wait a week,' I scoffed, probably doing myself no favours.

'Manage, own, *and* operate many bars do you, Miss Atkinson?' He said my name in a way that made the hairs on the back of my neck stand on end. Forever the smart-arse.

I simply glowered up at him.

'I didn't think so,' he said, spinning me around and giving me a slight nudge through the opening. He closed the door before I had a chance to turn around.

Bastard.

Chapter Nine

Of all the arrogant, self-centred, smart-arse, big-headed . . . I mumbled each insult as I stormed down Arcadia Lane.

Well, he could just shove his bar right where the sun don't . . . I stopped dead in my tracks, overcome with an absolute dread. 'Shit-shit-shit-shit,' I said, as I about-faced and started to quickly make my way back in the direction from which I had come.

I'd left my bloody bag in Dean's office. First my bra (which I'd never got back, mind you) and now my bag. Dean's office was the Bermuda Triangle for possessions.

I stormed straight past the Irish girl out front, skirting around the edge of the room so as not to be detected by Cassie the barmaid. I climbed the stairs, knowing he would see me coming through the glass. I didn't even bother to knock, I just turned the handle and entered. Much to my surprise, I found myself standing in the middle of Dean's empty office.

He was gone, and so was my bag. Bloody hell, I wasn't in the mood for this. I made my way down the stairs. Maybe he'd put my bag in a lost-and-found cupboard or something?

I moved over to the bar, waiting eagerly for Cassie to finish serving her customers, a couple who were agonising over the cocktail menu.

Come on, come on, come on.

I couldn't wait anymore. 'Hey, Cassie, Dean didn't happen to drop my bag here, did he?'

Cassie shrugged, semi-distracted. 'Sorry, haven't seen him.'

Great.

'Listen, I really need my bag, do you know where I can find –'

'Look, just go up and knock on the door,' she said curtly, tipping shots of vodka into a shaker.

'He's not in his office.' I wanted to stomp my foot in frustration.

'His office?' Cassie's brows pinched together as she shovelled ice into the cylinder. 'I wasn't talking about his office.'

Oh my God, how did he employ such people? Cassie might serve a cocktail with impressive speed but she wasn't the sharpest tool in the shed. 'So, umm, where do you suggest . . .'

Cassie turned her full attention to me. 'His apartment,' she snapped, 'that's where he'll be. Jesus.'

Wait: apartment?

'Upstairs, to the last door on the right. Make sure you knock.'

Cassie pushed a button, flinging the till open, slipping in some notes and counting out coins as change for her thirsty customers.

My eyes slowly lifted upwards.

So Dean lived here.

I thought of the balcony out front and wondered if that was part of his 'apartment'. Guess I would find out. 'Okay, I'm just going to head up and –'

'Knock, make sure you knock, and I didn't send you.' She gave me a pointed look.

I nodded. 'I was acting purely of my own free will.'

Sort of, kind of.

Okay, last time up these steps, I thought, then I could just get my stuff and be done with this place once and for all. I got to the top of the landing, veering to the right, seeing a long, dark hallway that had a series of doors on either side leading to who knows where. All I was interested in was making a quick, determined line to the door down the end of the hall. I don't know what I expected, a plaque on the door saying 'Dean's room' or 'Boss man'? But there was nothing to indicate that this was any different from the rest.

I stood before the door, taking a calming breath that did little to steady the beating of my heart. Was this going too far? Maybe I should have had Cassie call up here, got him to meet me down in the bar. That would have been the smart thing to do. Was it too late to turn around and double back? I was just about to when I heard a creak of a floorboard from within and I wondered if he could see my shadow from the sliver of light under the door.

Crap!

I don't know why I was even nervous. He had my property. Of course I would come back for it. If anything, Dean should have come chasing after me, but I doubt he'd ever chased after anyone in his whole life.

I knocked on the door with a businesslike tap-tap-tap. When there was no response I knocked again,

Was he ignoring me? Pretending not to be in? Maybe he had monitors in his apartment too and the second-guessing had my eyes skimming around for a hidden camera until I told myself to stop being stupid. I was all but ready to give up and turn back down the hall in defeat when something did very much grab my attention. And it wasn't the sound of footsteps or the opening of the apartment door. No, this was far more significant because, muffled beyond the thick wooden door, I could hear the sound of my mobile phone ringing.

Without thinking, I opened the door in a panic, and ran towards the noise, scrabbling to answer it before it stopped ringing. At first disorientated, I turned, honing in on the sound that was coming from the table where my bag had been placed. I found my mobile in the depths of my bag and pressed the button. 'Hello? . . . Hello? Shit.' I pulled it away, glowering at the blank screen. I had missed it.

But as it turned out a missed call was actually the least of my problems. As I grabbed my bag to leave I was stopped by a voice calling out from the balcony.

'Dean, I'm going to go, let me know if . . .' The words fell away as a set of wide blue eyes locked onto me, a pair of eyes I remembered with the very same horror from the last time I had seen them. It was a look I would never forget, a look that still haunted my dreams. This certainly felt like an awful dream. There, standing in the doorway leading from the balcony was Ballantine's mum, who was obviously Dean's mum, too.

'Lexie?'

'M– Mrs Ballantine.' I nodded, trying to keep my voice even.

My first impression of Mrs Ballantine had been under much different circumstances. I was the mysterious new girl that had brought out the better part of her son's character; she had even gone so far as to praise me for being the very reason Ballantine had stopped skipping school. But then I had turned into the girl who had purchased the pregnancy kit from her. Ballantine had said she knew the truth, that it had been for Amanda, not me, but standing in her oldest son's apartment, brought the feelings of guilt flooding back. Just as I opened my mouth to speak, I was saved from having to by the sound of steps that neared, and there, turning the corner into the large, expansive living space of the apartment, was Dean, his eyes almost popping out of his head when he saw me.

'I forgot my bag,' I blurted out, which really only sounded worse. What was my bag doing in Dean's apartment? What must she think? As soon as Ballantine is out of town, I start hanging out in Dean's apartment? Oh God, would she tell Ballantine? This had to be clarified immediately.

'I had a job interview,' I said quickly.

'I see,' she said.

'Well, I better get going,' I managed with a small smile, one that I hoped didn't seem too false as I side-stepped away, turning to face Dean, who looked at me with guarded amusement, as if he thought this awkward exchange between me and his mum was funny. Trust him to take joy from my torture.

'Well, I'll wait to hear from you then,' I said, holding out my hand to shake his, old-school style.

Dean looked at my hand and I thought he might leave me hanging there for a second, until he slowly reached out and took it, in a warm, firm embrace, squeezing to the point of being uncomfortable. I tried not to react. Instead, I dug my nails into his skin and, seeing the brief flash in his eyes, I felt vindicated, thinking I would be leaving my mark.

'Oh, I'll be in touch,' he said in a way-too-sexy voice, considering his mum was right there. I could feel my cheeks burn as I took my hand back, still feeling the warmth of his skin on mine like a hot brand.

'Bye, Mrs Ballantine,' I said, turning before I could take in the true scepticism of her curved brow.

God, what must she think of me? I clutched my bag close and walked out the door of Dean's apartment. This time I really wouldn't be coming back.

Chapter Ten

I never fooled myself into thinking Dean would actually give me the job. In the final days narrowing down to D-day, my lack of prospects was clear.

No Ballantine; no job; nowhere to stay.

I had failed on so many levels and now I had one last obstacle to navigate before my parents arrived and broke out in an 'I told you so' dance with beaming smiles and jazz hands.

In two days Aunty Karen and Uncle Peter would take the not-so-heartbroken Amanda away.

Having been subjected to a full-scale cleanathon, it got to the point where there was nothing else Aunty Karen could possibly scrub, rub, disinfect or paint. So now, in the final days, there was nothing else to do except wait it out before it would be 'Goodbye Paradise City' for everyone, even me. So what was there to do? You throw a farewell party.

After a last-ditch journey to dump a bag of clothes to the Salvos, we travelled back down the freeway at warp speed.

'Call it a combined bon voyage and happy eighteenth party, so invite any friends you like, Lexie,' suggested Aunty Karen from the front seat of the car.

'Pfft, what friends?'

'Amanda.' Aunty Karen flashed her a hard look.

'I'm kidding,' Amanda said with a yawn, as if completely bored by life. I wondered if I could glower at the back of her head long enough it would set her hair on fire. There was one positive thing to come out of this; I didn't have to put up with Amanda anymore.

'Won't having a party kind of trash the place?' I asked, thinking back to waking up the day after my dad's fortieth, with cans and empty beer bottles strewn over the lawn, a few deck chairs on their side, a table filled with half-eaten food and paper plates, stale bread and flies feasting on the crusty remnants of pav.

'Oh, don't you worry about that. Just think about who you might like to invite. You leave the rest to us,' Aunty Karen said as she steered into the driveway.

I really didn't want a party because apart from Laura, who would I invite? Boon? Oh God, that would be a disaster, I don't think I could subject poor Boon to that. Amanda was right. I had no friends.

I really was tragic.

•

'What do you mean you can't come? You have to.' I slid the laundry door closed, leaning against the washing machine, trying to steal a moment of privacy in a house buzzing with caterers – that's right, there were caterers. It was a full-fledged posh party with a tower constructed of champagne glasses, and white linen for the food tables, so not like Dad's fortieth at all. In fact, there would be no Aunty Karen and Amanda wandering around with black garbage bags the next morning, no siree, there was a clean-up crew for that. No wonder Aunty Karen was not stressed about getting the place dirty.

'I'm sorry, Lexie, but I just started my job and I can't go asking for time off already.'

Wait, what?

'Job? You have a job? You never told me that.'

Silence.

'Sure I did.'

'Ah, no, I am pretty certain you didn't.'

Laura seemed to make a habit of forgetting to tell me the important things, first Ballantine leaving now this.

'Aw, um, yeah, I started at Video Ezy.'

My heart sank: even Laura had a job. I wanted to feel happy for her and be all understanding about why she couldn't make it to the party, but as much as I tried I could feel my frustration and jealousy bubbling their way to the surface. I was the one who needed a job right now, to prove myself to my parents. I wished more than anything that I could miss this party because I had to work – if only!

'Sorry, Lexie, maybe we can catch up tomorrow or something. Go down to Arcadia and get matching tats for your eighteenth.' Laura was trying for lightheartedness but I was far beyond any point of being cheered up. I had never dreaded my birthday more. At a time when I should have been living it up and counting down the hours to the milestone, I was instead going to be stuck at a pretentious party with no friends – literally.

'Maybe,' I said, knowing full well my parents would arrive tomorrow and that I would most likely be busy packing my bags.

I cleared my throat, trying to steady it as I said goodbye to Laura, knowing that we wouldn't get a chance to head back to school together and hang out like we had last year.

'Have fun at work. Talk later!' I said all too quickly, before slamming my thumb on the end button.

•

Did I mention it was a cocktail party? And I don't mean mini frankfurts on toothpicks, oh no-no-no. I was dressed in a midnight-blue strapless number with a layered lace, tulle-like skirt just above the knee. I looked like an evil ballerina, and I kind of felt like one, too.

Amanda had gone emerald green, silky and way too short, and her BFF Lucy wore a devil red dress – how appropriate, I thought – but one thing that helped was they were too busy fussing with themselves and their friends to notice me and my lack of friends. I was just a thing in the corner, the birthday girl slash wallflower for the evening, and that was fine by me. I saw the pity in Aunty Karen's eyes when I told her I hadn't invited anyone. I thought she might break down and cry uncontrollably or something. It made me feel even worse, especially when Aunty Karen tried to pacify me by buying me this dress.

Despite my sarcasm-laden musings about such an over-the-top party, I couldn't help but appreciate how beautiful the backyard looked, adorned in fairy lights and lanterns with everyone dressed in their best, and bowtied waiters circulating delicious bite-sized snacks and, HELLO, champagne!

Aunty Karen click-clacked her black heels across the tiled floor with two champagne flutes in her hands, still managing to walk with the utmost grace even in her glittering black dress. She looked like Grace Kelly. I was glad my mum wasn't going to arrive until the next day. This kind of scene was not what we were accustomed to. Kenny Rogers was not singing

'The Gambler' in the background, and no-one was going to light a bonfire. Oh, how different two sisters could be, and as beautiful as all of this was, I would have preferred a piece of pav and some Cold Chisel any day.

'Here.' Aunty Karen passed me the champagne. 'I know you're not of age until tomorrow but I think you can have a sneak drink with your favourite aunty,' she said with a wink.

'Thanks,' I said, reluctantly taking it from her. When Uncle Eddie had given me a sneaky drink of beer when I was sixteen it hadn't been an enjoyable experience, and as I sipped on the elegant crystal glass I prepped myself for the same kind of bitterness, but it didn't taste like that at all – it tasted worse.

I tried not to wince as I clinked Aunty Karen's glass with mine. 'Cheers,' I said, hoping the aftertaste wouldn't linger too long. Oh, what the hell: I took another sip. Maybe I'd get used to it. Ugh.

'Try to have some fun tonight, Lexie.' Aunty Karen patted my upper arm sympathetically.

When Aunty Karen had left me so she could attend to a kitchen emergency, I downed the last of the fizzy amber, smacking my lips together with fake appreciation. I studied my empty glass with interest, wondering why people drank this stuff; surely it was just to get drunk, it couldn't possibly be for enjoyment.

I wasn't sure why Uncle Eddie did. After a night's heavy drinking he woke up the next morning with a case of amnesia, not recalling anything about the people he had offended or the things he had accidentally broken. Give me some of that, I thought. I wouldn't mind waking up without any knowledge. Just for one night I wanted to forget, forget about all my failings, forget about Ballantine, forget about the fact my parents were going to be here tomorrow for my birthday to 'discuss' the reality of me staying here. A handsome waiter with a boyish smile lowered his tray. 'Champagne, ma'am?'

Ma'am?

'Why, thank you,' I said, taking the flute with enthusiasm, saluting him.

Another glass wasn't going to hurt anyone.

Chapter Eleven

'Speech, speech!'

There was a clinking of glasses and cheers as Uncle Peter sheepishly went to stand beside Aunty Karen.

Were they serious? Was I at a wedding? They were renting their home out, they weren't signing up to be enlisted. I watched on as Uncle Peter gave a heartfelt, witty speech that had me rolling my eyes. I took another sip from my glass, looking out over the pool, thinking how I would have given anything to have Uncle Eddie here, drunk and screaming 'CANNONBALL' while bombing in the pool, dousing everyone in a tidal wave of water. The very vision of it made me snort. I covered my mouth with my hand to stifle the sound, earning me a glare from Amanda. Seeing as everyone was so engaged in Uncle Peter's speech, I took the moment to flip Amanda the middle finger with a smile.

Yep, one last day of putting up with you.

Amanda turned away from me, focusing on her parents once more.

Pfft, whatever.

I tilted my glass back, only to find it was empty, damn it. The magical, nasty-tasting liquid was working a treat. I was far more fascinated by the layers of my skirt and how the fairy lights picked up the faint sparkle of the material than my uncle's boring-arse speech.

'And we just want to wish our beautiful niece a happy eighteenth for tomorrow.' Aunty Karen's voice rung out over the partygoers. Standing on her tippy toes, she called out, 'Where's Lexie?'

O-oh.

I edged back a little, hiding behind a potted palm near the house.

No sudden movements, Lexie, be stealth like a jungle cat.

'There she is!' Lucy's shrill voice rang out and everyone turned in the direction she pointed . . . Could it get any worse?

'Happy birthday to you . . .'

Oh God, Aunty Karen was singing, waving on the crowd to join in. And they did.

'Happy birthday, dear Leeeexiiieeee . . .'

I smiled weakly, wishing the ground would just open up and swallow me whole. This champagne was pretty good but not enough to numb my senses entirely. Where was a fucking waiter when I needed one?

'You know, it seems like only yesterday that Lexie was running around naked under our sprinkler,' laughed out Aunty Karen.

Oh dear God, make it stop.

'Or that one time she went over her handlebars at Christmas time and ended up in Emergency,' added Uncle Peter, causing people to laugh. Yeah, the two of them were a regular stand-up comedy duo.

I had to get out of there, and as soon as the topic shifted to their beloved, smart, beautiful, kind and loving Amanda I knew that was my cue to leave. Skimming along the back wall now everyone was looking at Amanda with doe-eyed affection, I took my chance to step inside the kitchen, taking a moment to casually lift a bottle of champers off the ice and continue my merry way with champagne flute in hand, through the lounge, into the foyer and out the front door.

•

Dressed up and nowhere to go be damned! It was going to be my last night in Paradise and I wanted to party. Bottle in one hand, heels in the other, I walked along the beach, thinking if I followed the long half-moon sweep to those sparkling lights of the city in the distance, that would lead me to where I had to be. I zigzagged along the edge of the water, the waves at times surging forth and riding a little too high up my legs, causing me to squeal and laugh as I nearly lost my footing in the sand.

I walked forever, even the unopened bottle in my hand was starting to feel heavy. I aimed to rectify that situation as soon as possible. I stopped, juggling my shoes, glass and bottle. Squinting at the top with the aid of streetlights on the embankment above the beach and the fullness of the moon, I cursed when I realised it was a bottle with a cork. Crap, how did you get these things out and not take an eye out? I was seriously not very worldly, even now on the verge of . . . wait a minute. What was the time? Surely it was past midnight? Could it be? Was I officially eighteen?

No watch, no mobile: I had no way of knowing. I spotted a flickering mass further up the beach where a cluster of people were enjoying some music and a bonfire on a summer's night.

I trudged on, excitement clawing at my soul. I neared the circle of party-goers, approaching tentatively. 'Does anyone have the time?' I cringed, having interrupted a group conversation, causing them to stop and turn to me.

'Lexie?'

I turned to the voice from across the opposite side of the group. Boon approached, his eyes shifting over my cocktail dress, half drenched from the ocean, heels, champagne flute and bottle in my hands.

'Everything okay?' he asked gently, as if he was afraid to spook a wild animal, which wasn't too far from the truth.

'I'm just fine and dandy, thanks.'

'Where are you going?'

'There.' I used the bottle to point towards the sparkling city lights; the glowing, bright lights of the Ferris wheel were a beacon in the distance to guide my way.

Boon breathed out a laugh. 'Do you have any idea how far that is?'

I squinted in the distance. I had been walking forever and yet it still didn't seem like I had got any closer. It felt like a cruel optical illusion.

'Is it more than a bottle of champagne away?' I asked.

'I think it would be a good crate of champagne away, maybe two. And by the time you arrived you'd need your stomach pumped.'

'Yeah, well, I don't even know how to open this bloody thing so I think I'm safe,' I said, tugging and twisting at the cork. 'Ugh, can you open this for me?' I pouted, holding it out to him.

'Do you think that's really a good idea?'

'Well, how else am I going to make my way there? I'm going to need some sustenance.'

'A drunk girl wandering off into the night – yeah, that's a good idea.'

'Are you going to open it or not?'

'Or not,' he said, refusing to take it from me.

'Thanks for nothing,' I said, shoving it under my arm and turning to continue on my journey.

'Lexie, wait.'

Boon caught me by the arm, moving to stand in front of me. 'Where do you wanna go? I'll give you a lift.'

My ears pricked up. 'Really?'

'Come on, I'll take you home.'

'Home? I don't want to go home.' That was the last place I wanted to be. I wanted to make this night, my last night, count.

'So where are you going then?'

'I was going to drop into Video Ezy,' I said, to give your sister a piece of my mind, I thought.

Boon stopped, causing me to run into him. 'Geez, watch it.'

'Video Ezy? Why?'

I shrugged. 'I need to return a video.'

Boon eyed me sceptically. 'You don't look like you need to return a video.'

'Well, I'll have you know this dress is very deceptive.'

'Is that so?'

'It's like a Swiss army knife.'

'Really? That's impressive.'

I lifted my chin defiantly.

'I'm still not taking you there.'

'Why not?'

'Because it's quarter past twelve, they're shut,' he said, continuing to walk up the sandy embankment.

'Oh,' I said.

Wait a minute, quarter past twelve.

'Holy shit, Boon,' I yelled out.

Boon paused at the top of the track, looking back at me with a sigh.

'I'm eighteen!' I laughed, lifting my hands to the night. 'Wooohooo!'

Boon shook his head. 'God help us.'

Chapter Twelve

Seeing as I couldn't take my frustrations out on Laura, the winner of the worst-supporting-friendship award, I had to take my frustration out on the next best thing, and seeing as I was now safely twenty-one minutes into adulthood, I couldn't wait to give Dean Saville a piece of my mind. I had nothing to lose. In fact, I had lost everything I had ever really wanted because of him. He existed purely to make my life miserable without even really trying.

'All right, birthday girl, you'll have to leave the bottle here.'

'Fine, you can have it, it's warm.' I passed it to Boon, who grabbed it from me and walked to the skip across the car park, turfing it inside with a clank and a smash.

'So who are you meeting here again?'

I cleared my throat, momentarily forgetting what I had said. 'Oh, um, Cassie. I'm meeting Cassie.'

'Behind-the-bar Cassie?'

'Yep!'

Please don't come in, please don't come in.

'So how are you getting home?'

Oh my God, Boon was worse than my parents. 'Cassie's going to give me a lift. Stop worrying. Geez, do you give Laura the third degree when she goes out?'

'Laura is home reading books in her bedroom like a good girl.'

'You hope,' I scoffed.

'I know my sister.'

I was going to say that my aunty and uncle probably thought they knew me, yet here I was standing out the back of the Wipe Out Bar tipsy, barefoot and ready to party. I patted myself down as if I was searching for car keys. 'Crap!'

'What's wrong?' asked Boon, not really wanting to know the answer.

'You don't have any money, do you? I left my purse at home.'

Boon sighed. 'Bloody hell, Lexie, I thought your dress was like a Swiss army knife.' Reaching into his back pocket and flipping out his wallet, he flicked through his money, choosing a golden note over the orange. I smiled, bless his soul. 'Here,' he said, handing me the fifty.

'Aww, thanks, Boon, I'll pay you back.'

'Yeah, well, just don't go skipping town.'

My smile fell away, my heart clenching at how real that was, that I would be skipping town tomorrow, no doubt. I shook off the feeling, instead embracing the lively, warm buzz the champagne had afforded me.

'I better go. Cassie'll be waiting.'

'Just lay off the champers maybe for a bit,' he said with a smirk.

'I'm eighteen now, remember?' I said, smiling and wrapping my arms around him, hugging the life out of him. 'Thanks, Boony, you're a legend.'

Boon laughed, causing his toned warm frame to vibrate, as he gently unlinked my vice-like grip from around his rib cage.

'Wow, high praise, indeed,' he said.

'No, seriously, you are. Amanda was a bloody idiot to break up with you.'

And just like that, all the humour drained away from Boon's face; I inwardly cursed my big mouth.

'Um, anyway, thanks for the ride,' I said, backing away and heading towards the flashing lights and pounding music.

•

'That will be fourteen dollars.'

'What?'

'Fourteen dollars,' yelled the barman, shouting over the music.

I snatched the menu off the bar, my eyes frantically searching for the cocktail I'd just ordered. 'Holy shit, fourteen dollars. Are you serious?' My horrified gaze lifted from the menu to the barman, who looked like he was losing patience.

I begrudgingly handed over my fifty-dollar note, mentally calculating how far it would get me, and added 'ridiculous prices' to the list of things I was going to have a go at Dean for – a noticeably absent Dean, mind you.

It was a pumping Friday night but I didn't recognise anyone. The bar staff were different and there were no tables of families dotted around at this late hour. Only groups of people, and girls on a hen's night squealing and laughing at a nearby table. The massive open space on the far side of the bar that just looked like a big square of parquetry flooring during the day was now transformed into a giant dance floor with a sea of flailing bodies getting down to a live band. Things were certainly different from how I had seen it before. Maybe the Wipe Out Bar was the place to be.

The barman dumped my change into my hand.

Bloody rip-off.

I struggled to find a place to put my change, mostly my coinage, so being the classy beast that I am, I opted to wedge it into my bra. I took my cocktail, ensuring that I would sip slowly on it. It tasted much better than the champagne. I turned, lifting my eyes to the office upstairs, wondering if that's where the ogre was right now, hovering over the monitors.

The heat in the bar was overwhelming, and the bodies vying for the bartenders' attention were aggressive in their pursuit as they mimed numbers with their hands and shouted their orders. Service was always fast and efficient, but tonight they were literally running up and down the bar, their hands working like lightning. I chewed on my straw, watching, thinking there was no way I could do that. How could they remember all the ingredients in the drinks? Maybe Dean had done me a favour by not employing me. Not that I'd ever admit that to him.

With my elbows tucked in I attempted to move against the flow of bar traffic. 'Excuse me, sorry, excuse me.' Even though I was still feeling the buzz of bon voyage champagne with a layer of a vodka cocktail I still felt a little out of my depth and woozy on my feet. A combination of booze, heels and limited space and it was like I was in a pinball machine, losing my balance then slamming hard into someone's back and spilling my drink on me and him. He was tall and tanned and . . . hello.

'I'm so sorry, I'm such a klutz.' I shook my hand and wiped at my dress and at the boy's shirt before thinking, yep, okay that's probably even worse. I cringed at the now dark blue stain.

'Hey, it's okay,' he laughed, hitting me with a blinding smile that was almost more overpowering than the alcohol

I had consumed. 'What's your name?' Mr Tall, Tanned and Blond asked. He looked like one of those fitness fanatics you see running along the beach at some ridiculous hour of the morning.

'Lexie,' I shouted above the music.

'Oh, sexy Lexie, hey?' he said with a wide grin.

Ugh. He just lost major points there.

He must have read as much on my face as he quickly changed his tune. 'So, what are you drinking? Or should I ask, what am I wearing?' He glanced down at his shirt.

'Look, I'm really sorry, I'll grab some serviettes.'

'Don't worry about it, it's cooled me down.' He laughed; he had a nice laugh. 'I'm Dan,' he said, extending his hand.

'Dan the man, hey?' I quipped.

'Ah, yeah,' he winced, rubbing the back of his neck. 'How about I buy you a drink, make up for that little embarrassment.'

'I think I should be buying you a drink,' I said with a laugh, and then instantly regretted it, thinking about how expensive the drinks were.

'I insist. Wait here. What are you having?'

'Oh, um, a Midori Illusion.'

Dan took my empty tumbler and winked. 'Back in a sec.'

I felt my tummy flutter with butterflies watching Dan cut a clear path towards the bar, his big imposing frame making his way through the crowd with ease as he manoeuvred into a spot against the bar and lifted his hand up, grabbing a bartender's attention straightaway. He was the kind of boy who would grab your attention too, and he was buying me a drink – happy birthday, indeed.

Dan motioned from the bar to move over to a less crowded area, which I was happy to do, nudging my way to the edge of the dance floor where high round tables and stools were dotted.

'Here you go, one Illusion.' He placed the tumbler carefully in front of me.

'Thanks, I'll try not to spill it on you this time.'

'Oh, I don't know, I think I could go for matching sleeves.' Dan smiled, his elbows leaning on the tabletop. 'So what's a girl like you doing in a dive like this anyway?'

I was a bit taken aback by the question. 'I don't know. Is it that bad?' It was really the only bar I had been to in Paradise. As much as I had dreaded walking through these doors on various occasions, there was a part of me that felt a little defensive of that statement.

'The band's good,' I said, just in time for a cover of a Eurythmics classic to start blaring out of the speakers. 'Oh my God, I love this song.'

Dan laughed, taking my drink from my hand and placing it on the table. 'Well, let's go burn up this dance floor then.'

What? I looked at my drink being left behind, 'Oh no-no-no, I don't have to dance to it, I just said I liked it.'

Dan took me by the hand, dragging me onto the dance floor. 'Come on, Lexie, live a little,' he said, spinning me around. 'Come show me what you got.'

It was useless to fight against his strong hold. He flung me around like a rag doll. He was built and at least six foot, so he towered over me.

'I didn't take you for a dancer,' I yelled above the music.

'Well, I have to dry off my shirt somehow,' he said with a laugh.

Yeah, that joke was getting kind of old.

I did love to dance. At any gathering I was always the first to stampede towards the dance floor to do the 'Nutbush' or the 'Time Warp'. I loved the freedom of it, feeling the music and having fun, but this wasn't really dancing, there was nothing freeing about this. Dan kept twisting and flinging me around on the floor. I felt dizzy and powerless to break away from him. He turned me before yanking me towards him, hitting his chest hard, almost knocking the breath out of me as he caged me in his arms, circling my waist as he changed the tempo to slow.

The multicoloured hues from the lights flashed across his face, casting it into shadows, and all of a sudden he didn't seem so friendly anymore. The way he looked down on me was predatory and the way his hands slid across my back made my skin crawl.

'I think I'm going to sit this one out. My feet are killing me,' I said, trying to pull away.

'No problem,' he said, picking me up so I stood on the top of his giant feet. 'Problem sorted.' He laughed. I could smell the alcohol on his breath, the bitter tang of it made me cringe and now I felt even less in control as he danced me around like a puppet.

'I like you, Lexie, and I don't care if you don't like it, I think sexy Lexie suits you just fine.'

'Thanks, but I really don't want to dance anymore,' I said, my hands pushing on his upper arms, trying to pry myself away, but he only laughed and held me tighter.

'Relax, Lexie, just go with it.' I felt his breath on my neck and I started to panic. We were among a crush of bodies on the dance floor, all too preoccupied to see the panicked look in my eyes, the music too loud for them to hear my scream. My heart was racing, my efforts to fight against him were failing. I tried to knee him but he was too clicked on for that and my struggle only seemed to encourage him.

'Let me go,' I gritted.

'Is that how you repay someone for buying you a drink?'

'Shove your fucking drink,' I snapped.

'Oooh, kitty got claws,' he crooned as he slid his hands lower, grabbing my butt. The shock of it instinctively drew my hand back before slapping him so hard across the face it almost dislodged my arm from its socket.

He finally let go of me as he grabbed the side of his face, his mouth gaping as he winced. 'Son of a bitch, what the fuck?' he yelled. His face was like thunder as his eyes bored into me. My palm stung so badly I could literally feel it throbbing, my hands shaking as I moved to back away, but it was too late. He caught me by the wrist, his grip so crushing I thought it might break the bone.

'You little bitch,' he spat, dragging me towards him.

I went to scream, but before I could brace myself for what was to come, Dan went flying, crashing into the upright table, sending drinks and glasses smashing everywhere. People screamed and dived out of the way.

My mouth was agape, looking at this huge bloke blinking, dazed and confused at what had just happened. I was doing the same until I turned to see Dean beside me, his chest heaving with a silent rage.

Chapter Thirteen

'You all right?' he asked.

'Um, yeah, I –'

He didn't wait for the answer; instead, Dean strode forward, grabbing Dan by the back of the hair and dragging him out towards the exit as a sea of people parted to let them through.

Dan was pleading. 'Okay, okay, I'm going . . .'

Dean stopped short of the doorway, slamming Dan against the wall, glowering at him. 'If you ever darken my doorstep again, you won't make it out next time, you understand?'

Dan was bright red, fighting for air, a smear of blood across his cheek.

'Do. You. Understand?' Dean repeated.

'Yes,' Dan croaked, his eyes watering, a vein pulsing in his temple.

'Good. Now get the fuck out of here.' Dean grabbed him with both hands and tossed him out the door.

Dan stumbled and fell on the street outside, gasping for breath, clasping at his throat. 'You're a dead man,' he said in a raspy voice, struggling to find his feet. 'You hear me? Dead!'

Dean smiled. 'Run along now.' He turned to the big, burly security guard near the door. 'Think you can remember that face?'

The guard didn't answer, he simply tapped his temple as if it were in the vault.

Dean nodded, pleased, until he turned and saw me standing there, wringing my hands together. He stormed a determined line towards me, his expression dark. He grabbed me by my upper arm and marched me back into the room and up the stairs.

'Dean!' I yelped as he dragged me up the steps so quickly I pretty much tripped the entire way.

We burst through the door of his office, Dean letting go of my arm so as to slam the door behind us.

I stumbled against his desk, using it as a means to gain my balance as I turned towards him, catching my breath and taking in his fiery eyes. They were heated with such anger I wanted to move further away from him but the desk stopped me from doing so.

'What the fuck are you playing at, Lexie?' he shouted.

I blinked, shocked at his outburst. 'I . . . just came to . . .'

He closed the distance between us, standing before me and glowering down at me. 'This is not a playground. You're not giggling with school boys in the canteen line here. Men come here to drink and they pick up, and they fuck in alleyways and they don't offer friendship rings or promises of forever. You want to have some fun, save it for your girlfriends' slumber parties.'

I could feel my cheeks burning, my chest rising and falling heavily. I should have looked away from him. He was dressing me down, putting me back in my place and trying to intimidate me into being the little girl he pegged me for, so when

I breathed out a laugh and shook my head, a new level of anger flashed across his face.

'You are such a hypocrite,' I said. 'Don't act like you're some kind of saviour, because you're not. Remember your last words to me when I left? "Let me know when you're tired of playing with school boys." Well, maybe I am tired – tired of being treated like a stupid little sheltered farm girl, tired of not being taken seriously or given a bloody chance to prove myself, tired of being set up to fail and never being given the benefit of the doubt. Maybe you don't get anywhere in this city unless you're an Amanda or a Lucy, treating people like shit. So excuse me for wanting to be in the real world, for going about it any way I can because as far as anyone else is concerned, everyone has been nothing but a fucking hindrance to me, especially you.'

Dean's eyes ticked over my face as he crossed his arms across his chest. 'You finished?' he asked.

I stepped forward, lifting my chin defiantly up at him, looking straight into his eyes. 'Not yet.'

Dean smiled a slow wolfish smile, inching closer to me. 'Do you really want to be in the real world, do you really want to know what it's like?' he asked quietly, his voice warm and hypnotic. I could feel my uneven breathing and a new heat was burning across my skin.

'Yes,' I breathed, feeling his breaths burning my cheek.

'Do you think you could handle it?' he whispered in my ear.

I could feel myself quivering as I swallowed, closing my eyes and running my tongue along my bottom lip. 'Yes.'

What was he doing? Was he going to kiss me? Oh God.

I fought for breath. He was trying to push me into being afraid, but instead he was doing the complete opposite, which was frightening me. I straightened, feeling his heat burn against me standing so close as I lifted my gaze to him, looking him directly in the eyes. 'I can handle it.'

Dean's expression grew darker, and just as I thought I might hold my breath for what was to come, Dean stepped away from me.

'You better go,' he said.

My legs felt shaky, and I panicked for a new reason. 'Go?'

Dean looked surprised by the disappointment in my voice. It was something that surprised me as much as it did him. I felt cold now, and exposed and embarrassed.

'It's late, I'll call you a taxi,' he said, moving towards his desk, making sure to give me a wide berth. He passed the long row of monitors that were flickering with moving images from below. This is where he would have been sitting, watching on, guarding his manor with a watchful eye, and the realisation of what he had done hit me as I turned to him finishing up his phone call and setting down the receiver.

'Thank you,' I said. 'Thanks for saving me before.'

'Yeah, well, I don't want anyone to sue me,' he said. He was trying to lighten the mood, but it didn't really work.

I gave him a small smile. 'Well, thanks anyway,' I said, moving towards the door.

I heard him sigh wearily. 'Lexie, wait.'

I paused with my hand on the door handle.

Dean moved from behind his desk to stand next to me, taking his wallet out and thumbing out some cash. 'For the taxi,' he said.

Something broke inside me: more disappointment, and thinking maybe he had called me to stop for another reason – not sure what I wanted it to be, but a taxi fare sure wasn't one of the possibilities. 'It's all right, I have a little money.'

'Yeah, well, a little is not going to be enough.' He picked up my hand and placed a fifty in my palm then closed my fingers to envelop it. Great, all this night had produced was me owing both Boon and Dean money now. I should have just stayed home and saved myself a hundred bucks. 'I'll pay you back.'

Dean breathed out a laugh. 'Consider it a birthday gift.'

'Goodbye, Dean,' I said, stepping through the door and trying to pull it closed behind me. But it wouldn't give. I turned to see Dean holding it open.

'Goodbye? I didn't bar you for life, just maybe for twenty-four hours,' he joked.

I canted my head, not sharing the joke. 'I'm going home tomorrow.'

'Home?'

'Home to Red Hill.'

Dean frowned, confused.

I sighed. 'I had two weeks to get a job and find a place to live before my parents took me home again,' I said.

Dean's eyes studied my face.

I smiled thinly. 'That's why I needed a job.' Shrugging, I started down the steps.

'Hey, Lexie, wait . . .' Dean called after me.

'I'll send the money to you,' I said without looking back. I just couldn't. Saying what I just had made it real. This was it. I was eighteen and had failed my agreement. Tomorrow I was going home.

Chapter Fourteen

I closed my eyes behind my sunnies, willing the breeze to blow over my skin on the warm summer's morning. The hum of the pool pump soothed me in an odd way as I tried to settle myself into a semi-coma, hoping the painkillers would kick in any second. I inhaled deeply. Mum and Dad would be here tonight and there would be a reunion slash farewell dinner and then we would be gone, away from Paradise.

Don't think about that, Lexie. Just close your eyes and wait for the pain to subside.

My stillness and lack of thoughts were working a treat: calming breaths, the trickling of water and silence, beautiful, blissful, sile–

'Where the hell were you last night?'

Ugh.

I flicked up my sunglasses to squint up at Amanda standing there with her hands on her hips, blocking my sun,

'Why, whatever do you mean?' I asked innocently.

'I mean, you accidentally elbowed me in the head when you crept into bed smelling like passive smoke and stale alcohol, and there's sand ALL through my bed.'

I smirked.

'Look, Lexie, I don't know what's going on with you right now but you are not going to win any friends behaving like this.'

My eyes snapped up. 'What? Win friends like Lucy? No, thanks.'

'Shhh!' Amanda glanced towards the house. 'Lucy's just inside.'

'Of course she is. Does she ever bloody go home?'

'Yeah, well, I doubt you will run into her living with Principal Fitzgibbon's family.' Amanda looked smug. I wanted to punch her in the face.

'Over my dead body,' I said.

'Well, I'm sure that can be arranged.'

'What can be arranged?' asked Lucy, coming to stand beside Amanda, looking at me as though I was something to be disposed of.

I was ready to shout the fact that no thanks to Amanda and her parents upping and leaving to give their precious daughter a new start, I had to go back home and suffer a fate worse than death . . . home schooling.

But just as Amanda was about to open her mouth, Aunty Karen's heels clicked along the concrete.

'Lexie?' she called.

We all turned to see Aunty Karen approaching cautiously. 'Honey, there's someone here to see you,' she said quietly, her gaze flicking back towards the house.

I peeked over my shades, following my aunty's eyeline, and slid off my recliner to stand, rather inelegantly, in seconds.

Dean Saville, wearing Ray Bans, skimmed his way through the sliding glass doors. He never once turned his attention away from me as he came to stop before us.

'Lexie,' he said, nodding his head with a smirk.

I don't know what he found so amusing – maybe it was my gaping expression, or maybe it was because I looked like death warmed up and he was delighting in my pain. Maybe he just wanted his money back? Whatever the reason, I failed to voice the obvious.

What the hell was he doing here?

I shifted nervously, hoping Dean wasn't here to unveil my whereabouts last night, or to share my awkward account of how he saved me from sleazy Dan. But anything that brought Dean Saville to my door could never be a good thing.

'Hi, Dean,' chirped Lucy, blinking once, twice.

Dean turned as if seeing her for the first time. 'Lucy,' he said with another head nod.

Ignoring Amanda altogether, he turned his attention to Aunty Karen. 'It's a lovely home you have here, Mrs Burnsteen.'

'Oh, please, call me Karen.' Aunty Karen laughed.

Oh my God, was she blushing? Gross.

Dean smiled. 'Well, Karen, if you don't mind, I just need to steal Lexie for a bit. If that's all right by you?'

All eyes turned to me.

'Oh, um, I have no problem with that, I mean, if that's . . . and you and her want to umm . . .' Aunty Karen was flailing, dancing between the awkwardness of being asked permission and granting approval. Jesus, it wasn't like he asked for my hand in marriage or anything.

'Lexie, do you want to go for a drive?' Dean asked.

My hangover seemed to miraculously melt away. Or maybe it paled in comparison to my confusion and the utter shock of Dean being here and above all wanting me to, what did he just say? Go for a drive? I could see in my peripheral vision the stunned looks on Amanda's and Lucy's faces.

Even my Aunty Karen's surprise was evident. After all, what would some hot boy be doing on her doorstep seeking my attention? The whole vibe rubbed me the wrong way and regardless of whatever Dean really wanted, it didn't matter. I suddenly felt powerful, thinking about what it would be like for me to walk out of here with Dean Saville.

'Sure,' I said, placing my sunnies on top of my head, looking directly up at him.

I don't know what your game is, Dean Saville, but what you are about to do for me in front of these two idiots is more than I could hope for.

'Back soon,' I said, kissing my aunty on the cheek and managing a last-minute fuck-you glance at Amanda and Lucy, who were still staring at me in disbelief. I put on my sunnies and Dean stepped aside as I glided past.

•

Dean drove a sexy, immaculate-looking dark blue Holden Kingswood with tan leather seats and not a speck of dust on the shiny, oiled dashboard. It even had that new car smell even though it was a model from the '70s. Dean's apartment had been immaculate too. Maybe he was a bit OCD? Seemed plausible.

We travelled in silence along a winding coastal road I had never been down before. It had me wondering how well I actually knew Dean. By all accounts he could have my body buried in a shallow grave before the day was out, but as we petered off from the desolate stretch of road and travelled to an intersection, Dean turned left and his Kingswood thundered down the road where I started to see familiar landmarks. And once we'd veered off the busy main drag and into the narrow alley's back entrance that led into a car park, it was clear that it was the very same one Boon had dropped me off in last night at the back of the Wipe Out Bar.

Without a word, Dean plunged the gear stick into park, turned the thumping motor off and slid out of the car, whistling like he didn't have a care in the world. I watched on through the windshield, genuinely perplexed as to what he was doing. I opened the car door and slowly stepped out from the passenger seat, pushing my sunnies upwards to divide the folds of my hair. I didn't need them so much here in the concrete jungle. The back of the Wipe Out Bar looked so different in the daytime. It was tagged with graffiti, the skip bins overflowing with rubbish. There was a small alleyway that led down the side towards the front of the building, and an entrance out the back that led down to the basement, which brought back memories of my first time here. Ballantine had led me here, introduced me to that very basement, which turned out to be the pool hall for lost youths and delinquents. I felt a pang of nostalgia hit me. I would give anything to go back to that night, to be led by Ballantine into the dark again. Ballantine. Now was not the time to think about him. Coward.

My eyes shifted to where Dean was making his way up the back fire escape to the second storey. Once he got there, he inserted a key into a thick army-grey fireproof door. Assuming that he wanted me to follow, I made my way towards the fire escape, rickety and rusted at best. Like most of this building, it left a lot to be desired. It was something I had even thought about in regards to its owner. I came to stand beside him, watching on as he jiggled and twisted the dodgy lock, until the magical click sounded.

'Seems like you need a new lock,' I mused.

Dean looked at me, his eyes unshielded by his sunnies that were now hooked into the pocket of his shirt. 'Why?' he asked, frowning.

'Well, seems a bit dodgy, that's all,' I said with a shrug. I'm convinced he would argue any point. If the sky were blue he would swear it was green.

'There's nothing wrong with it,' he said, stepping back and tilting his head at the flaky gunmetal grey door with its wonky, hard-to-open lock.

He yanked it open, the heaviness of it straining the muscles of his inked biceps, muscles that I averted my eyes from because, well, it seemed wrong to stare.

I stepped into a hall, long, narrow and dark, suddenly feeling enclosed and hot until Dean started making his way down it. I couldn't see much except the outline of his tall frame as he led me along where it became lighter. Then we turned a corner and passed a familiar door to Dean's apartment. At the end, in the opposite direction, I could see the door to Dean's office and just as I thought that was our intended destination, double stepping to follow, Dean stopped, causing me to slam into his back.

'Ow, Jesus, what are you doing?' he hissed, turning around to look daggers at me.

I winced, rubbing my forehead. 'What am I doing? What are you doing? What is this?' I snapped, tired of the cloak-and-dagger behaviour.

Dean laughed, actually laughed, shaking his head and looking down at me with a devious spark in his green-brown eyes. Without saying anything and without taking his eyes off me, he twisted the handle of the door we stood in front of and pushed it open.

Chapter Fifteen

I didn't know what to think.
 I didn't know what to do, so I just stood there and stared at the bed, a single bed against the wall of a small, stuffy room that had nothing more than a wardrobe, a chair and a washstand in a corner.

Okaaaay.

Dean tilted his head. 'Go on.'

I looked at him as if he were mad; maybe he was. But I wasn't going to walk into that room, not in a million ye–

He pushed me. Actually pushed me inside so that I stumbled a little. I spun around, glowering at him. 'Hey, what the –'

'The rent will come out of your wage . . .' Dean walked casually to the window, lifting the blind to reveal a brick wall. He coughed, quickly lowering it down again before spinning around.

'W– wage?'

He sighed, crossing his arms and leaning against the windowsill. 'Wage,' he repeated.

I stood there, stunned into silence. Was this some kind of cruel joke? He said wage, but had I heard rent, was he saying what I thought he was saying?

'Cassie will show you the ropes, give you a feel for things on a slower day shift and we'll go from there.'

My vision blurred, and there was nothing I could do to stop the emotion that flooded me when I looked at Dean from across the room. A dank, horrid, small room that probably housed a rodent, and, yeah, had a brick wall for a view, but it was mine for the taking, mine if I wanted it.

Dean plunged his hands deep into his jean pockets. 'Look, I know it's not exactly the Taj Mahal or anything, but –'

'It's perfect!' I said quickly, shaking my head and grinning from ear to ear.

Dean looked taken aback. 'Well, I have never actually heard this room referred to as that before but if you say so.' He shrugged, walking past me until I stopped him. Grabbing him by the arm, he looked down to where I touched him and it was enough of a reminder for me to remove my hand. I swallowed.

'Thank you,' I said, for once wanting him to see how sincere I was, my eyes boring into his.

A crooked smile creased the corner of his mouth. 'If you say so.'

'I do, I really do.'

Dean reined in his smile, masking it like it was something that wasn't meant to be there, before walking from the room and heading down the hall.

•

I couldn't care less about the view, or if I had to spoon a rat on a flea-infested mattress. This meant one thing; no, two things! One, I wouldn't have to board with Principal Fitzgibbons and two, I wouldn't have to go back to Red Hill. I had won, fulfilled my end of the bargain, albeit not knowing my hourly rate or how many days a week or really anything other than I had a place to stay and a means to keep it. Sure, there was no pool or Axminster carpet or imported tiles but still, the bed was mine, all mine. I squealed, throwing myself backwards on the springy single bed. A cloud of dust poofed into the air, which caused me to break into a coughing fit.

Minutes later, just as I was learning how to breathe again, my mobile rang. 'Hello,' I croaked.

'We're heeeere,' singsonged my mum's voice. I flinched, looking around before realising how stupid that was.

'Ah, where?'

'We've just pulled into Karen's driveway. Where are you?'

Oh shit.

'I'm out.'

'Out?'

'Um, yeah, I'm just settling into my new place,' I said, biting my lip and waiting for the response. What I got was silence, long, drawn-out silence, before Mum spoke.

'Place?'

'Yeah, I've found a place. Isn't that great?'

'W– where and when exactly did this happen?'

I could hear my dad whispering in the background, 'What's going on?'

Mum put her hand over the receiver, muffling her voice but I could hear her clearly enough.

'Lexie's found a place.'

I could almost visualise my parents' faces, the looks of sheer horror.

'Where did you say this place was again? Is it near here?'

Uh-oh, here it came. The twenty questions, the third degree, finding fault with my decisions. My excitement from before was quickly diminishing as my eyes wandered around the dank, dusty room that no matter how much cleaning and attempting to put a feminine touch to, wouldn't help it look any better. It would do me because I was desperate, but what would my parents make of it?

'Where are you? We'll come to you.'

Oh shit-shit-shit . . .

'No!' I said a bit too loudly, standing up. 'Um, I was just about to come home. Aren't we going out for tea tonight with Aunty Karen?'

'Yeah, I think so. Is it far? What suburb are you in?'

Oh God, I could imagine Dad getting the map out of the glove compartment already. There would be no stopping them. They'd soon be pulling up out the back, their horrified eyes skimming over the skips, graffiti and dodgy, prison-like back door leading into a darkened hall.

Welcome to Paradise!

If that was to be their introduction, if this room was what they saw, then it wouldn't matter if I had the best paying job in the world. None of it would matter. They would take one look and frogmarch me back to their car in a heartbeat. I knew my parents too well.

'Lexie, are you there?'

'Arcadia Lane,' I said with a heavy heart. 'It's called the Wipe Out Bar – you can't miss it.'

•

I hovered at the entrance to Dean's office, biting my lip and wringing my hands together. He was focusing on the papers on his desk with deep concentration, concentration that was about to be interrupted as I gently knocked on his door.

'Yes?' he said.

'So, um, I may have done something really stupid,' I said, wincing.

'You haven't broken the back door?'

'What? No.'

Dean's shoulders sagged a little. 'Well, what could you have possibly done already?'

I stepped forward, taking the seat in front of his desk.

Dean watched on with guarded interest, intrigued by my anxiety. 'What did you do?' he deadpanned.

'My parents have hit town.'

Dean swivelled from side to side in his chair. 'Right?'

'And they're coming by here now. And they might have freaked out when I said I was living in the city . . . above a bar.'

'Go on . . .'

I bit my lip some more; it was a terrible habit when I was really nervous. 'And so I may have described my living arrangements,' I said.

'And they didn't approve?'

'Well, actually, they seemed really impressed, a little excited even.'

Dean's expression changed, his brows lifting into his hairline. 'Really? Well, good,' he said, moving forward and focusing his attention back to his paper as a means to dismiss me.

Good? No, it was not good, far from it, and this was what I was leading up to. 'The thing is, they were impressed when I described to them the apartment I had found.'

Dean froze, his gaze slowly lifting from the desk. 'Apartment?'

'Yeah, I may have mentioned that it was really large and airy with an industrial galley kitchen and a balcony overlooking the –'

'No,' he bit out.

'Dean, please . . .'

'Absolutely not. Jesus, Lexie.' He stood, pacing the room and running his hands through his hair, exasperated.

'Look, I will work for nothing, I will scrub floors, toilets, mop up vomit, hose down urine, I don't care. I just need one small favour.'

'You've been under my roof for two point five seconds. I have given you a job and a room to rent and you want a favour?'

'Just hear me out. I don't want your apartment, I just want to borrow your apartment, quickly show my parents around – put on a show so they don't want to kidnap me and take me home. They'll be gone by the morning and all will be as it was before.'

Dean stood across from me, his stare hard and dark. Although I wanted to retreat from that stare, I met his eyes dead on, and tried for my best pleading expression.

There was no change in his demeanour, not an inch of him willing to move on this. I couldn't really blame him, but even so I felt a sinking sensation in my heart.

'Okay.' I nodded. 'If it's meant to be, it's meant to be.' Standing up and making my way towards the door, I heard him swear under his breath.

Dean pushed past me. 'When will they be here?' he snapped, standing in my path.

'Fifteen, twenty minutes,' I said quickly, fingers crossed.

He exhaled. 'We'll have to get rid of the obvious things: photos, aftershave, shoes, anything that makes it look like a bloke's apartment,' he said, walking down the hall. I trotted after him.

'Dean, I swear to God, I owe you big time. Like, seriously, I owe you.'

He stopped before his door and glared down at me. 'Owe me?' he scoffed. 'Sweetheart, you have no idea.'

As much as his chuckle was all kinds of scary sexy, I was starting to get worried. What on earth had I done?

Chapter Sixteen

I had never been so appreciative of someone living so minimally. With the few personal items, like shoes and cologne and photos, removed and stashed under his bed, there was nothing obvious that might suggest anything untoward. Sure, the wooden floors and sharp, modern lines of the apartment looked masculine, and the dark navy blue plaid of the bed cover was extremely manly, but there was nothing in the apartment my parents could object to.

I had nightmarish flashes of Mum and Dad nearly getting barrelled over by skateboarders as they passed the tattoo parlour, with 'People are Strange' by The Doors playing in the background, walking among the local freaks and tourists in a part of the city they would never normally visit. I knew they had to be absolutely wooed by this apartment. They had to think it so utterly amazing that they could see past all the depravity, grime and graffiti; they had to love it in a way that had them wishing they lived here, and as I stepped out onto the balcony taking in a salty sea breath of air, I knew that they would approve, because standing on the big, sweeping corner balcony outside of the Wipe Out Bar, looking beyond, was undoubtedly the best view in all of Paradise.

There was the long stretch of the dark blue sea, the backdrop to the boardwalk that stretched along the shoreline leading out to a huge pontoon and an impressive hall and amusement park; then there was the Ferris wheel, the jewel in the crown of the seaside park. Laughter, chatter and sounds of people living and enjoying themselves against the delicate wash of the ocean was intoxicating. This was a view of Paradise you just couldn't see in suburbia, with all its perfect, clean lines, manicured trees and concrete driveways. Suburbia was stifling in all its unnatural polished, bleached surfaces. Here was the reality, here was where it was at. I sensed Dean standing beside me, looking out towards the horizon.

'Not bad, huh?'

I turned to him, smiling like a kid on Christmas morning. 'It's amazing.'

'Yeah, well, Mummy and Daddy better like it, because there's no penthouse to show them.'

'They'll love it, I guarantee it.'

I heard the jingling of keys, and turned to see Dean pocket his wallet.

'Where are you going?'

'I think it's probably best they don't find me here when they arrive,' he smirked.

Okay, that was a good point. 'So are you going out, out?' I asked, trying to seem nonchalant. I don't know why but I wanted to know where he was going.

'Yeah, I would rather not have to lie to your parents' faces, if that's all right.'

I felt guilt claw at my insides. I was telling a little white lie; okay, so it wasn't that little, but knowing them like I did there was no way they would ever see reason if they thought I was living in squalor. If they thought I had a deal too good to refuse with this apartment then surely that would win them over, wouldn't it?

'I'll get Cassie to send them up to my apartment . . . well, your apartment,' he corrected.

'Won't she ask questions?'

Dean paused halfway out the door, glancing back at me. 'The very first thing my staff learn here is not to ask questions,' he said in all seriousness. I took a mental note.

No questions.

'Oh, before I forget,' he reached into his back pocket and flicked open his wallet, thumbing out a small card and handing it over to me, 'my business card. Ring me when the coast is clear.'

He started down the hall. 'And try not to break anything,' he called back.

•

Okay, they would be here any minute now.

I used what time I had to do a last-minute sweep of the apartment, getting familiar with its layout and where things like milk, coffee and tea were kept, cups and such for when they would want a drink. There was nothing much to it, really, the apartment was like a giant warehouse. Large, open spaces, all open living, with a lounge and a huge TV at the far end of the room. There wasn't even a bedroom, just a bed in the middle of the room. The only thing that was separate was the bathroom, which was in its own little alcove, yet still quite spacious and decked out tastefully. The whole apartment was newly renovated, fitted out with a keen eye for great craftsmanship, completely in contrast to the rest of the building.

I glanced at the clock on the wall. They were late, but then I thought of them making their way cautiously through the arcade and thought it made perfect sense that they would be late. Knowing them they would probably conduct interviews with all the members of staff before they made their way up here. Even if they did love where I lived, there would still be questions – many, many questions. What's my job, how many hours, what does it pay? Will they do school hours, won't this be too loud, don't go drinking just because you're now eighteen. Wow, eighteen. I had completely forgotten it was my birthday today. Amid all the chaos it just felt like any other day. Well, any other day that you get given a job and a place to stay handed to you on a silver platter. After my rather intense standoff with Dean last night and all the trouble I basically caused whenever I was near him, he seriously was, and it really pained me to admit this, a good person. I smiled. Oh brother, I would never, ever tell him that. I'm sure my appreciation for his character will soon wear off after a few shifts working for him.

Working?

Real-life paid work and a place to call home. Things were looking up! And just as I was coming to terms with the new life I was about to begin, and the new leaf I was about to turn over, there was a knock on the door, causing me to jump even though I'd been expecting it, clutching my already pounding heart.

Oh God.

They're here.

Suddenly giddiness overtook all my anxiety and regardless of it only being a couple of weeks since I'd seen them last, I still missed my parents like crazy.

Another knock sounded and I ran across the huge space, closing in on the door, sliding sideways as I overshot the door in haste. I laughed, clasping onto the handle, twisting and yanking it open with an air of regal flair and enthusiasm . . .

'WELCOME TO MY APARTMENT!'

Oh my God I'm going to hell.

Chapter Seventeen

I barely had a chance to breathe before I was crushed by a bear hug from my mum. 'HAPPY BIRTHDAY, my beautiful girl.'

'Thanks, Mum,' I could barely get the words out.

I kept a close eye on Mum's expression when she entered the apartment, but then my gaze shifted to a red-faced Dad, who was busying himself carrying a large box. I think he was trying to say Happy Birthday, but I don't think he had the strength to speak as he mimed with his head to open the door wider and he staggered on through.

'Oh God, Dad, put it on the table over there, before you do yourself an injury.'

I padded after him, my excitement building thinking about what could possibly be in the box. Whatever it was it was really, really heavy. I fought the urge to dance on the balls of my feet, for the first time that day I had actually felt excited about it being my birthday. My thoughts returned to my mum as she circled around the apartment, a look of awe and wonder spread across her face.

'H– how much is this place costing?' she asked.

And here it began, question one of a million and one questions, questions I didn't have the answers to.

'Ah, what's in the box?' I asked, partly because I really wanted to know but mostly because I really wanted to change the subject.

'The box is for you,' said Dad, his face having turned back to a normal colour. He swept his hand out, encouraging me to inspect.

My smile returned, wrapping my arms around him and kissing him on the cheek.

'Happy Birthday luv.'

'I wouldn't get too excited if I were you,' warned Mum, but her words fell on deaf ears as I powered forward, pulling at the cardboard flaps, exposing what lay within. I paused, my smile falling away.

You have got to be kidding me.

I blinked, confused. I lifted my eyes to my parents. 'School books?'

Seriously?

Amid all the chaos and preoccupation with finding a job and a place to stay, I really hadn't put too much thought into starting school again. My future had been so uncertain, I kind of hadn't wanted to put all my hopes into everything actually working out, but then it suddenly occurred to me. My books were here, my parents had actually brought them here, which could only mean one thing.

'So, does this mean I can stay?' I asked, my expression imploring as I looked into my mum's blue eyes. 'I know you want to ask all the questions, and draw up pros and cons lists and analyse all the data while pulling every detail apart and finding flaws in all my answers, but, please, can you just let me have this, just this once?'

Mum looked taken aback. 'Is that what you think we do? Pick apart your plans?'

My silence said it all really, and Mum looked a little hurt by it. She looked at Dad.

'I worked really hard to do all the right things. I have a job and a place to stay.'

In a dingy, cell-like room, but who needed details?

Mum smiled. 'And we're very proud of you.'

'Really?'

'Of course we are,' added Dad. 'I mean, look at this place. Jen, have you seen the view?' Dad walked towards the window. 'Honestly, I think Karen and Peter leaving is the best thing that could have happened for you,' he said.

I tried not to let guilt override the unbelievable feeling of relief, fearing the worst and hoping for the best. I took the moment to strike as Mum followed Dad out the open doors to the balcony, dreamy expressions plastered on their faces.

'You mean, you're not going to take me back to Red Hill?' I asked tentatively.

Dad spun around from his view, a little smirk lining his face. 'Now if we were going to take you home, why would we have bothered to bring your birthday present all the way here then?'

'What?'

'It took a fair bit of arranging but we brought it with us,' he said, giving Mum a knowing look.

I slowly straightened, grinning broadly at the sheer weight my dad was putting on the emphasis of his words. 'You mean aside from the books?'

Dad laughed, 'Aside from the books.'

'What is it?' I asked, eyes big.

'Let's just say it's a means to get you from A to B,' said Dad.

'Don't spoil it,' warned Mum.

'Is it here?' I asked, a little bit too loudly. My heart was thundering against my rib cage. I was eighteen. A means to get me from A to B? Could it possibly be true? Had they bought me a car for my birthday? I couldn't hold in my excitement and Mum and Dad knew it.

Mum was hopeless at keeping secrets, so before she could burst with shared excitement she gestured to the door of the apartment. 'Outside.'

Chapter Eighteen

Okay, so it was most definitely not a car.

The two-wheeled, Tiffany Blue vintage bike with cane basket strapped on the back of Mum and Dad's Pajero was definitely not what I had expected.

'The best thing about this is you don't have to put your hand in your pocket for fuel,' Dad said, unravelling the rope.

'I bet no-one in Paradise has a bike like this. She's a real beauty, but I'd store it inside your apartment, Lexie, I wouldn't trust leaving it outside,' Mum said, warily looking around as if we were hanging out on the wrong side of the tracks. All I could think about was how this was going to make things in my room, my real living quarters, very cosy.

Finally the bike was free, Dad lifting it down with a groan. 'So, do you love it?' He swept his hand along it in a 'ta-da' motion, his chest puffed out with pride, and I smiled. I did love it and I could imagine myself riding along the boardwalk, the salty sea breeze in my face. There was many a time I could have done with a bike the last time I was in Paradise. Things were definitely looking up.

'I absolutely love it!' I said beaming, and clutching the handlebars. 'It's so beautiful.' I kissed my dad on the cheek.

'I'll put it away some place safe, I'll be back in a minute.' I started rolling it towards the Wipe Out Bar.

'Wait, we're coming too,' Mum said.

I paused, glancing back in confusion. 'I thought we were going out for dinner with Aunty Karen?'

'Oh, we have plenty of time.' Mum waved off my words. 'Besides, we're not going anywhere until we meet your employer.'

Wait. What?

'S– sorry?'

'Well, I think that's fair,' nodded Dad. 'If you are going to stay here, I think it only fitting we meet with the people who we are entrusting our daughter to.'

Oh shit-shit-shit.

I cleared my throat. 'Oh, I think it's safe to say that if they employed me then they're an excellent judge of character,' I said, trying to make light of the situation.

Panic was bubbling inside, as my mind flashed to a scowly, smart-arse Dean and I was thinking he was definitely not the kind of boy you would want to bring home to meet your parents. He kind of lacked the social graces most people have and I didn't know if he could be trusted not to blow my elaborate cover. Although he had been really good to me in the last twenty-four hours, I couldn't deny that.

My parents were giving me 'this is non-negotiable' stares and considering everything had gone surprisingly well thus far, I thought it best to meet them halfway.

Oh God, Dean was going to be so pissed, I thought, as I reached in my pocket and felt the sharp corner of his business card.

'Okay, but then can we get going back to Aunty Karen's? I would kind of like to spend some time with Amanda before she goes.' As far as lies went, that was the biggest one I had told to date.

•

'What?' came the rather blunt response from the phone. I smiled at my parents from the kitchen as I turned my back to mask my face.

'My parents want to meet you,' I repeated.

There was a long pause on the other end of the line, so long I thought he might have dropped the receiver and bolted, but then he finally spoke. 'I don't do parents.'

No shit, Sherlock, this wasn't my idea.

'Look, you're not seeking permission for my hand in marriage, they just want to make sure that the person who's in charge here isn't a whacko.'

'And you still want me to meet them. Are you sure?' he asked, amusement in his voice.

'Of course I'm not, but my mum isn't one to take no for an answer.'

'Ah, so that's where you get it from? Like mother like daughter.' Dean chuckled.

I straightened my spine. 'What do you mean?'

'Never mind. Listen, I have better things to do than cater to your constant demands.'

'Well, I am telling you right now, they won't be leaving until they meet you and that means sitting in your apartment drinking infinite amounts of your expensive coffee.'

I didn't have to imagine too hard the thunderous look on Dean's face. He was right. I had been under his roof for two seconds and I was already proving to be extremely high maintenance. With each favour I asked I just knew I was digging myself into a deeper and deeper hole, and that somehow, in some way, he was going to call back the favour, and owing Dean anything bloody scared me.

A weary sigh came down the line. 'You have five minutes of my time, and then you get them out of my apartment. Is that clear?'

'Crystal. Where are you? Do you want me to meet you in your office or –'

'I'll come to you.' The phone went dead. He had said it like a threat, one that made my skin feel all goosebumpy.

Yep, he was definitely not happy.

•

Waiting for Dean was like battening down the hatches for an impending hurricane. You knew it was coming but there was no real way of knowing how destructive the path might be. He had been charming enough to my aunty and uncle in the past. Would he deliberately try to make me squirm in front of my parents? As far as birthdays were concerned, this was by far the most stressful. Weren't eighteenth birthdays meant to be special? Welcome to the new world of special. There now always seemed to be an element of unexpectedness in my life, a constant not knowing. My thoughts were interrupted by the loud knocking on the apartment door.

Oh God.

My mum looked up expectantly from her position sitting lazily at the table on the balcony. 'That will be Mr Saville,' she announced.

Hearing Mum call him that seemed so wrong. It was as though she was expecting a balding, big-bellied man with oily skin and pants belted underneath his armpits to walk through the door, sniffing and pawing at his sweat-stained singlet that had bolognaise sauce down the front from his dinner the night before.

'His name is Dean,' I corrected, getting up from the table and making my way across the long stretch of the apartment towards the door, my heart pounding so loudly I was sure he could hear it through the thick wooden panelling. Taking a breath to calm myself, I opened the door.

There, standing before me, expressionless, was Dean, in his usual black t-shirt exposing the long line of intricately curved tattoos trailing down his right arm. He towered over me, his thumb casually hooked in a belt loop of his dark denim jeans. Obviously not one for any airs or graces even when meeting parents, and this would have worried me if I hadn't noticed a very clear difference. Dean was freshly shaven. His aftershave hit me first then the realisation that his dishevelled stubble from before was gone and his chiselled jawline was now smooth and clean. I don't think I'd ever seen him freshly shaven like this. He seemed so young, so innocent ... well, that was until a cocky eyebrow lifted and any thought of him being innocent went straight out the door and flew over the balcony. I saw the mischievous spark in Dean's eyes. There was nothing innocent about him, not by a long shot. His small smirk that lifted the corner of his mouth said as much.

'Can I come in?' he asked. It was then I knew he aimed to torture me in front of my parents, and there was nothing I could do about it. Because slamming the door now was not an option.

'You must be Dean?' my mother asked politely.

Dean's expression morphed into something unrecognisable. It was lighter and more carefree and I frowned at the unexpectedness of it.

'You must be Mrs Atkinson?' he replied, reaching out his hand, causing me to step aside.

'Please, call me Jen. This is my husband, Rick.' Mum turned her attention to Dad, who had reluctantly moved himself away from his comfy position on the balcony.

'We can't thank you enough for employing Lexie.'

Oh God. I cringed.

'Lexie was a worthy candidate, and I'm sure she will bring a lot to our team.' Dean nodded his head, his hands on his hips as if he was a PE coach addressing a sports team on the field. 'I have to say, Lexie, I really love what you've done with the place.' Dean looked around as if he was totally amazed by the space, as if seeing it for the first time.

Smart-arse.

'It's an impressive space,' added Dad.

'Best views in town,' agreed Dean. 'Have you been in town long?' Dean guided my parents back onto the balcony, beginning to point out the city view layout like an astronomer viewing the night sky, captivating my parents with such charm you thought it might have made me feel at ease, but it didn't. Not one bit.

Mum broke away from their conversation long enough to subtly mime a drink with her hand and a nod towards Dean.

Oh shit, yep, I was going to be awesome working in hospitality.

'Dean, would you like a drink?' I asked politely.

Dean broke away mid-conversation from my dad, glancing over at me as if seeing me for the first time. 'Thanks. Coffee, black.'

Like his soul I thought, smiling politely.

'Anyone else?'

Mum and Dad respectably declined, which was of no surprise after my disastrous efforts last time. Note to self: turn the bloody kettle on.

Chapter Nineteen

Laughter – loud, genuine . . . and sickening.

Who was this creature before me? Dean was polite, warm and, dare I say it, charming. I didn't have to worry. He was expertly easing my parents into letting me stay here because they believed he wasn't a whacko. How wrong could they be, I thought. I hid my smile, sipping my cup of tea. To my relief my parents' million questions were now being fired at Dean, questions that he answered without hesitation, even though I was sure he was making up half of the answers.

Mercifully, Dean managed the old 'look at the time, I best excuse myself while I tend to some important manager duties' announcement, which prompted Mum and Dad into scurrying into a panic about heading to Aunty Karen's.

We all walked Dean to the door, which felt a bit weird and over the top, and having zoned in and out of the praises and thank yous to Dean for giving their daughter a means to survive, their next question threw me completely.

'I hope you don't mind if we crash the night at Lexie's, Dean? My sister and her family are leaving in the morning and you can't so much as breathe at her house.'

Wait. What?

Dean's smiley, carefree facade froze as he stood in the doorway.

'Um, Mum, I haven't officially moved in yet,' I said.

'Well, they are leaving tomorrow, when were you planning to? Karen won't have time to bring you over with your things, and we could organise it tonight, if that's okay with you, Dean?'

'It's only one bedroom,' I interjected, panic spiking inside me as Dean's five minutes was morphing into a twenty-four-hour period in HIS apartment.

I was never going to hear the end of this.

Dean, for once, didn't have an immediate response to Mum's question. His reply came slower and his expression was more a grimace than a smile. 'You can stay in my office if you like? It's nothing fancy but there's a sofa bed and a mini fridge, you can even make a cuppa.'

'Sounds better than most shearing quarters I've stayed in,' said Dad with a laugh.

Dean smiled. 'Well, you're more than welcome.'

This must be really killing him. This may in fact kill me.

'Thanks, Dean, that's really kind of you, seeing as the thought of us staying in Lexie's massive apartment seems so unsavoury to her.' Mum gave me a pointed look and I just wanted to die. I wanted to be wrapped in plastic and at Aunty Karen's, making sure I didn't touch anything.

'Have you got your things with you? Bring them up now and settle in if you want. We'll get the room ready for you.' Dean glanced at me then back to my parents, his friendliness back in place.

'Thank you, Dean, good idea.'

'Yeah, thanks, mate, it will save us on a hotel room in peak season.' Dad slapped Dean on the back of the shoulder on the way out the door. I closed my eyes. Dad was always watching the budget – could he be any more embarrassing?

'No problem at all. Do you need any help?'

'Nah, we'll be right, we pack light. Well,' Dad glanced towards Mum, who was already out the door and walking down the hall to the staircase, 'I do anyway,' he said with a wink.

Dean and Dad shared a silent, knowing look, one that said, 'Ha! Women.' I had seen that look plenty of times before between men.

Dean and I stood in the doorway, watching as my parents made their way along the hall and down the stairs. I was ready to let out a sigh of relief and congratulate Dean on an Academy Award–winning performance when I felt him grab my arm and yank me into the room, slamming the door behind me, with my back pushed up against the door.

'What the fuck, Lexie?' Dean growled. Gone was all the humour and lightheartedness from moments before. Instead, there was now a steely, murderous gaze that bore down on me, one that I met dead on and unblinking. I had been all ready to kiss his feet for doing such a stellar job of convincing my parents that despite the rough exterior of the Wipe Out Bar, I was in good hands.

'Hey, I didn't invite them to stay, it was your suggestion to get them to stay in your office. I tried to get them to leave.'

'Not good enough,' he said, stepping back from the door and walking away, running his hands through his hair as if the weight of the world was on his shoulders.

'Don't blame me just because you're a charming bastard.' The words fell out before I had a chance to stop them, before I had a chance to open the door and run in the opposite direction, but it was too late.

Dean turned slowly, his narrowed, questioning eyes fixing on me before a slow, devilish smile lined his face. 'So you think I'm charming?'

I rolled my eyes. 'Trust you to take *that* from what I said.'

He shrugged. 'Everything else you say just sounds like high-pitched ringing in my ears.'

My brows lowered. 'You're such an arsehole.'

'I thought I was a bastard?'

'I thought you didn't listen?'

Dean's eyes sparked with amusement, as if he was enjoying my anger. He crossed the floor, then reached for the handle.

'Come on, we better get Mummy and Daddy set up for their slumber party.' His words were laced with sarcasm.

'Wow, if only they knew what you were really like,' I scoffed.

Dean paused, looking down on me, his eyes burning, a crooked smirk tilting his mouth, a mouth I tried not to look at as I lifted my chin.

'Do you want them to know the real me?' he said, leaning in, his voice all smoky and suggestive.

'No!' I blurted out, before clearing my throat in an effort to appear casual and completely unfrazzled by the fact his aftershave was still strong, and his eyes seemed almost luminous in the light streaming in from the balcony. A hot wind blew in from the sea, swaying the loose wave of his brown hair. I shook my head. 'Does anyone know the real you?' I asked, mainly to myself but he heard, I could tell by the way his expression changed – his brows lifted in surprise.

'And who are you, Lexie Atkinson? Are you a badass independent woman or a shy, mousey school girl looking for Mummy and Daddy's approval so you can stay and play with all the cool kids?'

I breathed out a laugh. 'You don't know a thing about me.'

Dean burst out laughing, the sound so loud and foreign I blinked, his sternness all but melted away by the lightness in him now as he looked back at me, twisting the door handle to open. 'Ditto, kiddo, ditto.'

•

Creepy monitors switched off, paperwork cleared from the desk and the foldout couch set up, Mum and Dad were as happy as clams in their free-room-for-a-night. For me, it was just bloody awkward as I left them to get ready for dinner and headed back to my fake apartment. Dean, who had managed his own amount of fakeness with my parents, didn't hold back on the deep scowl he threw me behind their backs as he headed down the stairs. It was a none-too-subtle you owe me, big time. And no doubt I did. As the day went on my hole was getting dug, deeper and deeper. I envisioned working twelve-hour shifts, seven days a week, shovelling coal into a fiery pit in the basement or whatever other kinds of hideous things my boss could think of. Actually, being Dean's personal slave was the worst thing I could imagine and after all the favours he'd done me, I was seriously worried about what I'd have to do in return.

Happy freakin' birthday, Lexie.

Chapter Twenty

One thing that I did get great pleasure from was seeing the look on Amanda's face when Mum and Dad talked about my impressive new apartment and job slinging drinks at the Wipe Out Bar. I reckon I could have cracked an egg and cooked it on her forehead she was so mad. I also knew she was thinking I was full of shit, which I kind of was in some ways.

'The Wipe Out Bar? Amanda, isn't that the place you submitted your résumé to?' Aunty Karen's brow crinkled in wonder as she spooned out some sweet and sour pork onto her plate and returned it to the Lazy Susan.

My eyes shifted to Amanda, who had gone a deeper shade of purple as she glowered at her mother. Amanda had applied for a job at the Wipe Out Bar?

Well, this is awkward.

'I wouldn't want to work in that dive anyway. Lucy said she quit because Dean was a psycho.'

Mum's and Dad's heads snapped up in unison from their combination chow meins. I inwardly prayed for restraint, as I really wanted to reach over the table and smash Amanda's face into her special fried rice.

'Dean? Why, he seems lovely. Isn't he lovely, Lexie?' Mum turned to me, her eyes pleading. She didn't want her only daughter to be working for a psycho. But lovely and Dean were not two words that ever went together in the same sentence.

I twisted the fork in my noodles. 'He has been very good to me,' I admitted truthfully.

Amanda snorted. 'I bet he has.'

My instant response was to kick her in the shin, resulting in an *oomph* and a scowl.

The last thing I needed was for my parents to be fed innuendos about my new boss. Oh God, the more I thought about the fact that Dean Saville was going to be my manager, with the authority to boss me around, the more it made me want to vomit. In fact, the thought of returning to the Wipe Out Bar tonight with my parents in tow made me feel ill. The morning couldn't come soon enough. Mum, Dad: as much as I've loved seeing you, it's definitely time to go.

•

It was late by the time we got to the Wipe Out Bar. The sign was still aglow out front but luckily it didn't have the same crazy dance party vibe or Dean throwing out some drunken creep; instead, Cassie was shutting down the bar, something that I would no doubt be learning how to do in time. My stomach did a little backflip just thinking about what my new existence was going to be like working here. If I just blocked out the minor detail of Dean being my boss, the thought had me . . . excited.

Mum yawned. 'What a day,' she said, as we took the stairs all the way up to the landing, pausing before Dean's office door leading to my parents' makeshift hotel room. Mum turned and cupped my cheeks. 'Happy Birthday, baby, did you enjoy dinner?'

'Yeah, I did.'

'Chinese, your favourite,' said Dad.

I didn't have the heart to tell him my favourite food was Mexican.

'We'll see you in the morning.' Mum kissed me on the head.

'Night,' I said, hugging and kissing them both. Feeling the warmth of their arms around me made me feel guilty for wishing them away. I thought now that maybe it would have been nice to have them stay around for a few days. Of course, that thought quickly slipped away when I found myself tiptoeing past a particular door, a door to what would eventually be my room – the dusty, dank, small room where Dean was forced to sleep tonight, something he'd made me painfully aware of earlier in the evening when he'd taken the key to his apartment off his key chain and slammed it on the bar for me as I waited for my parents to come down for dinner. Creeping past the door, the last thing I wanted to do was wake the beast.

I inserted the key into the lock, turning it slowly until I heard the magical click then I pushed inside. The first thing that hit me was a cool breeze from the opened doors. Dean never seemed to have them closed. He obviously didn't worry about people climbing up the guttering and getting into his apartment. Although thinking about it, the rusty, dodgy guttering would not hold a fully grown human.

Even though the sun had set hours ago, a glow still penetrated through the open balcony doors – orange and red lights from street lamps and the amusement park further in the distance. The dark stretch of the ocean was the perfect backdrop to the flashing, vibrant theme park. Curved wrought iron lamps lit the way to the domed old-fashioned building that served as a gateway into the park, but what stood out most was the light pink hues of the Ferris wheel, shining bright and beautiful. I could have stood there and soaked up the view all night, and watched the people down below. Even this late the area still buzzed with excitement, fuelled, no doubt, by alcohol. The distant boom of music from another local establishment pounded in the night and carried on the breeze along with the traffic and the shouted hollers of people in search of a good time. I smiled, thinking of how Dean would sit up here every night, staring down from the shadows as he people-watched and took in his surrounds, watching on as the townspeople went along their merry way around his kingdom. The vantage point would have been right up his alley, but unlike the people who skirted around like ants below, my eyes kept lifting to stare at the Ferris wheel, slowly turning and flashing. It was hypnotic.

'It's better in the night, don't you think?'

I jumped, yelping at the unexpectedness of Dean's voice behind me. I spun around, seeing the unmistakeable silhouette of him leaning casually in the balcony's doorframe.

'Bloody hell, Dean, don't do that!' I yelled, clutching my heart.

He chuckled from the dark, probably something that should sound unnerving but all it wanted to make me do was punch him in the face. He moved closer to stand beside me.

'What are you doing here?' I asked.

Dean did a double-take. 'I live here.'

'I– I thought you were sleeping in the other room.'

Dean breathed out a laugh. 'I'm not sleeping in there,' he said, peeling himself away from the balcony and heading back inside.

I followed him, hoping maybe he was going to just grab some PJs or something and head back to his room, or my room, while I slept in his room.

'What's wrong with that room? I'll be sleeping in it.' I had this sudden fear that maybe there was a family of rodents living in there.

Dean opened the fridge, grabbed a bottle of water and twisted off the lid. He took a big gulp, smacking his lips together in appreciation. 'So, did the birthday girl make a wish before she blew out all her candles?'

I folded my arms. 'There was no cake.'

Dean paused before sipping. 'What? Eighteen and no cake?'

I shrugged. 'I guess amid all the madness, they kind of forgot.'

'That's bullshit.'

I smiled. 'I didn't take you for a traditionalist.'

'Some things are sacred,' he said, before tossing the empty bottle into the bin. 'Night, Lexie,' Dean announced, brushing past me with a knowing smirk and heading towards the bathroom.

'Wait, where are you going?' I asked a bit too quickly.

Dean turned with interest. 'To brush my teeth. Oral hygiene is very important, Lexie,' he said, before stepping into the bathroom and closing the door behind him. I heard the tap going and I inhaled a steadying breath. Of course he would be brushing his teeth – this is where his toothbrush is. He would simply get ready for bed and then head back to the bed he was meant to be sleeping in. We hadn't come this far to take the chance of Dean being spotted coming from my supposed apartment at some ungodly hour. I really didn't need my parents thinking I was screwing Dean Saville.

The running water in the sink stopped, which had me stepping quickly into motion. I ran to the bed, casually sitting on the edge of it as a means to lamely stake my claim as I worked on taking off my shoes one at a time and setting them aside before pulling out my ponytail and unravelling it to flow long over my shoulders. The relief of my fingers massaging along my scalp felt like heaven and I was suddenly aware of how bone tired I was. Never could I have believed it would come to this, me sitting on the edge of Dean Saville's bed.

I inadvertently gasped as I heard the bathroom door open.

Chapter Twenty-One

Instead of bidding me goodnight and heading out the front door without so much as a backward glance, he headed directly towards the bed, a wry smile on his lips. He was delighting in making me feel uncomfortable, and, oh, how I squirmed as he came to stand at the end of the bed, casually undoing his belt buckle and shucking off his shoes.

'W– what are you doing?' I asked, my eyes wide.

Dean looked down at me as if English wasn't his first language. 'What does it look like I'm doing?' he replied, peeling his t-shirt from back to front over his head in the way that boys do. And, oh my God, the muted lighting in the apartment lit him up perfectly, the toned indentations along his stomach that I kind of wanted to run my fingers along, the hypnotic twists of the black ink along his smooth skin. He wasn't deeply tanned like your typical Paradise local, as he spent more time indoors peering at monitors, but there was something very raw about Dean, something almost animalistic about the way he held himself, in the way he moved around a space. He stalked around his bar like a jungle cat. He was different, exotic almost. I watched the rise and fall of his bare chest, his stone-like expression staring down at me as he casually twisted the shirt in his hands and threw it aside to hit the back of a chair. Looking up at him, there was one thing that came to mind as I stared at his body in the half light. Dean was *sexy*, whether I liked it or not. I had to admit, Dean Saville was something worth looking at.

I swallowed. I'd been staring for too long. Shit. 'What, here?' I asked, a bit panicked, my eyes shifting to the bed I sat on.

Dean cocked his brow. 'Well, it *is* my bed,' he said, his hand confidently reaching for his belt.

'Okay, okay.' I held up my hand, turning my head. 'You win. I'll go sleep in the other room.' I moved to stand, keeping my eyes averted as I went to walk towards the door, only to be stopped as Dean's hand snaked around my upper arm.

'Whoa, hold on a sec,' he said.

My attention moved from where he held my arm, up onto his face. He was looking at me intently, as if he wanted to say something, but then he finally blinked. 'Take the bed, I'll sleep on the couch,' he said, slowly lowering his hand from me, a hand that seemed forever to be encircled around my upper arm, pushing and pulling me in all directions. I was sure the heat of it was permanently branded on my skin.

'But what if my parents –'

'We lock the door,' he said matter-of-factly, as if it were simple, and I guess it was really.

'So you really don't want to sleep in that room?'

Dean shook his head. 'I don't much fancy confined spaces.'

'Is that why you keep your balcony doors open?' It was a question that simply slipped out, and yet I was still very much interested in the answer.

'Maybe it is,' he said, breaking away and heading towards the plush leather couch. 'Good night, Lexie.' He said it with no enthusiasm. He didn't even look at me as he peeled a throw rug off the back of the couch and punched a scatter cushion into the shape of a pillow.

'Night,' I said, turning away as I heard him peel the denim off one leg at a time. I moved to rummage through my bag, distracting myself from thinking too much about Dean being merely metres away and only partially clothed. Grabbing my toiletries bag and nightie, I glanced over, seeing only a lumpy shadow on the couch. I couldn't see him but no doubt he could see me. I clutched my possessions to my chest and quietly padded my way towards the bathroom, closing the door and snipping the lock behind me. Only then could I give myself permission to let my shoulders sag in relief as I set my back against the door, thinking how incredibly surreal this moment was. If anyone had told me that upon coming back to Paradise City I was going to be selling my soul to the devil and be sleeping in his bed, I wouldn't have believed it – no way, no how.

I brushed my teeth, cleansed, toned and moisturised my face, entwined my hair into a topknot bun and nodded at myself in the mirror with a sense of finality. Time for bed.

Dean's bed.

In Dean's apartment.

With Dean.

I shook the thoughts from my head. There was no need to obsess about the details.

I opened the bathroom door and the light spilt into the room. I quickly clicked the switch off, realising that the only light now in the room was that of a bedside lamp. My eyes blinked, adjusting to the change and quickly trying to fathom what else had changed, and then it was obvious to me. The doors to the balcony had been closed and the blinds drawn, plunging the room into darkness.

Could he see me lingering uncertainly near the door?

I used the lamp light like a beacon. Making a beeline for it, I quickly turned it off, plunging the room into such complete blackness that spots in my vision danced. It was so dark, thick and suffocating, I could feel my heart racing as I scrambled to peel back the covers and lay under the sheets.

I was in Dean Saville's bed, the soft black sheets that smelt like crisp linen, which kind of disappointed me because I expected them to smell like his aftershave.

I tried not to think how weird this was, that lying in the dark just over there was Dean. I would simply just let sleep claim me . . . but it didn't. Instead, what felt like hours passed with me tossing and turning, sighing, punching the pillow, and then the worst thing happened: my mind started to wander, and the questions started to build up and before I knew it I rolled onto my side staring into the blackness, towards the direction of Dean's couch. Only the sounds of the city, sirens and traffic still audible through the thick glass could be heard but apart from that I heard no snoring, no shifting from Dean, just darkness and silence.

'Dean?'

'Mmm,' came the sleepy reply.

'Why did you give me a job?'

The leather couch creaked as he shifted. 'Whaaat?' he groaned, as if it was an overly complicated question.

I hitched myself onto my elbow. 'Why did you change your mind?'

Dean sighed, weary. 'Do not ask me questions.'

'But I want to know.'

'If I tell you will you go to sleep?'

'Yes.'

Maybe.

More silence. It went on for so long I thought he wouldn't answer, and then he spoke. 'I guess my black heart has a gooey centre after all.'

I waited for him to continue but he didn't. 'Is that it?'

'Yes, now go to sleep.'

Never a simple answer, I thought, as I spun around, punching my pillow in frustration and staring off into the opposite side of blackness.

'Lexie?'

I spun around expectantly, thinking maybe he had decided to elaborate. 'Yes?'

'No funny business, okay? I'm feeling rather vulnerable.'

I stifled a giggle, grabbing my pillow and turfing it towards him, having no real way of knowing if it was even anywhere near close to hitting him. The only indication I'd hit my target was the chuckle that pierced through the black. 'Night, Lexie.'

'Good. Night,' I said, rolling onto my side and tucking myself into the sheets. I closed my eyes with a smile creasing my lips.

'Lexie?'

'What?'

'Happy Birthday.'

Chapter Twenty-Two

It was still dark out when I felt the warmth against me, the feel of lips softly pressed against my shoulder as I stirred from my sleep. I turned to see Dean's face hovering above mine, his eyes full of promise, his smile curved knowingly.

'I can't sleep,' he whispered against the lobe of my ear, nipping playfully, my fuzzy thoughts stirring to life as other parts of my body did the same.

Breathing was hard, thinking was hard, and oh God . . . he was hard! I felt him push against me as he cupped my chin, turning my head to the side so that his lips were close to mine.

'What are you going to do?' I breathed out, my heart drumming fiercely as excitement coursed through my body, barely believing this was happening.

Dean smiled slow and wicked as his eyes traced along the lines of my face.

'First, I'm going to start from here.' He popped the top button of my nightie, followed by a second and a third. 'It's going to be slow,' his hand slid down my exposed stomach before gripping the elastic edge of my panties, 'and then hard,' he whispered against my now gasping mouth. I felt his fingers delve beyond the delicate pink bow of my undies and push inside me, eliciting a deep groan from me. Dean smiled against my lips. 'And very, very . . . thorough.'

•

BANG-BANG-BANG!

My body jolted awake at the foreign sound, the sound of insistent knocking at the apartment door.

'Lexie, wake up!' Mum's voice yelled through the door. 'Oh, Rick, it's locked, why would she lock it?' Mum's voice rang out like a shrill nightmare as her and Dad argued in the hall while rattling the door handle in a bid to get in.

'Lexie, open up!'

Oh shit, oh shit, oh shit.

I sat up in bed, still hot and flustered from my mortifying dream. That's right – a dream. It was just a dream, I reasoned with myself, fighting desperately to get my bearings. Looking around, just to be sure, there was definitely no Dean in my bed; I looked down to see the buttons of my nightie all perfectly aligned and together. I breathed a calming breath.

Just a dream.

I dived out of bed, scurrying towards the couch to wake Dean, but it was empty, cushions aligned and the throw rug perfectly folded. I spun around, expecting him to be watching my rather rude awakening with amusement, but he was nowhere to be seen.

'Lexie, come on! Karen and Peter will be waiting to say goodbye,' Dad's voice rang out.

I blinked, sweeping wisps of hair from my eyes. Had I dreamed that Dean was here last night?

'Coming,' I called.

Unlocking the door, I prepared myself for the onslaught of nervous mania that was always present with any farewell, and today would be twice as bad, because it was going to be a double farewell. Goodbye to Aunty Karen and Uncle Peter, and goodbye to Mum and Dad. Double the tears, double the emotion. Was it wrong that I simply wanted to guide them quickly to their cars and wave them bon voyage? Only then did I feel like I could take a breather, start my life working and settling into where I was supposed to be. I could feel my gut twist every time I thought about it.

Dean was nowhere in sight; I hadn't even heard him leave this morning, and he had made himself deliberately scarce, much to my mum's dismay.

'Oh, we wanted to thank him for his hospitality, he seems like such a nice young man.'

'He has his moments,' I mumbled under my breath as we descended the stairs. I was ever watchful in case he appeared from somewhere, but he didn't and I was quite relieved, and I escorted my parents from the Wipe Out Bar towards awkward, sobbing farewells.

•

Ugh! Of course Lucy would be here. Why did I ever doubt that she would? Considering she was about to lose her BFF, she didn't seem too upset about it. In fact, she looked almost giddy, whispering and giggling with Amanda on the kerb as Aunty Karen and Uncle Peter packed the car. I tore my murderous gaze from them.

Freaks.

'So, Lexie, we have some pretty exciting news for you.' Aunty Karen's heels clicked against the concrete. 'Or has Amanda told you?'

'Told me what?'

Maybe she was back with Boon?

'Well, she had to do some convincing,' Aunty Karen glanced at Uncle Peter who was too busy poring over a road map with Dad, trying to work out the best route to take, 'but Amanda is going to stay in Paradise for a while.'

'WHAT?'

'Oh, that's wonderful!' chimed Mum. 'I can't tell you how much of a relief that is to me, knowing you girls will be there for each other.'

'Sorry, what?' I turned to Mum, bemused by what was going on. 'What about the family that's renting your house?' I asked Aunty Karen.

'Oh, that will still happen, but Amanda is going to stay with Lucy. I'm no fool; I mean, I was young once too. And they might as well get all their partying out of their systems before uni starts, right?' Aunty Karen winked at Lucy like she was one of the gang. It made me want to be sick.

'We'll look out for each other, Mrs Atkinson. We can hang out and have movie nights at your apartment, Lexie,' smiled Lucy sweetly.

This was bad news. Paradise was just not big enough for the three of us. The one thing I had been looking forward to the most was waving Amanda goodbye and never having to put up with Lucy again. Although how hard could it be to avoid them? I'd be at school and they wouldn't. And it was not like we had to be under the same roof now.

'Can we go now?' I asked impatiently, thinking never in my right mind did I ever assume I would look forward to heading back to the Wipe Out Bar, that it would become my place of refuge.

How quickly things could change.

•

After watching my parents' Pajero become a speck in the distance, swallowed up by the city traffic, my fake smile slowly evaporated as I spun on my heel and stormed my way through Arcadia Lane. No longer did I feel like a timid farm girl excusing herself through the mass of sunburnt, pudgy tourists with knee-high socks, bum bags and Canon cameras hanging around their necks, I simply pushed past the hordes, ignoring the screaming, misbehaving kids who were chucking tantrums over wanting an ice-cream. None of it made me even blink, because I was afraid if I took my focus off the very direction I was headed that I would lose it. I was actually relieved to see the Wipe Out Bar up ahead, the imposing double-storeyed faded structure on the corner was now something I strode towards instead of fought against.

Home sweet home.

•

My finger traced the dripping line of condensation against my glass. I sat at the bar, my chin resting on my palm. I had tried to ring Laura to tell her my good news – that I was still very much here and ready to take Paradise by storm, but in typical Laura style she never answered. Never had I felt more alone, more disenchanted. I thought once I got my independence I'd feel better, but I didn't. I just felt alone. And just as the misery was ready to consume me, a pink little carton was placed on the bar in front of me. My eyes flicked up to see Dean standing behind the bar.

I took in the handsome line of his jaw, those eyes that were always looking at you like he was ready to devour you. A girl would have to be blind not to appreciate his appeal. I didn't even want to know how many notches he had on his bed post. My gaze shifted warily from his boyish smirk to the little pink box.

'What's this?' I asked, straightening on my bar stool and looking rather sceptically at the frosted pink box tied with a silky white ribbon. I studied it as if it were about to explode.

'Open it,' he said.

I tentatively unlaced the white ribbon that was holding the box closed. I was thankful for the distraction as my mind flashed back to my dream the night before. I quickly shook the images from my head and concentrated on the task at hand.

'Diamonds?' I suggested, raising a small smile.

'Better,' he said.

I opened the box to look inside. 'What is this?'

Dean rolled his eyes. 'A puppy. What do you think it is?'

I reached in, carefully picking up the most beautiful, delicious-looking cupcake, a smile spreading wide across my face, my mouth instantly salivating as I admired sugar-laden perfection.

'White buttermilk cupcake with pineapple filling and cream cheese frosting,' Dean said as I peered at it from all angles.

'Definitely better than diamonds,' I said, grinning from ear to ear. It was then I noticed a circular sticker on the side of the carton that read *Paradise Cakes.*

'Where is this magical place and why have I never been there?'

Dean looked at me like I was crazy. 'Paradise Cakes? It's a national treasure down on the boardwalk.'

I winced as I licked the frosting from my fingers, not from the taste of the creamy, sugary treat but from a rather embarrassing admission. 'I've never been down to the boardwalk,' I said, shrugging.

Dean paused, still smirking as his eyes studied me, waiting for me to say, 'Just kidding.' But I was deadly serious and now he really knew I was. Dean frowned, disbelief lighting his face. 'You have never been down the boardwalk?' he repeated.

'Nurvurh,' I managed through a mouthful of cupcake.

'Oh, hell, no,' he said, scooping up the empty carton and turfing it in the bin.

'Hey!' I protested, 'I wanted to keep that.'

Dean walked a long, sweeping line around the bar to stand directly next to me.

I swallowed my mouthful. 'What?'

'Eat up.'

'W– why?'

'I can't have you not knowing what makes this city tick. We're going down to the boardwalk.'

I almost choked on my cupcake. 'What, now?'

'Got anything better to do?'

I thought about it. I thought about the feeling I had had a moment before and now all of a sudden I had a purpose. I'd always wanted to go down to the boardwalk, but only ever ventured as far as the beach where the surfers were. It was also my chance to get Dean away from the Wipe Out Bar and get some answers. He seemed to be in a rather jovial mood and I wanted to take advantage of it.

'What are we waiting for?'

Chapter Twenty-Three

It was a strange thing walking in the sun; the boardwalk was awash with colour, life and laughter and here I was beside Dean, dressed in his usual black jeans and black t-shirt, looking nothing like sunshine and happiness. He was completely not suited for this, and by the pained look on his face he certainly didn't enjoy it. I wasn't exactly feeling it either, after last night, but it was definitely better than sitting in the gloomy Wipe Out Bar with too much time on my hands. There was hope that at least I would start work soon and that would help, and until then, this was perfect.

I laughed, actually laughed.

'What?'

I shook my head. 'Cakes, impromptu visit to the boardwalk. It's true. Your black heart does have a gooey, soft centre, Dean Saville.'

Dean scoffed. 'Bullshit.'

I spun around to walk backwards so as to watch him squirm. 'Putting a roof over my head, giving me a job, helping convince my parents they could leave me in Paradise. Admit it, Dean, you are a nice person.'

'I wouldn't get too carried away, you haven't started work yet,' he said.

'How bad could it be?' I asked, turning around so I could see the crowd become thicker as we neared the main attraction. The boarded walkway for pedestrians overlooking the beach was swarming with people. If Dean had replied, I hadn't heard him. Instead, I was too focused on my surrounds – the distant screams from the amusement park, vendors with delicious-smelling treats from their carts, artists drawing cartoons of tourists and face painters for the kids. I licked my lips, remembering the juicy chunk of pineapple when I had taken a bite of the fluffy, light cupcake.

'Where's Paradise Cakes?'

Dean laughed. 'So I'm guessing you liked it?'

It was then it occurred to me that I hadn't even said thanks.

I smiled, squinting against the sun and looking up at Dean who was a good foot taller than me.

'Liked? I loved it! What's the occasion? Happy first day on the job? Does every employee get one when they start?'

'No. It was more along the lines of a belated birthday cake you never got for your eighteenth.'

It was a thoughtful gesture based simply on my rather sooky admission that no-one had thought to provide a cake for my eighteenth. I felt like such a diva now. As always, things seemed to revolve around me and now I just felt embarrassed I had mentioned anything at all, although it did score me the most amazing cake I had ever tasted in my life, so there was that to be thankful for.

'It was worth the wait,' I said. 'Thank you.'

'Yeah, well, we will definitely go with that. If the other staff find out they'll all want one,' he said, walking on, plunging his hands in his pockets as he glanced out over the beach.

Silence fell between us, but it wasn't awkward. It only became awkward when he asked the next question.

'So, are you homesick already or are you pining for my baby brother?'

We walked up to lean on the railing overlooking the pristine, silken sand of the beach speckled with sun-tanners, a family playing cricket and young teenage girls in bikinis flirting with the edge of the waves, squealing as the water lapped up too high and they ran away, then back again. We rested our elbows on the top barrier, Dean flicking his Ray Bans on as he looked out over the beach. I wished he hadn't. I really wanted to see his expression when I told him what I was about to. I gripped the railing, taking in a lungful of salty sea air as I turned to him.

'Well, I'm definitely not homesick.' I selected my words carefully, churning them around in my head before voicing them, something I didn't tend to do much.

Dean didn't say a word, he simply waited, and watched, his silence urging me to continue.

'And as for Ballantine . . . well, that didn't end so well.'

Dean turned, pressing his back onto the railing and resting his elbows as he took in the view of the boardwalk. 'Yeah, Ballantine's always been sensitive.'

'Were you two ever close?' I asked. Shielding my eyes from the sun, I watched the wind shift his thick hair in the breeze. Depending on the direction of the wind, I would get a hint of his aftershave. I looked at Dean, trying to figure him out.

Are you bad or good? A sinner or a saint?

I really wanted to believe that he was good, that above all, inside he really was about being good. I mean, he was giving out cupcakes, come on.

Dean sighed. 'Why do I feel like you want me to lie on a leather couch and confess my fucked-up childhood?'

'Was it fucked up?'

Dean flicked back his sunnies, his eyes flashing. 'I love it when you talk dirty.'

I rolled my eyes. 'Answer the question,' I said. I could feel the butterflies in my stomach. I had never seen Dean so unguarded before, so open. Maybe it was the feel of the sun streaming across us, or the fresh salty wind against our faces, but I thought that if I kept him talking, I would have an insight into why Ballantine had done what he'd done, and why he'd left.

Dean smiled lightly. 'We had different childhoods,' he began. 'Mum had me when she was really young: seventeen? She fell in love with a handsome bar owner who had a passion for women and the horses, and all the things in between.'

'Your dad.'

'Mick Saville, by all accounts, a terrible husband, but he was a great father.' Dean looked at me when he spoke, as if it was important for me to believe it. 'He was no angel, but he tried, and he raised me when my mum couldn't. Dad took care of me, brought in nannies while Mum went and finished her Ph.D, even though they weren't together he still did it, he took care of what belonged to him.'

'So you grew up at the Wipe Out Bar?'

'Yep, I'd walk down Arcadia Lane with my school bag, hop on the bus and off to school I would go. I soon got jack of that, dropped out in Year Ten and started running the business fulltime.'

The plot thickened; this was how he had acquired the bar at such a young age. He was born into it.

'Did you always want to be a businessman?'

Dean laughed. 'Never. I was always dreaming of being someplace else, to travel, with the least amount of responsibility as possible.' Dean looked far away, as if he was still dreaming of being someplace else.

'So your mum remarried?'

Dean snapped out of his daydream, shaking his head. 'She did. Carl Ballantine is a nice man, a sensible, straight-laced businessman with a good head on his shoulders. He's everything my dad was not. Good with money, monogamous, a family man. I lived with them for a little while, but suburbia is not for me. There's no substance, it's all glitz and glamour. Arcadia may not be glamorous, but it has substance.'

'So where's your dad? Did he give you the business?'

Dean fell silent, a darkness overshadowing him as he clenched his jaw. 'He died when I was seventeen.'

'Dean, I'm really sorry . . .'

'It's fine. He always said he was here for a good time, not a long time.'

My heart ached for Dean, for the rawness in his face when he spoke of his dad.

'So I inherited a rundown bar and a lot of debt. Dad had put all his assets in my name long before he died to ward off the bank taking it from him, and thanks to Carl and Mum, they helped straighten out my finances. I got my flat refurbed and I've finally saved up enough to start renovations on the building.' He smirked, a lightness returning to him.

'So you and Ballantine are just from different worlds.'

'Maybe it's mostly my fault, but when I see Ballantine skipping school, bumming around, taking for granted how good he has it, what Mum sacrificed for him to be able to live the life he has, it pisses me off.'

'Jealousy?' I pressed.

'Maybe. I don't want his life, but I want him to appreciate it, and I don't think he does.'

The wind blew my hair in my eyes. I brushed it away, because it was important that when I asked him the next question I could see his reaction. I stepped forward, reaching up and taking the glasses away from his eyes. He stilled, his eyes looking down on me, curiously flicking over my face.

'I'm going to ask you something,' I said.

'Well, that's a shock.'

'The trouble Ballantine has with you feels like more than sibling rivalry. When he left,' I swallowed, having not thought back to that day in a while, it still conjured up the same raw emotions, 'he left thinking there was something happening between you and me, and it never seemed to matter how much I told him that there was nothing happening, he still didn't believe it.'

Dean gave me his undivided attention.

What I didn't dare ask was, was Dean like his father? Was he a product of his childhood?

Dean broke into a wolfish smile. 'I told you my little brother, Ballantine, is a sensitive soul.'

'Has he reason to be?' I raised an eyebrow.

'I think the one thing he believes I have taken from him is the only thing he has ever truly wanted.'

'Oh, and what was that?'

Dean shrugged one lazy shoulder as he looked down on me with his serious eyes. 'You.'

'Me? B– but you don't have me, you've never had me,' I stumbled, getting all flustered.

'Yet,' he winked, making me all the more flustered.

'Oh be serious, just for a minute.'

Dean chuckled, 'Why do you care so much?' He sobered, looking at me for a long moment. 'If he doesn't believe you, trust you, then you have nothing. I can't help it if I'm the thorn in his side. It's not my life's mission to involve myself in Ballantine's affairs.'

My mind flashed back to Boon and his cagey response that Dean and Ballantine had a shit history, alluding to it being more than stealing his Tonka Truck. There was a burning jealousy that had existed long before I came along and considering Ballantine had a charmed life compared to Dean, there had to be something more to it. I had to know what girl had been entangled with these brothers before me and whose heart got broken and why.

'Who was the girl?'

Dean looked confused, genuinely so, as he tried to work out what I was talking about, and then the seriousness morphed into an outburst of laughter. 'Oh my God, surely he's not thinking of –'

I interrupted. 'Was it Lucy? Is that why she doesn't work at the Wipe Out Bar anymore?' I blurted it out without thinking, but it was my worst fear.

Dean did a double-take. 'Lucy? I let her go because she had a bad attitude, she was bad for business. I certainly didn't want to make her my business.'

I felt relief, but I still had to know. 'Well, who then?'

Dean sighed. 'Sherry. He'll be referring to Sherry.'

My blood ran cold; that was a love triangle I didn't need or want to find out about. I felt sick.

'I see,' I said, thinking now I had to deal with the Ghost of Sherry?

Dean grinned. 'Relax, it's not as sordid as it seems.'

'Yeah, well, that's all I need to know. We should probably head back now.' I went to move but Dean grabbed my arm, stopping me in my tracks.

'Now just wait a minute, you asked, so let me tell you.'

I tried to remain calm now. 'I said, I don't want to know.'

'And I think you do.'

Dean pulled me back as if I weighed nothing. I sighed, crossing my arms and giving him my best pissed-off stare.

'Once upon a time there lived a prince who owned and managed a bar . . .'

'Don't be a smart-arse.'

Dean cleared his throat, stifling his smile. 'All right, all right.'

I'm glad he was finding this so bloody amusing.

'It's rather simple. Ballantine was skipping school, failing. Mum asked if I could help so I had him come work for me, gave him some responsibility and tried to straighten him out.'

Now it was me who was hanging on every word. I could almost feel myself holding my breath.

'He got better, still a little shit, but he improved. Then Sherry came along. He liked her but . . . she liked me. He blamed me and I took him from out the front and put him in the kitchen and he's had a massive chip on his shoulder since. And that's it.'

I looked at Dean sceptically. That couldn't be it.

'And is that why Sherry left? Because of all the drama?'

Dean's good humour fell away. 'Sherry doesn't deal with drama and she certainly doesn't run away from it.'

His defence of her was somewhat admirable if not . . . annoying. 'So, how did Ballantine deal with you and Sherry?'

'Me and Sherry? There was no me and Sherry, it was never like that.'

'Never?' I found that hard to believe.

'Never.'

Dean stepped forward, so close I could feel his breath on my face. Reaching down he slid his hand over mine, unhinging my fingers from around his sunglasses, taking them from my grasp, before flicking them out and placing them back on his head.

'Any more questions?'

I shook my head.

'Good. You, me, bar, tomorrow.' He said flipping on his glasses and heading back towards Arcadia Lane.

Only when I saw his dark figure get swallowed up by the crowd did I allow myself to deal with the reality.

'Tomorrow? Fuck.'

I spun around to grasp the railing only to find a lady with a pram next to me, giving me daggers.

'Oh, sorry.' I grimaced as she strapped her child in and stormed off in a huff.

I didn't have the brain capacity to care as I stared out over the beach. There was no betrayal, not really, and as much as all that other stuff was good to know and provided clarity, there was also something else that was very clear: I was in way out of my depth.

Chapter Twenty-Four

This was the first night in my room, my *real* room, and it was everything the apartment was not. It was small but cosy, no sweeping views or even so much as the modern convenience of a toilet or shower – I would have to use the bathroom down the hall for such luxuries. The sounds were different on this side of the building. My room faced a brick wall, which gave me an attractive view of the alleyway. There were only muted traffic noises and certainly no sound of the ocean. I had thought to open up the window to try and let some air into what was a pretty stuffy room, but the window would not budge, and try as I might, the damn thing was painted shut. Probably just as well. As memory served, the alley was lined with skip bins and smelt nothing like the ocean. The plastic frosted laminate placed on the window for privacy made me feel claustrophobic and I think I would have preferred to look at a brick wall.

Geez, Lexie, ungrateful much?

Yep, even I was getting sick of my own whingeing. Honestly, I had a room, a job, what more did I need? And with that very thought my tummy grumbled. Food. Nope, a cupcake alone was not going to cut it. I unpacked the last of my schoolbooks, converting my windowsill into a makeshift shelf. My room was more cramped than ever, filled with additional boxes of things my parents brought up for me, including some creature comforts like my own pillow and dressing gown. It felt like some demented form of Christmas, locked away in my tiny room unpacking cherished items from home. Looking over the mass assortment, I smiled. What if I hadn't found a job? They had packed the car regardless with the intent of me staying on, so either they had incredible faith in me after all or the thought of escorting me home against my will was something they didn't want to subject themselves to.

Untying a black garbage bag, I peered inside. The contents gave me a good, solid dose of reality as I reached in, pulling out a folded square of fabric with an unmistakeable blue and white checked pattern.

My school uniform.

Getting up from my bed, I made my way to the calendar I had lovingly rehoused on the wardrobe door. Yep, there it was, circled with a big smiley face – school went back next Wednesday. Who the hell starts back at school on a Wednesday? Among all the insanity and uncertainty I was not prepared for this. I wanted to pace my room but there was not enough space for that so I opted for standing still and biting my thumbnail, as anxiety bubbled inside me. For some strange reason the thought of going back to school with no Amanda, no Aunty Karen or Uncle Peter around kind of made me nervous. They had been, and it was strange to admit this to myself, my go-to people. Who did I have now? Dean? Oh God I felt sick, or maybe it was just the hunger pains. And as if summoning the very image of my unsettling reality, a loud series of knocks sounded on my door.

I navigated my way to the door, pausing to brush my fingers through my hair and straighten my clothing until I caught myself and wondered what I was doing. Pushing my thoughts aside, I whipped the door open.

There he stood, all tall and menacing as if being here at my door was the last place on earth he wanted to be.

I lifted my brows in a silent 'can I help you?' expression. This only seemed to irritate him all the more.

'Making yourself at home, I see.'

'I'm getting there.'

Dean nodded, and a long drawn-out silence stretched between us. Well, this was awkward. What did he want, for me to thank him every moment of the day? Did he want to come in? Should I invite him? No, that would just be weird.

'You hungry?'

My eyes snapped up. Yes! But before I could answer, he continued.

'Come down to the kitchen. I'll tell Bernie to make you what you want,' he said, before turning and striding down the hall.

'Thanks.' I managed, but if he heard me he didn't acknowledge it. He simply walked on, without so much as a backwards glance, into his office and shut the door behind him.

•

I felt like I was in *Charlie and the Chocolate Factory* following Bernie into the cool room.

'We have lasagne, Guinness pies, parmis all made fresh this morning,' Bernie called out as he grabbed a huge tub off a shelf and carried it back into the kitchen.

'Great, whatever, I'm starving,' I said, stepping out of his way and following him back out.

Bernie was a tiny man with black hair, dyed by the look of it, under a hair net. He had a pencil-thin moustache and a tattoo of Popeye on his bicep.

'So, whatever?' he repeated.

'Surprise me, cook whatever you like. I'll eat anything.'

'Well, thank God for that. Cassie keeps me on my toes with her "vegetarian" requests,' Bernie air-quoted vegetarian as if it were a fancy word, causing me to laugh.

'You think if I were a vegan it might tip you over the edge?' I teased.

'Don't even go there,' he said, rolling his eyes.

'Do I wait or –'

'Go sit down in the bistro, table 27 is the staff table. I'll get someone to run it out.'

'Okay, thanks, Bernie,' I said, leaving the chaos of the steamy kitchen behind, glancing at the boy at the sink powering his way through the pile of dirty dishes, just like Ballantine had no doubt done when he worked here. I brushed the thought quickly from my mind as I pushed through the door of the kitchen, walked down the hall and turned into the main bar area to make my way through to the bistro.

Table 27, table 27? My eyes skimmed over the golden numbers that were mounted on the tabletops, all the while smiling politely at people enjoying their meals. The restaurant wasn't full, so it would make for a quiet dinner thankfully. It didn't take me long to locate my table . . . it was the one that Dean sat at, tucked away in the far corner of the bistro.

Great.

I inhaled a deep breath and weaved my way through the tables, coming to a stop before Dean. In true Dean style his serious gaze was cast onto a heap of paperwork before him, something that seemed to always captivate his attention.

'You work down here too?' I asked.

Dean's eyes lifted from what he was reading. 'Oh, you know me, I'm everywhere . . . like a nightmare,' he said, with a crooked little grin. He was everywhere all right. In every corner, every room, every door. He was very much a presence in this place, and being the owner-operator, I guess he needed to be.

'Mind if I sit here?'

Dean didn't answer, he simply moved his paperwork over, making some room for me to sit opposite him. Sliding into the booth, I was suddenly aware that even though we were sitting in the family bistro, surrounded by several tables of people, it still felt very intimate. I wasn't sure if it was due to us being tucked away in the corner, or the subtle lighting, but I kind of wished my meal would hurry up and get here so it would give me something to do with my hands, hands that I clasped together on top of the table as I peered over at what had Dean so entranced.

'Homework?'

'Never ends,' he said, filling out a form with a black pen. He pressed hard against the paper, and his writing was messy and small.

I smiled. Writing was such a personal thing, giving an insight into a person. I pushed myself against the vinyl of my seat and folded my arms across my chest.

Dean's eyes flicked up, troubled by my sudden movement. 'What?'

'You have the writing of a serial killer.'

Dean's brows pinched together, as he cocked his head to look at his handiwork. I thought he might argue the point, be a bit offended. Instead, a small smirk appeared, one that he desperately fought against. 'I'd like to think I have the penmanship of a doctor, thank you.'

I shrugged. 'Whatever makes you feel better.'

'It's called hours and hours of paperwork,' he said, clicking his pen, then scooping his pages together and tapping them into a neat pile. My comment seemed to have given him a complex, although I doubted Dean would have a complex about anything.

'When every spare minute of your free time is dedicated to paperwork, let me know,' he said, now seemingly pissed off. The lines of his face showed his fatigue, as he scratched his head, weary.

I scoffed, 'Hey, you don't have to tell me, I'm doing Year Twelve this year so I know a thing or two about homework.'

Dean stretched his arms to the ceiling, groaning as his bones clicked and popped from their stiffened state. His t-shirt lifted, exposing a flash of chiselled stomach, a glimpse of flesh I actively forced myself not to look at.

'Bloody hell. School, when does that start?' he asked, his arms falling down to his sides as he sat back into his chair.

'Next Wednesday.'

'Wednesday?'

'I know, right?'

'Well, do you want to run through some bar drills after you start school?' he posed the question with a massive amount of uncertainty as if the cogs were turning in his brain, as if school was something he wasn't exactly counting on having to worry about.

I didn't want it to change anything, I could do both, no problem. 'No, I want to learn the ropes, the sooner I start the better, besides I have to earn my keep.' I nodded with a sense of finality.

Dean looked at me for a long moment, a quizzical set to his eyes. 'I thought you would have wanted to enjoy your last bout of freedom with your friends before school started.'

It was a legitimate thought to have, but I wasn't your run-of-the-mill Paradise girl. Laura, who was also working now, was really the only friend I had, and that was when her parents weren't being extra strict on her.

'I really have nothing else to do,' I admitted, as much as I had desperately wanted to come to Paradise, to experience my passage into adulthood, the reality was a whole lot different. I was now living in a world of responsibility, where I had to work to earn my keep. When I wasn't at school, I would either be studying or working, but I was okay with that, they were pretty good fillers for someone who didn't exactly have a jam-packed social agenda. And now that Ballantine was no longer around, what else was there to do? Anytime he popped into my head I shook him from my thoughts. Yep, the sooner I was kept busy the better. I rubbed my hands on my thighs, nodding to myself before watching Dean gather his things and stand.

'So, tomorrow right?' I said, perhaps a bit too eagerly as Dean looked at me like I was a freak.

'Tomorrow,' he nodded, and just as Dean left, a plate was slid in front of me by the waitress, a huge bowl of creamy chicken and sundried tomato pasta with a pile of grated cheese on top. My mouth instantly watered.

'Chef's special,' said the girl as she placed some cutlery on either side of my bowl.

'Did you need a drink or anything?'

I bit my lip, thinking about the reality of this possibly being my last night of freedom for a while. Should I, could I? What the hell.

'Can I see the drinks menu please?'

Maybe just a sip.

Chapter Twenty-Five

I woke up the next morning in a world of pain, pain that was about to increase tenfold as I lifted my face from the mattress, fully clothed and squinting at the blurry figure leaning in my doorway, sipping a cup of coffee and shaking his head.

Dean.

'Oh God, make it go away,' I groaned, rolling away from him and clawing at the blanket to pull over my head.

'Big night?'

Was that a question? I couldn't deal with questions. What did I drink last night?

'Don't worry, I'm sure you'll feel a lot better after a nice big glass of OJ.'

That's when it hit me, the very sound of that word instantly churning my stomach as the memories came flooding back. I had ordered glass after glass of the cheapest nastiest concoction available: Moselle and OJ.

'Yep, OJ and a big greasy fry-up should do the trick.' Dean spoke before taking another sip of his coffee.

He was here to torture me. He was put on this earth to make it his goal in life to be around at times like this.

'What time is it?' I croaked.

'Time to look alive.'

'What?' My head swivelled around, which was a baaad idea. Head spin. 'Ugh, you sound like a drill sergeant.'

'Trust me, this is a gentle wake-up call compared to that, but if you don't move within the next five seconds . . .'

'Okay, okay, I'm moving.' I snapped, attempting to sit up. Not my finest hour.

'Hope it was worth it,' Dean said, pushing himself from the door and heading down the hall. 'You have twenty minutes,' he called back.

'Twenty minutes?' I scrambled for the clock on my bedside table.

Craaaap.

I scurried my way out of bed, cursing the day, cursing Dean.

This was a test. Bloody hell, I was a girl. No, girl could get ready in twenty minutes, no way, no how.

•

With five minutes to spare I was standing woozily behind the bar, not completely convinced I wasn't still a little drunk from the night before. Here I was, ever present as I lifted my smug gaze to the camera near the bar and only hoped he was watching as I lifted my chin, smiling. There was something to be said about being surrounded by passive, stale beer smells when you have the mother of all hangovers.

The bar phone rang. It's shrill, high-pitched ringing had to be stopped, it felt like a jackhammer to my head as I made my way as quickly as possible to answer it.

'Hello?' I answered, my mouth feeling like cotton wool.

'That's not how you answer the phone.'

My mouth gaped, trying to even recall what I had just said.

'Okay, how should I be answering it?' I asked, knowing that I would have to put every ounce of patience into this day.

'Just don't worry about the phone right now.'

'But what if it rings?'

'Cassie will answer it.'

'But Cassie's not here.'

'What?' There was movement on the other end of the phone that had me imagining him swivelling around in his ridiculously large chair staring at the monitors. Ha! Guess he didn't have his finger on the pulse like he thought. I looked directly into the camera, giving a little wave.

'I'm coming down.' The phone went dead.

'Great.' I slammed down the phone, moving myself down to the other end of the bar, until the phone started to ring again, sliding me to a halt as I doubled back and picked up the receiver. 'Good morning, Wipe Out Bar, Lexie speaking.' I singsonged with great pride.

'I said don't answer the phone.'

My shoulders slumped. 'Well, stop bloody calling me!' I slammed down the phone. 'Jesus!'

I was not looking forward to continuing this day, nauseousness and blinding headache aside. Having to deal with Dean's snappy demands was going to bring a whole other level of pain.

I sighed, leaning against the bar, massaging my temples until I saw Cassie come tearing through the front door, juggling her jacket and bag. She looked frantic, stressed like she might have slept in her clothes. 'Sorry, I'm late, I just –' Cassie's words fell away as her eyes fixed to where Dean stood, halfway up the stairs.

'You're late,' he said, continuing down.

'I'm so sorry, Dean, Holly was up half the night with a temperature and I just –'

'Go home.'

'W– what?'

'Go home, Cassie, be with your baby.'

'It's okay. She's with my mum, she just –'

'I'm not asking, Cassie, I am telling you.'

'But I was going to show the new girl the ropes today.'

It suddenly felt very clear that I was eavesdropping, that obviously the new girl was me and that I hadn't even cemented myself into the fold long enough to even be known as anything but the new girl. It was like high school all over again.

'I've got it,' he said.

Cassie's eyes widened, flicking from Dean to me. 'What? You're going to show her?'

I didn't much like the look of horror on Cassie's face when she said that, I didn't much like it at all.

'Don't worry about me.'

Cassie looked at Dean. 'It's not you I'm worried for.' I could tell she instantly regretted the words.

'Cassie,' Dean warned.

'I'm gone, I mean I'm going,' she took the moment to quickly make her exit before pausing at the front door. 'Are you sure you don't want me to stay?'

Dean pointed. 'Go. You would be no use to me anyway.'

Something flashed in Cassie's eyes, a glimmer of hurt although she masked it with a thinly veiled smile. 'Thanks Dean,' she said, pushing through the front door.

Dean sighed, rubbing the back of his head like he did anytime he was nearing the end of his patience. He turned to me and took in my serious gaze. 'What?' he asked.

'That wasn't very nice.'

Dean looked confused, doing a double-take towards the doorway. 'What? Sending a mother home to be with her sick baby? Yeah, I know, I'm a bloody monster.'

'You could have been a bit more tactful, I think she felt a little –' I shrugged.

'A little what?' Dean snapped.

'Unwanted.'

'Oh for Christ's sake, what, because I said she wouldn't be any use to me anyway?'

I let my knowing stare tell him as much.

Dean scoffed, shaking his head as he came closer, then leaning against the bar. 'Let me tell you something, Lexie, managing staff 101. I don't have time to mollycoddle my staff and hold their hands. They can either work, or they can't. Their focus has to be here a hundred and ten per cent or they might as well just go home and not waste my time. Make no mistake, I expect nothing but the best from the people I pay.'

I simply nodded. It wasn't a subtle explanation from Dean. He had made his point.

'Which brings me on to my next point,' he said.

Oh, God here we go, he was on a roll. I took in a deep breath and steadied myself for what was to come next.

'Your school work.'

My brows lowered in confusion. 'What about it?'

Dean looked me straight in the eyes. 'It always comes first.'

I didn't know what to say. It was such an unexpected thing to come out of his mouth I must have just looked dumbfounded.

'You'll be working split shifts most weekends, with some shifts after school depending on what your homework load is like, we'll work it out. But your school work must always come first, that's non-negotiable.'

My eyes flicked over his face, so serious and almost angry as he delivered his set rules. The man was a complete and utter mystery to me.

'Okay,' I said, a bit uncertainly. You just never knew what was going to come next.

Dean's harsh exterior slipped from his boss man stance as the tension melted a little. 'Look, Lexie, I don't care what you get up to in your down time, just be here when you're here, and take your education seriously.'

I smiled. 'A hundred and ten per cent.'

Dean smirked. 'You were listening.'

'How else am I going to learn?'

'All right then,' he said, tapping the top of the bar as he made his way from the front around behind it to stand beside me, with a wicked look. 'Show me what you got.'

Chapter Twenty-Six

Crap.

When it came to bar work I knew jack. Well, that wasn't entirely true. While I was floundering under the watchful eye of a very smug-looking Dean, he did have a request that he and I both knew I could handle.

'How about you make me a Moselle and OJ,' he asked, flashing me a smile I kind of wanted to wipe off his face with my fist.

I straightened my spine, returning his smile. 'Coming up!' *Arsehole.*

Yes, admittedly after ordering one too many drinks last night I was indeed familiar as to how the devil's brew was made. I had seen often enough the cask of Moselle being lifted out from the left mini fridge, and the OJ taken from the juice and soft drink section of the bar, next to where the glasses were kept chilled. I carried out each step with an air of confidence and speed. Scooping the ice into the tumbler I was doing fine, but when I squeezed the tab on the wine box and the passive fumes hit me I had to swallow deeply, trying not to think about the chunks that wanted to rise. I could feel Dean's eyes on me, watching with delight as I broke out in a cold sweat and the colour drained from my face. I cleared my throat, trying to think of anything that would distract me from the drink I was creating, of how the yellowy wine trickled and melted over the ice.

Don't think about it, Lexie.

Next I grabbed for the OJ, topping up the glass and leaving a little room to add a dash of raspberry cordial. I plunged in a straw and gave it a little stir so it resembled a sunset, albeit a cheap and nasty one.

'Here you go!' I sat it with an air of smugness before Dean on the bar, quite proud of myself for not vomiting all over his shoes.

Dean picked it up with disdain, holding it up to the light, examining it like a squished bug underfoot.

'Where the hell did you learn how to make that?'

I shrugged. 'It's what everyone drinks in Red Hill.'

Dean scoffed. 'You don't say?'

I regretted it the moment the words fell out of my mouth. It wasn't enough that everyone already thought I was a country bumpkin, I really didn't have to remind them of it.

'Well, are you going to drink it?' I was thinking how much I was going to enjoy this.

Dean shifted, as if the very thought appalled him. 'I think you should taste it, check that it's the right consistency.'

'Oh, don't worry, it's a foolproof recipe.'

'Maybe, but remember what I said about commitment?'

I laughed, knowing it was one thing for chefs to taste their food for flavour, but this was a bit ridiculous. He was testing me, testing my dedication, or was he desperately trying to make me sick? The thought of tasting the Moselle made my skin scrawl and my stomach twist violently. Still, the way Dean's eyes were staring down on me in challenge was infuriating. He held out the drink to me. 'Go on, just a sip,' he taunted.

If I didn't I would be deemed a lightweight, and I couldn't be that, I had to dedicate myself a hundred and ten per cent. Plus I'd like to see the look on his face when I did do it, I took the glass from his hand and saluted him with it.

'Bottom's up,' I said, before moving the girly straw aside and taking a deep gulp of the absolute foulness that it was. Oh God, it was bad, and it took everything I had to not go running to the sink, my eyes were watering and all I wanted to do was gag, so instead when I smacked my lips together in appreciation and sighed, 'Delicious,' I felt more smug than ever. Ha! Take that, Dean Saville. I held the drink out to him expectantly, until I saw his dark expression, one that wiped any moment of smugness away.

He sighed. 'The next rule you will learn working behind a bar,' he said, taking the drink from my hand and pouring it down the sink, 'is to not bow down to peer pressure. If I ever catch you drinking on the job it will be an instant dismissal.' Gone was all of Dean's playfulness from before, instead replaced by a cold, boss man facade that slammed down.

He crossed his arms. 'So you have failed a few telling tests so far,' he said, looking rather grim.

I could feel anger building, a raging furnace of outrage that burnt my cheeks, mostly because I felt foolish for letting him goad me into drinking that bloody drink. I wanted to yell, to scream, to argue that he had tricked me into it; that he was setting me up to fail at every turn. Instead, I did something so incredibly painful, so completely out of character. I muttered, 'I guess I have a lot to learn.' The admission almost killed me and it wouldn't have been worth it had Dean not been completely surprised by it, so unexpected was my response he didn't know what to say . . . until inevitably he thought of something.

'You're as raw as they come. You sure you don't want to get a job at the ice-creamery down the road?' he asked, sizing me up.

Little did he know with every smart-arse quip he was actually stoking a fire inside me, one of steely determination. I squared my shoulders, ignoring the bait he so desperately wanted me to take. 'What's next?' I asked.

Dean snorted. 'I'm a very busy man, I don't exactly have time to be holding your hand with the nitty gritty.'

I cocked my head. 'Why, Mr Saville, are you giving anything less than a hundred and ten per cent?'

Dean's mouth twitched. 'I didn't say I wouldn't show you, I just don't have the time to.'

'Well, my heart bleeds for you, it really does, but as you so subtly pointed out, I need to learn, and someone has got to teach me.'

Dean looked at me for a long moment, the cogs turning in his mind, probably searching for ways to get out of this. Eventually, a slow smile spread across his lips. 'Okay, less yap, more work.'

And just like that my induction through the meat grinder began.

•

For someone who wasn't very wordy, Dean sure had a lot to say.

'The main bar is the hub, you'll have orders coming in for the bistro, people coming in from the pool room, plus the social drinker at the bar. During peak hour the bar will get smashed, you have to know where everything is, how much it costs. Everything should be stocked and prepped before the rush. No empty glasses on the bar, no thirsty customers, got it?'

I followed Dean around the bistro as he straightened up crooked tables. I almost wished I had a pen and pad in hand.

'So why don't you put a drinks bar in the bistro? Spread out the traffic a little.' It seemed like a pretty reasonable solution, one that had Dean in deep thought for a moment.

'Don't worry about that, just worry about the job at hand.'

He seemed annoyed and it was very clear that it was his way or the highway. So typical, I mused.

'With Cassie gone, we'll cover the lunch shift in the bar.'

I stopped moving, my eyes wide as saucers. 'We will?'

'We have to,' he said with a pointed look, 'Come on, we have a bar to prep.'

•

What was the saying? When you get chucked in the deep end you either sink or swim? Well, I had concrete boots, because try as I might I could do nothing right. With every quick shift to get to an empty glass, I misread or wasn't looking and either slammed into or stepped on Dean. To my surprise, he never chastised me in front of anyone. He stood beside me patiently at the till as he walked me through all the buttons. He answered each and every one of my thousand questions with surprising calmness. And even though he was diligent in his teachings, there was really one thing that was cemented in my mind.

I couldn't do this.

The lunchtime shift morphed into mayhem and I felt like more of a hindrance than a help, knowing that even though Dean was cool and calm on the surface, every one of my mistakes would be noted. I was psyching myself up to head down to the ice-cream parlour after my shift to beg for a job.

By two o'clock Dean allowed me to knock off. I sheepishly pulled the straps from my apron loose and folded it up neatly, paying great attention to it so I wouldn't let the tears of humiliation come. This was just a lunchtime shift. How on earth was I going to do the night-time? How was I going to do school and this when I was exhausted already? I felt like a big fat failure.

Dean came to stand next to me. 'Lexie –'

'I really don't need a rundown of my weaknesses right now,' I said quietly. I couldn't bring myself to look at him, I knew it wouldn't matter what I wanted. He would tell me anyway.

Dean sighed. I didn't know if it was a means for him to work himself up to the whole, 'Look, this isn't going to work out' speech and demote me to washing dishes, which I didn't think my ego could take. I steadied my nerves, sliding aside the apron and turned to fix my gaze on his face, his serious business face.

'You gave a hundred and ten per cent, Lex.'

I waited for him to continue, for there to be a 'but' in the conversation, but there wasn't. He looked at me with deep sincerity, no cockiness or arrogance. This was his way of complimenting me.

'So I did good?' I asked, eagerly.

Dean scoffed. 'Let's not get crazy.'

Chapter Twenty-Seven

A new day meant a fresh start and a chance to put the horrors of my rather ordinary crash test in the bar behind me. Making my way slowly, yet confidently, I walked past Dean's closed office door, swinging around the banister and heading down the stairs, ever aware that if Dean was at his desk he would be able to see me through the one-way glass. There never seemed to be any real privacy in a place like this and I guess that was the way it was designed. The big, imposing structure sat at the top of Arcadia Lane overlooking the arcade and the boardwalk. I slid onto one of the bar stools, looking around the eclectic get-up of the bar with its over-cluttered shelves of spirits and multicoloured cocktails.

This place was in good need of an update, and judging by the dusty bottles on the very top shelf definitely needed a damn good clean too. In fact, the whole place needed a really good scrubbing. Nancy, the cleaning lady, bless her soul, was about four foot, and at a guess, a hundred years old. She had a huge job to do for a little lady and based on the thickness of her glasses, I was pretty sure she missed a lot of the dust simply because she couldn't see it. The very last time I came here with my family for dinner, Dean had made reference to renovations but I had yet to see any changes.

There wasn't a whole lot going for the place in the light of day. It looked a bit tired, and by night the patrons were usually too drunk to care. My thoughts were interrupted by a loud thud next to me on the bar counter.

'Dean wants you to study this while he's gone,' Cassie said, leaning against the bar.

'What is it?' I slid the tattered folder towards me.

'It's the Holy Grail of cocktails we serve here. Read it and commit it to memory.'

'Oh, thanks,' I said, 'How's your daughter feeling?'

Cassie's demeanour changed at the mere mention of her daughter; it was like a spark of pride ignited in her as she straightened.

'She's much better,' she said with a nod of finality that had me mirroring her smile.

'Excellent!' I replied, as I flicked through the pages; some were stained, pages smudged, dog-eared, all from being studied by the bartenders before me, no doubt. It had me thinking. 'Hey, Cassie, did you work with Sherry?'

'I didn't work with her per se, I replaced her,' she said, and my curiosity was piqued.

'Why did she leave?' I asked, suddenly more curious about Sherry than ever.

'Her mum got sick, so she had to leave and work some personal stuff out.'

'Oh, do you think she'll be back?'

Cassie shrugged. 'I think Dean hopes so. Like he keeps reminding everyone every day, we've got huge shoes to fill.' Cassie tapped the folder, 'So study hard. We'll run through some stuff tomorrow.'

I opened up the folder again, studying it closer. The last thing I wanted was to be a failure, well, an even bigger one.

And the last thing I needed was for Dean to let me go because I was useless to him.

'You should think yourself lucky. You get the grace of a few days to study properly without Dean breathing down your neck.'

I cleared my throat, remembering how intently he watched me behind the bar, how his jawline clenched with barely controlled frustration every time I bumped into him. 'So where is his lordship, anyway?' I asked all casual, thumbing the pages.

'Who knows? He usually grabs his keys and disappears with no real indication for what or when he'll be back. Sometimes I think he just gets cabin fever and needs to get out.'

Ha! Didn't we all. And in that very moment it gave me an idea. 'Am I okay to take this with me?' I asked Cassie, holding up the folder.

'Sure, but for Christ's sake, don't lose it.'

'I won't,' I promised. 'Listen, I'm going out for a bit, I'll be back later, okay?'

'Lucky you,' Cassie said unenthusiastically. 'Have fun.'

'Thanks,' I said, sliding off my stool.

I ran up to my room to stash the Holy Grail of cocktails under my pillow. I could study later, I thought, but for now with Dean away I was going to live it up a bit, and by living it up I meant taking a certain Tiffany Blue bike for a spin – very cool.

Luckily I didn't have to keep the bike wedged in my small room. There was an alcove where all the cleaning products were kept out the back of the kitchen that led out into the back alleyway. Apparently the alcove was safe and out of the way enough so no-one was going to break their neck tripping over a wheel, which was always a bonus. Wheeling the bike out the back I craned my neck to the sky as I walked along, basking in the open elements. I wondered if Dean really had business to attend to or was this his way of avoiding me? I couldn't imagine Dean shying away from a challenge. He wasn't some naive school boy. I had seen the scars lining his knuckles, and the small one just above his left eye. He had been in a few altercations and working in a place like this, it was no wonder. As soon as I left the dark, dingy alley and turned the corner, the sun hit my face and my spirits soared as high as the sun. Today was a new day, the first day of my independence and I had never felt more alive. I swung a leg over my bike and slowly began to shakily pedal along the concrete path, leading out towards the arcade.

I didn't put a whole lot of thought into where I would be headed, how far I would go or how long it would take me. Whizzing along the path like a bat out of hell was so incredibly freeing. The blur of my surroundings and the ever-changing scenery occupied my thoughts and I wondered how long I could stay on the bike, because for the first time in a really long, long time I had nothing to decide except which path to choose, quite literally. And when I veered down a road that led me towards the beach, I lifted my legs out and let the roll of the hill take me down at an incredible speed. A fearful squeal escaped me as I steered to the right, down the very end of the hill, zooming around the curve of the road, grateful that there were no oncoming cars. What was oncoming, though, was the view of the ocean.

As I sped along the path's barrier I glanced at the long blue stretch foaming and cresting along the yellow sand. The path petered out into a large car park. I stood up onto my pedals, pumping my legs up and down more slowly but feeling the burn in them, before sitting down once more and pedalling like a mad thing. I jilted my handlebars up a tiny lift to bounce over the guttering and into the cark park, pedalling, pedalling, until my eyes locked onto the ocean, peppered with tiny little flecks on the horizon: *Surfers!* A big goofy grin lined my face as I cycled past, lost in a moment of nostalgia, until I turned my attention forward, realising I was rolling into a direct line with a parked car.

Oh shit!

I swerved at the last minute, blindly panicking and clenching my handbrakes, screaming as I went sailing over the handlebars and somersaulted into a bush, which rather painfully broke my fall, if breaking my fall meant being stabbed with thousands of tiny needles, that is.

Oh my God, I groaned. Was I dead? Surely you wouldn't feel this much pain in the afterlife? I tried to pull myself out of the bush as I heard the sound of voices nearing. Here I was spread-eagled, whimpering and bleeding – not a good look. There was no way of moving quickly, but I had to, I had to suck it up and limp on out of there with my bike. Oh shit. The front wheel of my poor beautiful, brand-new bike was buckled by the impact. There was no getting back in the saddle this time and I cursed myself for going so far afield as I squinted up at the sun high in the sky burning down on my battered and bruised body. I surveyed the damage – there was skin off my knee, a stream of blood running down my leg and a grazed shoulder that I couldn't see but which stung like a son of a bitch. As quick as I could, and it wasn't very quick, I picked up my wonky bike and hobbled out of the car park, wishing I could slink away into the shadows. Everything was bright and exposed and everyone who walked past me looked on with interest, and a whole lot of horror. I seriously considered hitchhiking my way back to the bar, but I didn't fancy ending up in a shallow grave so I simply put my head down and limped the very long, long trek back to Arcadia Lane.

Chapter Twenty-Eight

'Seriously, Lexie? You go out for one afternoon and this happens?'

'Oh, geez, thanks for your concern.' I winced as I cautiously slid onto a chair. 'I'm okay, by the way.'

Cassie let out a little snigger. 'Look, I'm sorry. Are you okay?'

'Well, if you must know, I wasn't mugged or anything, I just fell off my bike.'

'I kind of figured that,' said Cassie, walking out from behind the bar. 'I'll get the first aid kit. You're lucky Dean's not around, he'd have a hissy fit if you bled on his floor.'

Yep, I was grateful he was not around, I couldn't have stood his amusement at my mortifying predicament; yep, eighteen years old and still falling off my bike.

It's amazing how much bonding can be achieved through applying ointment and bandaids. Cassie, to my surprise, was actually a country girl too, more partial to horses than people, but working at the Wipe Out Bar while she studied TAFE part-time had really helped her come out of her shell. Looking at Cassie's cropped bleached hair and dark eye makeup gave me a little hope that working here would give me some worldly confidence too.

As Cassie opened up about the difficulties in juggling, work, TAFE and a baby, and she dabbed at my wounds with ointment, I kind of realised how good I actually had it. In the scheme of things I only had to look after myself, and sure, taking in my skinned leg and ripped shorts, I wasn't doing the greatest job of that. For the first time in, well, forever, I was actually clear on what I needed to do. It was like a Eureka moment and I smiled widely.

Cassie looked up at me, having applied the last bandaid to my shin. Her curious gaze flicked over my scary smile. 'You okay, Lexie?' she asked.

'Okay?' I repeated, looking down at my dishevelled, dirty clothes and bloodied, grazed skin that would no doubt bruise nicely by the morning. I laughed, actually laughed, as my mind worked overtime with my new set of ideas. 'I have never been better.'

•

Sure my bike was buckled, and my body was a little broken – I made a very slow and pained climb back up to my room – but my mind was determined. I knew exactly what I had to do to get my life back on track, and in order to do that I had to offer the best of myself. And if by doing that I had to build up my confidence and become an independent person, then all the better. A little surge of satisfaction pulsed through me. This genius plan was also about proving Dean wrong. I'd show him I could do this job and do it bloody well. I wanted to prove to all the Amandas and Lucys that I wasn't this tragic country girl they remembered from school. Nope, I was determined to make this count, make it all count. I had been given an opportunity and I was going to grab it with both hands and run with it. Well, for now, limp with it.

•

I got stuck straight into it by studying the cocktail book with deep concentration. I knew I could do this. I'd memorised complete formulas for exams before, plus it took my mind off the aches and pains in my body. During the quieter times over the next few days, I got Cassie to run me through the motions of cocktail drills, watching the speed with which she worked and took in her interactions with the clients. I studied everyone: the waiters, kitchen hands, bar staff, door people and even the night-time security.

In order to work in this place to the best of my ability, I needed to find out how it ran, so I threw myself deep into observational study with some after-hour prac work with Cassie. I took notes on the things that worked well, the things that needed improvement and what didn't work at all. And from what I observed, it was really clear that there was a lot that didn't work. It would take more than a pretty girl with a cute accent out the front to lure in tourists. I saw it in their faces as families loitered out the front, contemplating whether to come inside or not. It was easy to be confused as to whether this was a family restaurant or a nightspot for drunken tourists. There was no definitive vibe. The bistro said family, but the pumping, loud, edgy music blaring out front said come on in and party. More often than not I saw uncertainty plastered over tourists' faces as they smiled weakly and moved on, no doubt down the road to Flannigan's, the glitzy enemy. It was frustrating to see. And even more frustrating come night-time to see exactly what did come through the doors: drunken hordes of footy players on their season trips, hen's parties and creepers. No wonder Dean had security cameras. You really had to have eyes and ears everywhere. In

Dean's absence security was more prevalent inside and out, which was reassuring, but was this the way to run a business, I wondered, as I scribbled in my notebook?

Seeing as I hadn't officially been given the green light to work behind the bar, no doubt until Dean came back and pop quizzed me on my cocktail knowledge, I set out by using some employee initiative and followed old Nancy around the cleaning rounds, noticing all the places she seemed to miss as she continued her tried and tested routine. I didn't say anything to her, though, as she was an endearing old soul, who really should be enjoying retirement instead of cleaning up the previous night's vomit.

When I had casually asked if I could help her, her eyes had lit up in a way I didn't expect as she, without hesitation, hooked me up with some cleaning gear.

'The quicker I get through this the sooner I can get down to the club. They've got meat raffles being drawn today.'

I smiled, happily taking the cloth and disinfecting it for her.

Who doesn't love a meat raffle?

Not only did it pass the time, but it was also incredibly therapeutic. I worked on taking all the spirit bottles from the highest shelves and scrubbing off the caked-on dust from years gone by, and polishing the bottles. It created a snowball effect that had me moving on to the glasses and working on replacing the blown globes that lit up the shelves with some bulbs from the storeroom.

Once I had finished, the grime was well and truly transferred from the shelves to me as I wiped my brow with the back of my hand, proudly looking on the sparkling shelves of bottles that were now glowing and shone enticingly. They shouted, 'Drink me!'

Cassie stood next to me, nodding her head, impressed. 'I didn't even know there were light bulbs up there. It looks awesome. Can I take all the credit?' she asked, smiling with a devious glint in her eyes.

I laughed. 'Can we run through some more drinks tonight? I really want to tackle my imported beer knowledge.'

Cassie laughed. 'Are you always like this?'

I straightened. 'Like what?'

Organised, ambitious, structured.

'Anally retentive,' she answered.

My brows lowered, trying not to get offended. 'I just like to keep busy,' I defended.

'Well, surely you must have better things to do? Like going to the beach with your friends, enjoying your school holidays while you can? I mean, you're not getting paid for any of this, I just don't see the point.' Cassie shrugged.

I knew then that this was exactly why light bulbs never got replaced, because more often than not people only did the bare essentials. Did I want to admit that I didn't have any friends aside from Laura, who was also working, and that the one person I had wanted to be spending time with probably didn't want anything to do with me?

'I just think if I do all the hard yards now, it will only make it easier for me later, and then I can go have fun,' I said.

Cassie looked at me like I was some kind of creature from outer space. 'I've never met anyone like you, Lexie. You are wise beyond your years.'

'Yeah, well, don't tell my parents that, they'll put it down to a life of home schooling.'

Cassie grimaced at the thought. 'How are you not institutionalised?' she asked, moving back to the bar.

It was an interesting question. Maybe I was, maybe this was why I was not going out into the big, bad, wild world and getting drunk on my weekends. Instead, here I was, studying for my job. Don't worry, I knew how tragic I was. I looked down at my grubby attire. 'I'm going to have a shower,' I said, giving the glowing shelves one more look; tragic or not, those shelves looked shit hot.

Chapter Twenty-Nine

Maybe I had gone too far? By the third day of Dean's absence with no word on when he'd be returning, my cleaning rampage kicked into a whole new level.

'I can't believe you are doing this,' called Cassie from below as she held the ladder for me.

'Relax,' I said, trying not to think about how rickety the ladder felt underneath me. 'I heard him say he was going to get rid of it anyway.'

Stepping up the last step I could manage without getting too dizzy, I came face to face with my foe: Hank the inflatable shark, suspended by fish netting from the ceiling in the bistro. I shook my head. 'Dean, what were you thinking?' I said to myself, trying to wrestle the limp beast out of its net.

'I don't know, Lexie, you got some big balls doing what you're doing. I once moved Dean's car keys and he flipped his shit. I don't want to even think about what he might do if you rearrange furniture.'

'Dusting, light bulbs and moving this monstrosity is hardly anything,' I scoffed, finally freeing Hank, punching him to the floor like a beach ball.

'Oh God.' Cassie watched it float and sag to the ground. 'Okay, but I know nothing about it, capisce?'

'Don't worry, it was all my doing.'

'I mean it, Lexie, I didn't so much as hold the ladder for you, right?'

I rolled my eyes. This was exactly what was wrong with this place – nobody challenged Dean. He could have them all dressed in hot pink tutus and they would say 'Yes, sir, no, sir, three bags full, sir.' Well, not me. I would do my job, absolutely, but if he was going to lose his shit over an inflatable shark then he could stick his inflatable shark right where the sun don't –

'What are you doing?'

I nearly fell off the ladder, not from shock but because Cassie had jumped, shifting the ladder as we both locked eyes on the figure that was standing in the doorway of the bistro.

'Oh, hey, Sherry,' called out Cassie rather nervously.

Sherry didn't smile. She simply looked from Cassie up to me as if we had been caught with our hands in the till or something.

'Where's Dean?' she asked.

'He's gone away for a few days,' said Cassie, her eyes nervously shifting back to me.

'Did he ask you to do this?' demanded Sherry.

'Well, umm, not exactly, we were just –'

'No,' I said very clearly as I made my way down the ladder. Reaching the floor I kind of wished I had stayed up there, giving myself the advantage of Sherry looking up at me. Now I was looking up at her. She was tall and thin, with a liking for black clothing. I guess working at the Wipe Out Bar had rubbed off on her personal attire. It suited her though. She had long black hair and dark eyes; she was basically everything I was not and the thought of Ballantine liking her made something inside me pang, but I quickly wiped the thought away. She wasn't deliberately being intimidating, I think it was just her way. I had seen her smile at a good-natured joke and I had also seen her tear down a fully grown man with a raised eyebrow. As Cassie had quoted from Dean:

Huge shoes to fill.

Sherry looked over the scene as if what we had done was a big mistake, and it had me second-guessing everything. All of a sudden I wanted to grab Hank and climb back up the ladder.

'Did you want something to drink, Sherry?' Cassie asked, always the barmaid.

'Thanks, Cass, but I've got to go,' she said, turning her attention away from me. 'Can you just get Dean to give me a call when he gets back?'

'Sure, just on your mobile?'

'Perfect,' she smiled, something she didn't do very often. 'Good luck,' she said, as her eyes lowered to Hank, before heading out the door.

'Oh my God, Lexie, we are so dead. You saw her face. She thinks it's a bad idea too.'

'Oh, please, she always looks like that,' I said, trying to convince Cassie and myself at the same time.

'Why don't we just put Hank back up and ask Dean when he gets back what he wants to do?'

I sighed. 'No. Look, we'll put Hank and the net in the storeroom. The only way he will agree to keep it this way is if he sees the difference. Now, pass me that knife. I've got to get this net down.'

Cassie begrudgingly grabbed a steak knife from the cutlery drawer. 'Remember, I wasn't here,' she said, slapping the handle into the palm of my hand.

'And if he loves it?' I asked with a smirk.

'He won't,' Cassie said grimly.

'Guess we'll find out,' I said, beginning to, oh, so carefully, climb the ladder, as I clenched the knife in my teeth like Rambo.

'Hurld herh sturdy,' I said, before taking out the knife and starting to saw at the off-white net caked in dust and passive smoke from over the years. We moved the ladder from corner to corner until finally the last piece fell. Now there was absolutely no going back.

Chapter Thirty

Life was pretty good, I thought, as I brushed my teeth. Dean's prolonged absence had me steaming ahead with the freedom to familiarise myself with the Wipe Out Bar. I rinsed and tapped my toothbrush against the sink all smug, thinking about the look on Dean's face when he saw me at work next. He had been gone for a week now, and no-one had put out a missing persons report because as far as I could tell, he checked in with Cassie on the phone each night, the phone I wasn't allowed to answer – pfft. Apparently he was tending to some 'business' in Pascoe and would be back soon. Okay, Mr Cryptic. I pulled out the elastic band from my braid, unfolding the strands and letting my hair pool loosely around my shoulders. The sensation felt glorious as I ran my fingers along my scalp, stifling a yawn. The week had passed by quickly, busy full days and tomorrow I started back at school. I was giddy with excitement about my first day of Year Twelve and had every intention of heading to bed early, as I leant into the mirror and took in the dark rings under my eyes. I paused, hearing voices. I stood silently, trying to gauge where they were coming from and I crept over to my bedside lamp, which was only a very short three steps away. I clicked the room into darkness, although it wasn't really dark as a bright white security light shone in the alleyway, and that was where the voices were coming from. I edged my way to the window I couldn't see out of.

Bugger.

I pressed my ear to the window, but the voices were nothing more than inaudible mumbles, then I wondered if they could see my silhouette pressed up against the window and quickly backed away. Biting my lip, I began to worry. Glancing at the clock, I was surprised to see it was already one in the morning. So much for getting to bed early. The Wipe Out Bar was long closed and there really shouldn't have been anyone loitering in the alleyway. Well, not anyone who shouldn't be there, anyway. The voices elevated in pitch. Still unable to make out anything clearly, curiosity got the better of me and I grabbed the dressing gown Aunty Karen had bought me to match the lemon summer short PJs I had on. Slipping my feet into my Billabong thongs, I opened my door slowly, wincing at the painful squeak that sounded when I pulled it open.

Stupid, rickety building.

It was a miracle it was still standing it was so old.

I slid my feet along the carpet, pausing as I stood before Dean's door. I turned left down the hall. The green exit sign was aglow above the back door, a beacon lighting my way, making my venture seem less frightening until I got to the heavy steel door, which, much to my horror, wasn't even locked.

I shook my head. Mr Paranoia with all his security monitors and we could have all been murdered in our bloody beds! There was no delicate way of pushing this beast of a door open so I just had to stifle my moan as I put all my energy into shoving it ajar, the night breeze lapping at my cheeks as I left the stuffy dark hallway and stepped into the night at the top of the fire escape landing. Sure enough, a stale smell of rotten rubbish hit me, until the wind blew mercifully in the other direction. Phew. Leaving the door open slightly, I kept to the shadows, moving to the very corner of the balustrade. Leaning against the wall of the building, I waited, thinking myself crazy. Was I hearing things? Maybe the voices from the alley were gone now and just as I was ready to back away, I heard them, except this time very clearly and right below me. I froze, biting my lip as I edged forward, peering down to the ground below, and my breath hitched when I made out two figures. A man and a woman, except this time they were definitely not talking.

I knew I shouldn't be looking but I just couldn't tear my eyes from what I was seeing. Even in the darkness of the alley I could see them well enough to know I didn't know them, which was probably the reason I gave myself permission to stare. It wasn't personal. At least, that's what I told myself as I pressed myself further into the shadows. I watched on, fascinated, as the brunette woman kneeled down and took the blond-haired man in her mouth, his hands in her long dark hair, urging her on with dirty words, guiding her rhythm as his hips bucked. It was the most erotic thing I had ever seen. Two people, out in the open, groaning into the night. His head tilted back against the wall in abandon before looking down and watching her devour him with expert rhythm. I was aware of nothing but the scene playing out before me, as I watched from the shadows, not even aware of myself enough to be ashamed or sorry for not walking away. It felt so wrong and yet there I was staring down, feeling strange things stir inside me, hardly believing how brazen they were being – no-one in Red Hill would dare do anything like this. I thought for sure the couple would soon finish. If I knew the opposite sex I knew the guy wouldn't be able to endure that kind of torture forever, and just as the man gritted into the night air that he was about to come, he pushed her away, frantically yanking her by her wrists to stand, spinning her around to bend her over, her hands fixing to the edge of the skip bin as he hitched her skirt up over her hips. Oh my God, he was going to do her right in the alleyway – surely not.

But he did. It was hard, fast, hot and loud. If I hadn't have left my room I would have definitely figured out what was going on by this point in time. I think it was safe to say the whole of Paradise would have heard what they were doing, and as much as it was hypnotic and so very wicked to watch him take her from behind, I had seen enough. As I quietly edged back on the landing I bumped into something unexpectedly hard, something that hadn't been there before.

I spun around, ready to scream with fright, when a hand clasped over my mouth, smothering my voice. My nostrils flared and my eyes, wide with panic, locked onto a familiar set of green-brown eyes as Dean looked at me, lifting a finger to his lips, then his serious eyes moved from my face to over the balcony. His face was expressionless, unflinching as he took in the couple's moans down below. My cheeks were aflame, mortified that I had been sprung and of all people, by Dean, my employer. I desperately wanted to explain that I'd heard voices and come out to investigate, but instead I blinked wildly, feeling as though we stood in the dark for the longest time, until I heard the merciful sounds of the two strangers below giggling and straightening their clothes then moving on from their temporary love nest. I swallowed deeply, as I felt Dean's hand slide away from my mouth.

'Show's over,' he said, his voice was low and smoky, a knowing smirk lining his lips. And, oh God, if hearing him say that wasn't the hottest thing I had ever heard. I turned a deeper red, horrified that I could even be thinking like that. I blamed my rampant hormones, yeah, that had to be it.

I heard a low chuckle and glared up at him. This was most definitely not funny.

Dean shook his head. 'Honestly Lexie, loitering in alleyways, and on a school night and all,' he said, adjusting my collar as if worried I would catch a chill, when in reality I was more in danger of catching on fire. He was such a fucking smart-arse.

Dean moved to the back door, opening it up without effort as he swept his hand in front of him. 'Ladies first,' he said with a wry smile.

I eyed him sceptically as I moved forward, stopping before him, looking him straight in the eyes. 'I don't feel like a lady,' I admitted, still feeling the flush to my cheeks.

Dean straightened, still holding the door ajar. 'Would it make you feel any better if I told you I'm no gentleman?'

Against my better judgment I smirked, actually smirked. As if loitering in the shadows watching strangers do it in the back alleyway wasn't bad enough. Oh yeah, my parents had left me with who they thought was a saint, when really I was standing before a devil, a devil who looked as sexy as sin itself standing under the muted night lights. What was happening to me? Maybe it was the erotic live show I had just witnessed that was playing with me, making things stir in all the right places and clouding my judgment. I looked up at Dean and admired the perfect line of his bone structure, his bow-shaped lips, the very ones I felt pressed against my ear. I imagined him whispering wicked things into my ear.

I reckoned he would be the type, just like the couple down below. Dean would urge words of encouragement as he bent me over his desk and took me from behind. An image flashed in my mind of him doing exactly that to me in his office and I quickly broke my eyes away from his, my cheeks burning a deeper shade of red.

'Goodnight,' I said a little too loudly as I pushed past him, making my way quickly down the hall, cursing myself for thinking such ludicrous thoughts. I was clearly sleep deprived, I needed to go to bed – my bed.

Chapter Thirty-One

I had a dream.

I ended up painting the walls of the Wipe Out Bar hot pink, and decoupaging the bar with cut-out photos of flowers. I dreamed that instead of the giant surfboard at the entrance, I hung a picture of white horses – reminiscent of exactly how Mum had decorated my room back in Red Hill. And in my dream Dean loved it, absolutely raved about the changes, especially the bar with the flowers. He then shouted everyone at the bar a drink, which was definitely a sign that I was dreaming, because I could never imagine Dean ever doing something like that – there was more chance of him liking the colour pink.

I stirred awake, my eyes skimming the smoke-stained decorative cornice of my room, processing what was just a dream and what was very much a reality.

Dean was back.

I lifted the doona to my chin, like a small child warding off dark shadows in her bedroom. My worry was less about what Dean might think of my changes to the bar than with how I was ever going to look him in the eyes again. My mind flashed back to last night, the way Dean's eyes shifted from my face to over the fire escape railing, noticing the couple

I had been spying on. When his gaze had settled back onto me, it didn't take long for him to break into a devious little smile and come up with a smart-arsed comment.

I groaned, lifting the doona up over my head. I was never going to live this down. All I wanted was to hide away, to never cross Dean Saville's path again. My alarm sounded, causing me to jump at the unexpectedness of its shrill ringing. I peeled the covers from my head, rolling awkwardly to pound my palm onto the clock radio that was screaming at me to get up, get up and face the day. There would be no hiding from anyone.

I sighed, pushing myself into a sitting position. My eyes locked onto my school uniform and, despite everything else, a smile slowly spread across my face.

I had done it.

Today I was going to start Year Twelve. The full weight of that soon eclipsed all other thoughts. The day had finally arrived, and this was definitely not a dream, it was very much real.

Holy shit, I had really bloody done it.

•

It was a fantasy in most teenage girls' hearts that one day they would descend a grand staircase and make an even grander entrance into a room, where a boy, watching, would instantly fall in love with her. But I guess I had never been a lot like most teenage girls, and I certainly wasn't enjoying this particular moment. Especially as I stood on the landing, slowly stepping down, my hand gliding along the glossed, smooth finish of the bannister, the very last person I wanted to see was glancing up at me from the bar, breaking off mid-sentence to the man delivering stock into the cool room.

Dean turned fully towards me descending the staircase, a big grin lining his face as his eyes drifted over me, from my blue-and-white-checked school dress, to my white knee-high socks and T-bars. I shifted my backpack, filled with heavy textbooks, on my shoulders. He was far too amused by this, or maybe he was still thinking about last night? Maybe that expression was him silently judging me, wondering how he hadn't guessed I was such a deviant, or maybe that was just my paranoia. I tried to avoid making eye contact. The last thing I wanted was for him to say something smart to me; his expression was mocking enough. Instead, I walked a straight line towards the kitchen, trying my best not to do it too quickly, when all I wanted was to run out of view. I lifted my chin and walked on as if nothing was different. This was my first day of Year Twelve and I was off to conquer the world. I was aiming for this all along. This is why I had worked so hard to get back here, so I could finish my final year in a real school. Sure, things had turned out different from what I'd expected, but I was here.

Let's do this, Lexie.

I breathed in steadily. 'Morning,' I chimed cheerfully at Dean and the delivery man as I passed them. Caring not for their reaction, I forged on towards the kitchen.

Raiding the fridge, I wrangled up some fruit salad to fill my stomach before I left for my big day. It could have been hunger pains, but I suspect it may have been first-day jitters. So much had changed in my world since I'd last been at Paradise High, it was almost like going into a complete unknown. Without the likes of Ballantine to stare at from across the schoolyard, to share stolen moments as he brushed past me in the hall, flashing me a cheeky, knowing grin, who knew whether anything would feel the same?

I had prided myself on being Miss Independent by keeping myself busy and denying the hurt that lingered not too deep below the surface. I was afraid school would bring it all back, and I wasn't quite ready to face those emotions. There was also a certain amount of humiliation that went with it. At the last school social it had become common knowledge that there was something between me and Ballantine. We were no longer hiding it from the world, it was a new beginning filled with so much promise, a promise that ended all too soon. And here I was sitting in a booth at the Wipe Out Bar (my new home), munching thoughtfully on fruit salad and dreading my first day. At least it was Wednesday, not long and I would have the weekend to recover.

Having been in a form of holiday mode I was rarely up and about at this time of day. Seeing the bar and restaurant completely empty, and noticing there was still plenty of foot traffic outside – hungry strolling tourists on the prowl for a feed – I wondered if Dean had ever considered opening for breakfast. I made a mental note to ask although I may very well have overstepped the mark with what I had done so far. My eyes warily lifted up to where the hideous netting and Hank had once been and I swallowed. Shit, I wondered if Dean had noticed yet? He got back in the early hours; he probably hadn't.

I scooped the last mouthful of fruit into my gob and went to quickly scoot out of the booth. I really didn't want to be here when he discovered it. Grabbing the empty bowl and spoon I moved to make a quick exit from the bistro, rounding the corner straight into the path of Nancy, the dear old cleaning lady. I stepped back with a yelp of surprise.

'Oh sorry, Lexie, I didn't mean to scare you.' Nancy chuckled, probably because I was clutching my heart so dramatically.

'You're like creeping Jesus, Nancy,' I breathed out, trying to still my heartbeat.

'Sorry, dear.' Her big magnified eyes behind her thick glasses shifted to my breakfast bowl. 'Here, let me take that. You run along.'

'Oh, thanks, Nancy.'

'Ah, now, it's you I should be thanking. The shelves in the bar look beautiful. I just hope Dean doesn't like them so much I lose my job.'

'Oh.' I blanched. 'I think your job is safe, Nancy, especially once Dean finds out about his beloved Hank.'

Nancy squinted into the bistro. You didn't have to have twenty-twenty vision to notice that the hideous prop was gone. I had thought Nancy might have high-fived me, told me job well done. Instead, her tiny wrinkled face looked worried; deeply worried. 'Has Dean seen this?' she asked.

I suddenly felt very nervous. 'Um, I'm not sure, but I kind of was planning on not being here when he found out,' I admitted, thinking of an escape route from the building. Down the basement and out the back alley seemed like a sure bet.

'Ah yes, well, probably a good idea,' Nancy nodded. 'Well, hopefully by the time he gets back he will have calmed down a bit.'

I paused. 'Gets back? He's going again?'

He just got back.

I didn't much like the disappointment that my words were edged with. It was certainly not disappointment I felt. If anything, I was mostly incredulous. 'How can he expect to run a business if he's never here?' I scoffed.

'Quite easily,' came a voice from behind.

Oh shit.

My head and Nancy's snapped towards Dean, who was closing the distance between us. Nancy quickly shuffled into action, stepping away from me and heading into the bistro as if a tsunami was headed our way. And she wasn't too far from the truth. I sensed a mass of doom rolling towards me. I decided to meet him part way, stop him from looking into the bistro.

'Hey, Dean, have you got a minute?' I began. The friendly tone of my voice sounded unsettling even to me, and especially to Dean who openly scowled at me as if I were a stranger.

My shoulders sagged. 'You don't have to look so pained, Dean, it's only a question.'

'That's what worries me,' he said as he moved past me, picking up a newspaper from the table before making his way back to the comfort of the bar – not the bistro, thank God. I followed after him, two of my small steps equal to one of his long, confident strides.

'So, are you going again for the weekend?' I tried for light, carefree conversation at first, but there was no buttering up Dean Saville. He didn't do lighthearted, he only worked on two levels: scowling and smart-arse.

'Why, will you miss me?' He flicked me a knowing look.

Yep, there was the smart-arse.

'Terribly. Now listen, I was just wondering –'

'Son of a bitch,' Dean swore.

My mouth gaped, confused by his outburst until I followed his line of sight. Dean shook his head. 'Bloody revenue-raising pricks, the Shire's putting in parking meters all along Kirkland Avenue.'

'Oh, right, well, that's no good, but the thing is, I was just thinking –'

'The next thing you know they'll be metering our shopping centre car parks to make a quick buck, the bloody –'

'Dean!' I said, perhaps a bit too loudly, because his eyes flicked up to me, his irritation deepening as I interrupted him mid-rant.

'What? Shouldn't you be going to school?' He glanced at his watch, his already paper-thin patience wearing thinner.

'Yeah, soon,' I said, brushing away his words, 'Anyway, I was just wondering –'

'What happened to your knee?'

I frowned, glancing at the series of bandaids on my leg.

'Oh, I fell off my bike, well, actually I totalled my bike, but I'm okay. Now, I was thinking –' I moved on quickly before I got a lecture on road safety – 'maybe I could work the bar Friday night. I mean, if you're not going to be here, you could probably use an extra pair of hands, and I've studied the cocktail book and have been watching Cassie all week. I feel that I'm ready to give it a crack. What do you think?'

Silence.

Long, drawn-out silence filled the space between us as Dean's cool gaze rested on me, ticking over my face as if testing if I were serious or not. I was deadly serious. I had studied, pulled my weight in other ways, I was itching to work the bar, and, sure, there was a certain allure of doing my first night shift with Dean not breathing down my neck.

I swallowed. 'Well?'

Dean's fingers teased the corner folds of his newspaper as he studied me, as if he was weighing up a puzzle, a puzzle he finally had the answer to as he sighed.

'No.'

Chapter Thirty-Two

Dean turned back to his paper and smoothed out the lines seemingly without a care in the world.

'What do you mean, "no"?'

'I said, no.'

I stood beside him at the bar, taking in his bored, calm features as he read the paper. My hands balled at my sides as I could feel the anger lifting to an explosive level inside me. 'Why? Because you don't trust me?'

Dean chuckled. 'Now what makes you say something like that?' He looked up at me with interest, leaning his elbows casually on the bar top, waiting for my reply.

'Well, because obviously you don't.'

Dean's humour shuttered over into anger. 'Trust is earned, not granted, Lexie.'

'Well, what do I have to bloody do to earn it?'

'Oh, I think you have done quite enough.'

My cockiness slipped a little. I wasn't keen for a Dean argument first thing in the morning.

'Tell me,' he folded his arms across his chest as he leant back in his chair, 'did you use a knife or scissors to cut the netting? Because nothing thrills me more than the thought of you climbing a ladder in thongs carrying a sharp object. I mean, what could possibly go wrong?'

I wanted to explain that Cassie had actually passed me the knife, but thought better of it. The last thing I wanted was to implicate Cassie.

'And maybe the reason there were no light bulbs in the bar display is because they keep shorting out and are potentially not a great thing to replace near a shelf full of highly flammable liquids, but of course you know that too, right?'

I couldn't bite my tongue a minute longer. 'Well, maybe you should get that looked at, with a fair few other things that need to be brought into the twenty-first century around here.'

A smile formed across Dean's handsome face, a smile that didn't reach his eyes. 'You're not working the bar until I get back.'

'Yeah, and when will that be? You bang on about running a tight ship and yet you up and leave without so much as a word about where you're going or when you'll be back.'

Dean raised his brows. 'Wow,' he mused.

'Wow, what?' I snapped, shouldering my school bag, readying myself to leave him and his stupid bar.

'You really did miss me.'

I scoffed. 'Not bloody likely.'

Dean smirked. It was crooked and sexy and extremely infuriating, as was the fact he moved to stand from his chair, towering over me and looking down on me with a sparkle of amusement in his eyes. 'I won't be here by the time you get back from school, but I'll be back Sunday. Before I went away for business, this is for pleasure, is that okay with you?' His question was laced with sarcasm, and it only served to build my frustration against him.

'I don't care what you do,' I yelled, angry at his insinuation that I did, but more pissed at the fact that maybe, in some sick way, I did, because the way he said pleasure made something instantly twang inside me. I didn't know what that involved or with who but it did pique my interest in the worst way, so much so I desperately wanted to ask, but didn't dare.

As if he had some form of telepathic ability, Dean smiled more broadly, revelling in my anger. He rolled the newspaper up in his hands without taking his eyes from me.

'Don't stress, Lex, I am chartering a fishing boat with some mates for the weekend, not shoving twenties down a pole dancer's G-string.'

I blinked, once, twice. 'Why should I care?' I said, probably a bit too loudly and a bit too quickly, and then I decided suddenly it was time to go. 'Do what you like,' I said with a shrug, moving past him towards the front entrance.

Dean chuckled, rubbing his unshaven jawline. He was such a Jekyll and Hyde. One minute he was all broody and business-like, the next, teasing and smirky. He was impossible to gauge.

'Do you need a lift?' he called out as I neared the door.

I stilled at the doorway, turning to see him waiting expectantly. 'No, thanks, I'm going to hitchhike my way to school. It's what I like to do in the times I am not climbing ladders with sharp things and dabbling with electrical faults.'

Dean simply shook his head, I could tell he was trying to be serious but wasn't quite pulling it off. 'Nobody likes a smart-arse, Lexie.'

I breathed out an incredulous laugh. 'No, no they don't.'

•

The irony wasn't lost on me. Despite my rage I found myself smiling as I walked down Arcadia Lane, my thumbs hooked in the straps of my backpack. Here I was thinking Dean had a split personality, and yet I was going from rage to light-heartedness and then on to uncertainty. I pinpointed the change. Despite my adamant stance that I didn't care what he did, the admission that he was going away for a mates' weekend relieved me in the most unsettling way. I don't know what was going on in my head lately, but I quickly turned the relief into something else. It was obviously relief that he was going away, so I could clear my head from such absurd thoughts. Seriously, get your shit together, Lexie.

I wiped all thoughts of rage, and disturbing, unexpected twangs, and focused solely on watching and waiting for my ride, and just as if summoning them in my thoughts, a familiar powder blue vintage Holden emerged in the distance. I would have recognised Boon's car anywhere, even more so with Laura's arm flapping out the side, waving like a mad thing. The thumping VB motor purred like a big jungle cat as it pulled into the kerb.

Laura's arm rested casually on the open passenger window. 'Holy shit, you really are living at the Wipe Out Bar.' Laura laughed, shaking her head as if scarcely believing the reality. 'I thought you were shitting me when you said you were.'

'Of course I am. Why would I lie about that?' I frowned at her, moving to open the back door, shrugging off my backpack and sliding in the back.

'True, if you were going to make up a story, you wouldn't choose the Wipe Out Bar.' Laura laughed again, pulling down the sun visor and pouting her lips in the mirror. I glowered at the back of Laura's head, annoyed that she was bagging out the bar – it wasn't that bad.

I turned my attention to Boon, sitting sombrely behind

the wheel with his dark shades on, pulling the car into gear with a sigh.

'Hey, Boon,' I said gently, thinking how hard this was for him. If I felt nervous about my first day of Year Twelve, I couldn't imagine what the first day of repeating Year Twelve would be like. It certainly wasn't a conversational piece. 'Oh, before I forget . . .' I said, unzipping the side pocket of my school bag. I delved in, pulling out a crinkled envelope with Boon's name on it and tapped it on his shoulder. He took it wearily.

'Don't get too excited, it's just the money I owe you.'

Boon nodded in the rearview mirror at me as a way of thanks before he pocketed the envelope and readied himself to pull out onto the main road. 'So you working for the big boss man now. How's that working out for you?' he asked.

Speaking of a non-conversational piece.

'It's fine,' I lied. I was flawless in my delivery as if there hadn't been no heated argument only moments earlier.

Boon breathed out a laugh. 'Give it time,' he said.

I sunk back against my seat, tearing my eyes from the rearview mirror to look out the window, thinking if I was still in the honeymoon stage of my working life, then what the hell would happen in time? I didn't want to know.

•

Anxiety was replaced by a new feeling as the three of us walked through the ornate arch of Paradise High. I was flooded with nostalgia. Boon peeled away in the opposite direction, lost quickly in the crowd. I'm sure he didn't feel as nostalgic as I did, but there was also another very obvious change as we walked around the grounds. We were the seniors now, the top dogs, leaders of the school. No longer would I have to worry about the clusters of Amanda and her friends, or wonder where the Kirkland Boy surfers were. Nope, it was almost like a new power floated over us as Laura and I made our way up the concrete steps to the main building. I knew Laura felt it too, as we glanced at each other, smiling like goofballs as the electric first-day-back-at-school excitement reverberated everywhere. Reunions of friends dotted in the halls and in the yard, holidays and summer were nearing the end and the excitement of the morning would soon ebb into the usual humdrum routine for everyone but me. I always had the distinct feeling that I enjoyed school perhaps a little too much, that having been starved of normal schooling for most of my life made me a bit of an outsider. Even looking back at my stint last year – the disastrous start, the detentions – I wouldn't have traded any of it. It had given me the life experience I had craved and, more importantly, it had led me to Ballantine. I didn't have to work too deeply to shift my focus from him as the bell sounded, and the announcement rang out for assembly. I smiled to myself, thinking, yes, how different it would all be this time around. No entering late into school assembly this time. Nope, I was simply going with the flow, and that's what I planned to do, quite literally as I shuffled into the hall, following the masses. It was what I would do to survive all this: day and night I would just go with the flow, because things were different now, and if I could survive my final year of school I could survive anything.

•

Go with the flow, go with the flow.
I repeated the mantra in my head.

And I had been doing pretty well until I found myself paused in the doorway of the Year Twelve common room. Laura entered, turning to me, wondering why I wasn't following.

'I know it's probably not that big a deal to you, Lex, but I have been waiting five long years for this right.'

I smiled, cautiously entering the room. How wrong she was, this room *was* a big deal to me, but for all the wrong reasons. My attention flicked to the bright red door at the opposite side of the room, the very one Ballantine had led me through, the very room we had *done* things in. I hoped my complexion didn't match the deep red of the door. I quickly turned to study the hideous rainforest wallpaper.

'Isn't this cool?' Laura plonked herself on one of the couches, her eyes alight with excitement, matching the expressions of the other Year Twelves now piling into the room, looking like they had just walked into Willy Wonka's Chocolate Factory.

I sat beside Laura on the couch. Space was limited and it would be a fight every recess and lunch to claim a piece of furniture to relax on. Still, the boys had short attention spans and they were soon bored and heading to the cricket nets, leaving the girls to bitch and whisper all the more.

'So, are you working this weekend?' Laura nudged my foot, causing me to blink towards her. I was having difficulty staying in the present.

'Oh, umm, no.'

'Cool, we should do something then, I'm not working either. I'll come over and check out your new digs,' she said, wiggling her eyebrows.

'Don't get too excited, it's not much of a room,' I said.

'Room? I thought you had this flash apartment?'

My brows lowered. 'But I never said –'

'Boon overheard Lucy telling people at the beach.'

Ugh, of course.

I laughed. 'Well, at least it's a good rumour. What else did she have to say?'

Laura fell silent. Her big eyes were hopeless at disguising her inner turmoil. She cleared her throat, edging forward on the couch, cautious not to let anyone else overhear what she wanted to say.

'Is it true?' she asked quietly, leaning over.

'Is what true?'

Laura looked at me like I was crazy, like I should know what she was talking about. 'You know, that you're *fucking* Dean Saville, like, for real this time.'

Oh my God!

I rolled my eyes. 'Here we go again. No, no, I'm not, and honestly, have you not learned a thing from last time all this happened? No, I am not fucking Dean Saville,' I said a little too loudly as heads swivelled towards us, the room falling silent.

Laura smiled weakly, behaving like an embarrassed parent whose child was wreaking havoc in a shopping centre. Silence morphed into speculative whispers and judgmental looks, but what did I care, I knew the truth.

'Seriously, people in Paradise need to get a life,' I said, again a little too loudly but this time I wanted them to hear.

'Well, if you shack up under a hot barman's roof, people are going to naturally romanticise it.'

I laughed, genuinely laughed. Which only resulted in more death stares.

'I tell you what. Come over on the weekend and you'll see how romantic my life is.'

Laura straightened with interest. 'Well, maybe I will.'
'Do you want some words of advice though?'
'What's that?' asked Laura.
'Don't get your hopes up.'

Chapter Thirty-Three

I went from thinking starting back at school on a Wednesday was a stupid idea to thinking it was perhaps singlehandedly the best idea ever!

It had taken the edge off the first week back and before long I had the weekend before me. With my mind at ease and nothing better to do, I spent the weekend loitering around the Wipe Out Bar, itching to get in on the action.

Dean might have been mad about me tampering with his bar without permission but he had to admit how much cleaner and fresher the place looked. There was a glimmer that this was the case as I came down on Saturday morning to see an electrician working on the lighting panels above the spirit shelf. I stood there, grinning like a fool, until the electrician tore his gaze away from his job and looked at the creeper standing before him, smiling like the cat that got the cream. I nodded my approval and gave him a thumbs up.

'Good job.'

'Right. Thanks?' he said to the crazy girl.

As much as tampering with Dean's precious bar was deemed, in no uncertain terms, professional suicide, I couldn't shake the new day's determination: I was going to move some furniture around. Not much, just a little tweaking that would improve the flow of the room. Before her lunchtime shift began I enlisted Cassie to help, and although she was very accommodating in lending a hand, she was again very adamant that I not publicly acknowledge her involvement.

'So what are we doing today then?' Cassie asked, her hands on her hips, surveying the table and chairs I paced in front of.

I grinned at her. 'Well, I thought we could turn the chairs out like this,' I said, rearranging one chair, then the next before twisting the small square table so they were facing out to the streetscape. 'See, like this. This is how they have them in Paris. People can sit and watch all the street traffic go by.'

I knew from Cassie's smile she approved. 'I love it. Let's get cracking on the rest,' she said. 'You know what would also look good? Some tablecloths.'

'Do we have any?' I asked, excited.

'I don't think so, but it would really brighten the space up, don't you think?'

I looked at the tables. Now I couldn't envision them without tablecloths and that was just going to annoy me.

'Where do you suppose we could get some? Even if we just got them for the outside tables to begin with?'

Cassie's brows knitted together in deep thought for a long moment, and just as I thought we were both at a loss, she snapped her fingers. 'Nancy'll know.'

'Nancy?'

'She volunteers at the local charity shop, she'll know for sure.'

It was as if everything was falling into place. And how could anyone go crook over a tablecloth? Not possible.

'Okay, let's put that on the to-do list,' I said, moving to shift all the chairs out front into place.

Within the hour, Nancy had hooked us up with enough tablecloths to be able to rotate them when they needed to be washed. With a few minor adjustments and help from her expert hand the three of us were standing out the front, our hands on our hips, admiring how much more welcoming the entrance looked with the new display.

'I swear more people have come in today already,' said Cassie.

'See, it doesn't take much. A tiny change can make a world of difference,' I said, smiling from ear to ear.

'It looks lovely,' said Nancy, with a little tear in her eye. 'I'm sure Dean will be most pleased when he comes back.'

I wasn't so certain but all I knew was the Wipe Out Bar was coming to life, not only because it was literally shinier and cleaner than ever before, but also the bistro seemed to be slightly more occupied during the daytime.

Ha! You got this, Lexie Atkinson. This is how you should be all the time. Confident and capable.

'A job well done, ladies,' I said, turning to head back inside before I stilled, squinting and framing my eyes against the sun as I saw an unmistakeable figure coming – no, make that sprinting – up the arcade, dodging and weaving through the crowd. A small smile spread across my lips as I saw Laura gunning it towards us.

'Hello, stranger!' I laughed as she pulled up just before us, her hands on her knees as she regained her breath.

'Are you late?' I asked, glancing at my watch.

Laura shook her head, taking deep breaths so she could speak. Finally swallowing, she said, 'He's coming.'

My heart stopped. And I could tell that the same thing had happened to Cassie and Nancy too: the exact same feeling of fear swept over us.

'Dean? Where?' I asked, looking past her, my eyes searching the crowd, expecting to see the swarm of tourists part like the Red Sea as he stormed our way.

Laura looked at me, confused. 'Not Dean,' she said. 'Ballantine. Ballantine is coming to the Wipe Out Bar.'

Chapter Thirty-Four

'W- what?' I blinked, twice. What did she just say?

I stared at Laura, expecting her to start laughing, or tell me it was a joke, some kind of sick joke. But when her expression didn't change, it was like I could feel the earth fall away from me, heat creeping up my neck as the realisation sunk in.

Ballantine was back?

'H- how do you know?' I asked.

Laura tilted her head as if I was joking. 'How do you think?' she replied.

Boon.

My mind was racing; he was coming here, to the Wipe Out Bar. Holy shit. 'Does he know I work here?'

'I'm not sure, I think so, maybe . . . I don't know.'

Oh my God. I had clawed back some semblance of control, keeping myself busy and trying to find a means to prepare myself to be independent and strong, but the very instant the thought of Ballantine walking back into my life came to me, I could feel my resolve crumble. I was nothing more than that girl waiting under a streetlight for the boy to show, the one that broke my heart.

I inhaled a calming breath. 'When?'

'Tonight. Boppo, Ballantine and Woolly just got back from overseas so they're coming for a session with Boon.'

Oh God.

The Kirkland Boys from Paradise High were going to be here. Could I hide in my room? Could I disappear? I suddenly had a grand plan of sitting in Dean's office, hovering over the security monitors, taking in the scenes before me. And then, as always, the little voice inside whispered to my subconscious.

Get your shit together, Lexie. Face the music and be totally kick-arse!

I know I had planned to get to that point of being a total kick-arse in all departments of my life, I just wasn't sure I was there a hundred per cent just yet. Well, there was no better way to tell than by jumping in at the deep end. I glanced at my watch, calculating the usual time frame of arrivals for late-night partygoers. I should have a few hours, I thought, as my eyes flicked up to Laura.

'Okay, I'm going to need your help.'

'Okaaay. How so?' Laura asked, uncertainty lacing her voice.

'You have to help make me look bloody amazing.'

'Like Olivia Newton-John at the end of *Grease*?' laughed Laura.

My smile mirrored Laura's. 'Minus the stilettos!'

•

'Look, I don't know, Lexie, Dean seemed pretty adamant that you not do a night shift until he gets back.' Cassie's face twisted as if pained, which was pretty much every time we spoke to one another, seeing as it usually involved a hare-brained scheme like the one I was trying on right now. If

Ballantine was coming in with his mates I wanted to be behind the bar slinging drinks and showing them that I was more than some mousey school girl. I didn't know if he knew I was now calling the Wipe Out Bar home, but the fact he was even coming here made me feel so nervous, I needed to keep myself busy.

'Cassie, it will only be for tonight, I promise, and then there will be no more changing of any kind. I will simply sit quietly in my room and read up on cocktails.'

Cassie sighed. 'Seriously, you need to get a life; I have never met anyone who's practically begged for a shift.'

'Yeah, well, I'll get this under my belt and it will be one less thing for Dean to concern himself with when he comes back and sees what an excellent job you did educating me.'

Cassie's eyes lifted, a light of interest flickering in them before she nodded slowly. 'Okay, then, but only for tonight. I can swap Frankie to the bistro; he won't care but after that no more changes of any kind. I don't fancy Sherry taking back her job.'

'Sherry's left. She won't take your job.'

'You think? Why do you think she stopped by to talk to Dean?'

I went to speak and then paused. I hadn't thought of it like that.

'Make no mistake, Lexie, if Dean had to choose over two bar staff for one Sherry, he would always choose her.'

I swallowed, knowing that what Cassie was saying was the complete reality. Cassie, perhaps, but I, most definitely, would be out on the street. And what had I done? Learned the ropes, studied hard, thrown myself into understanding the place and tried to be a help, not a hindrance. The other thing

I had done was potentially piss Dean off epically. I wondered if it were too late to put Hank back up.

'You still want to help work the bar tonight?'

I blinked, meeting Cassie's questioning eyes. With Dean returning tomorrow, this could potentially be my only chance to learn the bar firsthand from experience without him present, and my one and only chance to see Ballantine. If it was the nail in my coffin and Dean fired me for Sherry, then so be it – I would move in with Principal Fitzgibbons and never darken Dean's doorstep again.

I nodded. 'I'm sure. If I lose my job, I might as well go out with a bang,' I said, smiling weakly.

Cassie didn't share the joke. 'Bloody hell, Lexie, this better be the last of your grand ideas, I don't think my heart can take much more.'

I scoffed. Mine either, I thought, mine either.

•

'So, what do we think?' I stood in front of the cracked mirror of my 1970s wardrobe, slowly turning to meet the wide-eyed stares of Cassie and Laura.

'You look smoking hot, Lex!' Laura chimed.

My eyes shifted to Cassie, who was smiling and nodding. 'Sex on legs,' she said.

I glanced back to the mirror to check they were both seeing what I was seeing, because as far as 'smoking hot' and 'sex on legs' were concerned, well, I had never been referred to as either of those . . . ever.

To fit in with the Wipe Out Bar vibe, I wore black skinny jeans, and a fitted black singlet top that made my boobs look deceptively big, which was a win. But what was most different was my face. Courtesy of Cassie I now sported smoky eye shadow that made my eyes pop, a cherry lip balm that made my lips shine and a delicate blush to my cheeks. I hardly recognised myself. My long blonde hair sat in a high ponytail that flowed over my shoulder. The outfit was tight, and accentuated all the right curves, all the ones I usually hid. I didn't even feel like me, and maybe that was what I needed? To channel some kind of alter ego in order to get through tonight, in order to face Ballantine and the Kirkland Boys. I took a deep breath. I felt like I wanted to be sick.

'I don't look too . . . slutty?' I asked, pulling my top up a little.

'Lexie, you look amazing. Seriously, every bloke is going to be ogling you, and Dean's booze takings are about to skyrocket. He is going to never want to let you go.'

'Ah, yeah, well, Dean will never know about tonight.' I cringed.

'What do you mean?' asked Laura.

'Well, he just can't know about me working the bar tonight.'

'Ha! And you think he won't find out? Are you serious?'

'Well, he might, but it won't be from any of us,' I said, glancing at Cassie, who nodded her head in total agreement.

'I think most people value their lives enough to keep it on the down low,' Cassie said.

Wow, everyone really was scared of Dean. I just didn't get it. Dean could be an arrogant jerk with a penetrating death stare like no other, but there was something that suddenly occurred to me. He didn't scare me, not in that way, anyway.

'You ready?' asked Laura.

I took one last look at the stranger reflected in the mirror as I inhaled a calming breath.

'About as ready as I will ever be.'

Chapter Thirty-Five

There were two things I didn't count on happening that night.

The first was just how really fast you had to be, even knowing every name and configuration of every alcoholic and non-alcoholic beverage in house, and knowing how to use the EFTPOS, cash register and volume on the sound system. Nothing could have prepared me for the chaos of a night-time full house of thirsty patrons.

The second and probably the most disturbing thing I hadn't counted on was the entire class of Year Twelve graduates being present at the Wipe Out Bar tonight. So many familiar faces in the crowd and at the bar from last year's Year Twelve. It seemed that everywhere I looked I recognised a face, and they recognised mine although their reaction was somehow quite different from my own.

'Hey, didn't I go to school with you?' yelled a cute, tall boy over the music. I didn't know his name but I knew he was in Chisholm House at school.

'Yeah, I was under you,' I yelled back.

The boy, who had a brilliant white smile, laughed as he shook his head. 'Now that would be something I would most definitely remember,' he said with a wink, as he grabbed his drink and headed back to his friends.

I blushed crimson, but had no time to let the innuendo take up too much time. As he left there were a million others to serve.

But even amid the chaos I was aware that I had yet to serve or spot Ballantine or any of his Kirkland mates. I had a sinking feeling that they might have changed their minds about coming, that maybe the last thing they wanted to do was hang out with a bunch of people they went to school with.

As the night went on the pace didn't lessen, not once I started scanning the crowd less and merely focused on the immediate line before me, at all the antsy, needy customers waving their money at me. And I realised I was loving every minute of it. The fast pace, the pumping music, the never knowing what was next, the witty banter from the boys who would shamelessly flirt with me. I could feel my alter ego soaring in confidence with every transaction.

'Lexie, go and take a break,' Cassie called from the other end of the bar.

'A break?'

Cassie rolled her eyes as she pulled a beer from the tap. 'You need to eat, take fifteen,' she said.

'No, it's okay, I'm not hungry,' I said, dumping change into a customer's hands with a smile.

'Lexie, a break is non-negotiable. Go! I'll get Frankie to cover for you.'

As much as I didn't want to I knew she was right. Breaks were forced on staff so as not to burn out, and as much as it pained me I served my last customer and untied my black apron from around my waist.

'Okay, back in fifteen,' I said.

'Good girl!' said Cassie as if she was amazed I had agreed.

Leaving the bar, weaving my way through the bustling crowd to head towards the back exit, I strode down the corridor towards the kitchen, which wasn't exactly the place you wanted to be as it had a different kind of chaos going on. There was a lot of yelling and clanging of pots and saucepans as orders flew up to the pass. I was supposed to put in a request for some dinner, but the last thing I had wanted was to eat. I was far too worked up to even think about food, so instead I slipped out the back entrance past the alcove where my poor bike lay crumpled and unloved, until I earned some real money to fix it. I walked down the back passage and through the screen door, where a set of milk crates sat next to a smoke bucket and a skip bin on either side. It wasn't the fresh air I was after, but it certainly was much quieter as I dragged up one of the crates and sat down, taking a moment to relax a little. However, the adrenalin that pumped through my veins was not an easy thing to tamper down.

Laura had promised she would be back tonight for moral support, but I hadn't seen her yet. It was now ten o'clock and I knew that the cool kids usually made fashionably late entrances but this was ridiculous. I then started to reason with myself. They were probably doing a bar crawl and seeing as the Wipe Out Bar was at the end of the arcade it seemed possible that this would be the final stop. In a way I hoped that was true. Maybe Ballantine would be a few beers in, to loosen up his inhibitions a bit, make our reunion less potentially awkward. It sure had helped me, I mused, thinking back to the night I had hitched a ride here. It seemed like a lifetime ago. A time when I wasn't sure if I would ever see

Ballantine again, and yet here he would be, close and yet so far.

I hated the forced break, with nothing but time on my hands. Old worries and insecurities crept back into my mind and made my heart ache in that familiar way. I didn't want to recognise that feeling, I wanted to be numb. I had no idea what I wanted out of this, what seeing Ballantine would do to me. My own plan had been so clear until now, to work to be busy, to take out my anger and frustration on Dean, whenever he wasn't gallivanting God knows where. I just wanted to be different from how I had been when I arrived in Paradise. I didn't want to be that whining, emotional girl anymore. And this week I had proven to myself that I could be different, and now I was determined to prove it to everyone else too. It was just the right frame of mind I needed to propel me back to the bar again. When I appeared, I saw the none-too-subtle look from Cassie, the one that read: 'That was not fifteen minutes'. But she didn't have time to argue the point. There were thirsty patrons to serve.

I got back into it like I had never left, and the criss-crossing rhythm Cassie and I had worked out so as not to run into each other became instinctual. I think even Cassie was surprised how well we worked together.

'I'm going to do a glass run, you okay here?' I yelled at Cassie over the music.

'Yeah, go for it. You read my mind,' she laughed.

I could never have imagined working with Sherry like this. Cassie was nice and very generous with information and compliments, so helpful and ready to help me learn or, like in the last few days, let me take some risks.

Stacking up glasses as high as I could manage from tables, windowsills and other creative places people tended to stash them, I made my way carefully back to the bar. The last thing I wanted was to have to explain to Dean why two dozen glasses were missing.

The rush of the crowd seemed to calm down as the night wore on and as eleven crept up, doubt crept in that the Kirkland Boys were going to show up at all and my heart sank. I desperately wanted Laura to walk through the door with an update, and just as if conjuring her out of my thoughts, Cassie called out from the other end of the bar: 'Lex, phone.' She held up the receiver. 'It's Laura.'

I blinked, wondering how I hadn't even heard it ring. My thoughts had been so far away. I was actually worried that customers might have gone thirsty on my watch for a minute, but as I surveyed my surroundings the coast was clear: no empty glasses and no waving money, phew. I made my way over to take the phone.

'Thanks, Cassie,' I said, pushing myself around the corner as far as the cord allowed me to reach. I placed my hand over my other ear to block out the thudding of the music.

'Where are you?' I shouted down the receiver.

'Shit, Lexie, I'm sorry, Mum's being a real bitch about me going out tonight. She says she wouldn't care but I have to work tomorrow morning, so I'm not going to make it.' She sounded sad.

'Yeah, well, looks like you aren't the only one who couldn't make it,' I said bitterly.

There was a long silence on the other end before Laura spoke. 'What do you mean?'

'Seems like the Kirkland Boys had better places to be than the Wipe Out Bar,' I said.

Laura scoffed. 'No way, Lexie, they left hours ago from here. They were heading straight there. They've got to be there.'

'Well, they're not, believe me. They must have changed their minds.'

'No, they were definitely going, Ballantine was really adamant about it.'

I frowned, starting to second-guess myself, before I shook my head. 'Laura, I swear they are not here.'

'Lexie.' Laura was starting to lose her cool. 'They said they were picking up Boppo at Woolly's and then heading to the Wipe Out Bar to play some pool.'

My blood ran cold. 'Pool?' I repeated, my mind racing at a hundred miles an hour as the details of a vague memory slotted back into place. The first time I had ever come to the Wipe Out Bar with Ballantine, he'd taken me around the back of the building and entered through the basement he affectionately called the 'Snake Pit'. A dank, dark room lined with pool tables and couches with a dodgy little bar in the corner – a haven where all the delinquents could shoot some pool away from the restaurant.

I closed my eyes. Surely not, surely it couldn't be true. Had the Kirkland Boys been here all along?

'Lexie? You there?'

'Yeah, I'm here,' I said, opening my eyes and shaking my head.

'Do you know where they are?' she asked, almost panicked.

'Yeah, yeah, I know where they are.'

•

After telling Cassie I just needed to grab something from my room, I made my way up the stairs, praying for one thing

– that Dean's office was unlocked. I didn't like my chances from the likes of Mr Paranoia, so when I tentatively twisted the handle and it actually turned the entire way I could have kissed Dean's feet.

I couldn't believe he had left it unlocked, but when I turned on the light it kind of became clear why he wouldn't care. Looking at the safe and the cupboards and desk drawers all locked up like Fort Knox, there was probably some kind of invisible laser beam criss-crossed over the room for would-be thieves. I had one purpose and one alone, as I quickly decided to switch off the light and close the door behind me. I really didn't want to alert Cassie or anyone down below of my whereabouts. I had to be quick, in and out and back to the bar before Cassie started to wonder about me.

After a skim along the panels it didn't take me long to work out what buttons I needed to press in order to bring the security monitors to life. One by one they blinked on, the grainy black-and-white screens painting a lively image of what was happening below. My eyes flicked along the screens and finally locked on the one that I wanted: the Snake Pit. One screen clicking from one angle to the next. I moved closer, leaning in to fix my attention on the changing images. A long shot of the pool room where all tables were visible, then a shot of the back door lingered for around five seconds before flicking inside again, this time to the couches where two groups sat, but try as I might I couldn't see Ballantine among them and I swear my heart was beating so fast I thought it was going to break through my chest. The image changed to the front door of the basement now, then back into the room and just as I was about to resign myself to the fact that the Kirkland Boys were most definitely not at the Wipe Out Bar, the monitor changed view to a corner of the room, making two pool tables very clear on the screen, clearer than any of the other images before and perhaps more meaningful than any could be, because as I squinted at what was before me, I felt my world fall away. In one five-second image, my heart shattered into a million pieces. Ballantine was most definitely in the pool room all right. He was there with his arm snaked around Lucy Fell.

Chapter Thirty-Six

'Lexie? Is everything okay?' Cassie called out to me. I had stormed down the stairs and past the bar with heavy-footed steps as I untied the back of my apron in one fluid motion and threw it on the bar. It was obviously hugely entertaining to see a girl storm through a crowd with steely determination because even over the loud thuds of music, as Australian Crawl's 'Boys Light Up' blared out of the jukebox, I could hear the cat calls and 'yeah baby!' heckling as I pushed through the drunken hordes towards the Snake Pit door.

I was beyond pissed, beyond enraged as everything over the past months came crashing back – all the silence, all the uncertainty of Ballantine leaving without even giving me the chance to explain and now he was back, laughing it up with his mates and Lucy Fucking Fell of all people, knowing how cruel she had been to me. If he didn't want to be with me then so be it, he just needed to insert a fucking sensitivity chip.

I burst through the door of the pool room. The dank, dark room was well and truly like a snake pit. I was backlit by the stream of light that flooded into the room, standing on the landing like a nightmare, staring in the direction of the Kirkland Boys. It had been a handy heads-up, thanks to Dean's security monitors. I saw Ballantine. His back was to me and he no longer had his arm around Lucy, but that didn't matter, I had seen enough in a ten-second flash for it to haunt me for years. Lucy was laughing it up on the couch with a couple of Year Twelves from last year, flicking her hair and blending in in a way I never could. Boppo saw me first, his attention snapping Woolly's head around, raising his brows in surprise before elbowing Ballantine, who turned, smiling, his eyes searching then locking on me, his smile slowly falling away, his eyes widening with disbelief as he turned fully and straightened.

My stony facade remained. Maybe I had learned a thing or two about working and hanging with Dean, but as I descended the stairs and moved to weave a determined line around the pool tables towards my captive audience, Ballantine shifted, moving forward, looking me over like he had seen a ghost.

'Lexie?'

I came to a stop right before him, close enough so when he looked into my eyes, he would make no mistake in comprehending my meaning. He reached out to touch my arm.

'Jesus, Lex, I can't believe –'

I dragged my arm away. 'Don't. Don't you bloody dare, Luke Ballantine.'

Everyone in the Snake Pit had turned their focus to us, the action in the room centred purely on me and Ballantine. This was not how I'd expected our reunion to be. I had visions of eyes locking from across a room, yes, but not like this, never like this.

Luke smiled and it was as I had always remembered, warm and completely disarming. I dug my nails into the palms of my hands to focus on something other than the familiarity of that smile.

'This is where we had our first date, remember?' His dark brown eyes never left mine, never faltered.

'Not one word, Ballantine. Not. One. Word.'

He sighed. 'Lex –'

'You didn't have the guts to say goodbye. You just believed what you wanted to believe, but I'm here to say that you were wrong. I would have waited for you, I would have waited for you forever.'

Ballantine's mood shifted, as the full weight of my words settled and gained traction in his mind. He was no longer the cock-sure, charming surfer, he seemed at a loss, searching desperately for the right thing to say, but the truth was, there was nothing he could say, nothing that he could tell me now that would wipe away or change the past. I don't know what I was waiting for, standing in front of him, hoping that by some magical force he would come out with the most profound speech, some completely acceptable explanation that would obliterate all the hurt inside of me. I squared my shoulders, preparing myself for the words that were to come, and just as he was about to speak, another voice interjected.

'Oh, for Christ's sake,' Lucy groaned, standing up from the couch. 'Take a fucking hint, he is not interested in you.'

I glared at her, a rage building inside me. I swear there were laser beams hitting her right between her eyes.

'Lucy, back off.' Ballantine cut her a dark look.

'What? Ballantine, she's fucking around with your brother, living with him, working for him. Who is she to act all high and mighty?'

'ENOUGH!' he shouted at her, so loud I swear she yelped. She was stunned, her eyes wide and shocked before they narrowed into something sinister.

'Pfft, what a joke.'

'You're the fucking joke,' came a voice, a voice I would recognise anywhere as my attention snapped to the corner of the room to where Amanda sat, her arms linked around Boon's neck. I hadn't even seen her before now. She slid off Boon's lap, moving to stand before Lucy. Amanda was taller and more athletic than Lucy's petite frame, and when Amanda threw daggers, she intimidated like no other.

'All your life you have been a dumb, rich bitch with a bad attitude. Now shut the fuck up.'

Lucy glowered at Amanda. 'Oh yeah, and what does that make you?'

'A smart, rich bitch with a bad attitude who has woken up to you.' Amanda stepped forward. 'You so much as even curve your stupid over-plucked eyebrow at my cousin again, you will be dealing with me. Got it?'

Lucy smirked, putting on a front of being anything but intimidated as she looked Amanda up and down like a piece of scum, until Boon stood up.

'And you'll be dealing with me,' Boon said, staring her down.

Boppo saluted. 'Me too.'

Woolly added, 'Me three.'

Lucy didn't seem so sure now, her gaze shifting from one Kirkland Boy to the next, before landing on Ballantine, who simply shook his head, which was all that was needed for the tears of fury to build in her eyes.

Ballantine turned back to me. 'Look, is there some place we can talk in private?'

I didn't know if I wanted to talk, now or ever. In my mind there was nothing to say, but as my eyes landed on Lucy Fell, I did have a definite feeling of how much it would piss her off if I left with Ballantine right now.

I tore my eyes from her and looked at Ballantine. 'Okay,' I said. I turned to lead the way out of the Snake Pit, relieved that there would be no more of a show, thinking I had made a big enough spectacle of myself as it was.

'You fucking bitch!' came from behind me, just before a full pot of beer landed across my back, drenching me in the ice-cold, frothy amber. I held my arms out, frozen in shock, my mouth agape as I turned to see Ballantine standing to my side, wearing part of the drink himself. We both turned in confusion to see Lucy standing in the middle of the room, glaring at me, and with a split-second decision . . . all hell broke loose.

Chapter Thirty-Seven

I had never been in a physical fight before. Never ever been involved, let alone instigated a bar room, or in this case, a pool room brawl. But as I took in the cocky smirk and infuriating curve to Lucy's brow after she hurled the drink at me, a Hulk-like rage spread through me like fire; it would be the last drink she would spill on me, ever. In a flash, it had gone from *The Bold and the Beautiful* dramatics between me and Ballantine to an episode of *Jerry Springer* as I lunged at an unsuspecting Lucy and wrestled her to the sticky floor of the pool room.

The Snake Pit erupted, the crowd milling around us as if they were watching two gladiators fight to the death, which in all honesty wasn't too far from the truth.

Fight, fight, fight, fight chanted the masses. It was like we were in a schoolyard.

I had gained pole position, overpowering Lucy, pinning her on the ground, just before I felt a steel-like grip around my waist, scooping me up as if I weighed nothing. Ballantine lifted me away, my arms flailing and my legs airborne as I kicked.

'Let me go!' I screamed, my arms imprisoned at my sides. Ballantine chuckled next to my ear.

'Not bloody likely.' He carried me to the back door, Amanda and Boon scrabbling to open it and escape into the night as pandemonium continued to break out behind us.

'Quick, go-go-go.' Boon held the door open for us as Amanda helped Ballantine drag me up the steps and dump me in the back alleyway. I fell inelegantly on all fours, fighting to catch my breath as the adrenalin worked to pump my heart so fast I thought it might stop.

'What the hell just happened?' said Boon, breathless.

'What just happened,' Amanda said, moving to offer me her hand, 'is Lexie just kicked serious arse.' She laughed as she pulled me to my feet.

I had aimed to be an arse kicker, but not in the literal sense. Ballantine shook his head at me like he was barely believing what he was seeing before him. It was exactly the response I wanted. I wanted people to start seeing me as anything but Lexie, mousey farm girl from Red Hole. And it had felt pretty amazing until the adrenalin wore off and reality sunk in. The door to the basement flew open, causing us all to turn to see Cassie skipping every second step into the alley.

'Lexie, what the hell?' she screamed. She stood before me, her voice shaking. 'I trusted you, and what do you do the minute I turn my back?'

'Cassie, I'm sorry, I didn't mean to –'

'Just don't,' she said, holding up her hands and stepping away. 'I am so fired. I hope you're happy,' she said, turning away and heading back inside.

When the basement door swung to a close, muffling the loud beat of the music and voices inside, the full weight of the situation dawned on me. Tonight I'd tried so hard to be responsible, and I had completely blown it.

I'd never felt like such a failure as I did now. I had let my emotions override my own wants, and this better person I was trying to build myself into, she was nowhere to be seen. Instead, in her place was some brawling, painted-up tramp. This wasn't me. But worse than that, I didn't even know who I was anymore.

'Hey, don't worry about Cassie, Lex, she'll get over it,' Boon said, trying to make me feel better.

I breathed out a laugh, taking in my drenched, dirty attire, the tear in my singlet top. 'She shouldn't have to get over it.'

An awkward silence fell over us until Amanda, who was about as subtle as a sledgehammer, elbowed Boon, motioning for them to leave with a nod of her head.

'Well, in light of tonight's events, I think I'll be crashing at your place tonight,' said Amanda.

A devious glint lit Boon's eyes as he looked at Amanda in the way he always had done – with complete adoration. 'Sounds good to me.'

Amanda turned to me. 'You okay?'

'Sure,' I lied. 'And thanks.'

Amanda grinned. 'Anytime. No-one makes my cousin's life a misery but me.' She elbowed Boon. 'Let's go.'

Amanda and Boon saluted their goodbyes and made their way out of the back alley, disappearing around the corner, leaving me alone with a very silent Ballantine.

'Hey.' Ballantine touched my elbow, but I shied away.

'Don't.'

Ballantine breathed out, as if praying for patience. 'Lexie, come on, talk to me.'

'Oh, what, so now you want to talk?'

Ballantine just stood there, looking at me as if an inner turmoil raged in his mind about whether to comfort me or not. Instead he surprised me by breathing out a laugh. A fucking laugh?

He shook his head, kicking at the ground. 'I'm not doing this, Lexie – not tonight, not any night.'

I scoffed. 'Well, run away then, it's what you're good at.'

Ballantine's eyes blazed.

'Did you even think about me when I left?'

Ballantine stepped forward, not touching me or looking me in the eyes. 'Of course I did.'

My heart was beating out of control. Despite all my reservations I still wanted to close the space between us, to forget about everything in between, but there was something that we weren't talking about, the same thing that would come up time and time again if we didn't talk about it now.

Dean.

I lifted my eyes to where the moon cast rays over the fire escape into an eerie glow against the back of the building.

Ballantine followed my eyeline. 'Home sweet home,' he said unenthusiastically, glancing up at the murky building painted in graffiti.

I shrugged. 'I work here, I have my own little room. It's okay.'

Ballantine reached out to grab my hand. I turned, seeing his weak smile as he laced his fingers with mine. 'Come away with me, Lex.'

'W– what?'

'We'll leave Paradise behind, just you and me,' he said, each word a promise.

I blinked, my gaze fixed on the fire escape. No-one was standing there, but a sense of unease swept over me, knowing how the back alley had eyes, and the things that people did here. I remembered the two strangers.

'We'll find our own paradise,' he said, as I felt his hand squeeze mine.

'Leave Paradise?' I repeated, trying to gather my thoughts.

Ballantine looked down at me as if the question was obvious. 'For the tour,' he said. 'I got sponsored, Lex.' He said it as if it was good news, and I guess it was, just not for *us*.

My mouth gaped, looking up at him like he was a stranger.

He shrugged. 'We don't leave until the end of the month.'

'The end of the month?' I placed my hands on his chest, pushing space between us. 'And then what? When were you going to tell me this?'

'I'm telling you now.' Ballantine shifted back a little. 'Lex, come with me, we can travel around from beach to beach, see the world.'

'You know what I had to do just to get as far as Paradise?'

'We can work it out.'

'I have school, I can't just leave . . .'

'Lex, come on, we don't have to have all the answers tonight. We have time.' Ballantine lifted my chin to look at him.

I shook my head. 'You can't not talk to me for weeks and weeks and then come into my life and expect me to leave it all behind,' I said, the tears forming in my eyes. 'You broke my heart.'

Ballantine's eyes were filled with sadness, his touch burnt against my skin. 'From here on in, Lex, nothing else matters, it's just you and me.'

Apart from the words of apology for abandoning me, *us*, those were the words I had so desperately wanted to hear. For all the times I cried myself to sleep, or wondered if I might see him today or tomorrow, if he would walk into my life again, and here he was, right here, and he was telling me he was mine.

Nothing else matters.

But something else did matter, and I couldn't quite put my finger on it. As much as I longed to be in Ballantine's arms again, things had changed. I had changed.

I looked into the softness in his eyes, noticing the way his fingers gently glided through my hair ... All I had gained tonight, all the familiarity I had felt in these past moments together were all for nothing. I looked Ballantine straight in the eyes, my chin trembling, as I took in a deep breath for courage.

'I'm so confused.'

Ballantine's eyes searched my face, his smile slowly disappearing as my words sunk in. He lowered his hand from my cheek. A coldness swept over him.

'It's an easy answer, Lex. Yes or no?'

'It's not that easy,' I snapped.

'Really?'

'Yes, really!'

We stared at each other for a long moment, tension building between us.

I looked him straight in the eyes. 'You answer me this then. What is this?'

'What is what?'

'This, here, now, you and me. Is it just some kind of quick hook-up in the night, some quick little fling? Tell me.'

Ballantine sighed as he pulled away. 'Jesus, Lexie, does it matter what I say? You seem determined to twist everything that comes out of my mouth.'

When I had no words for him, couldn't even bring myself to look his way, Ballantine sighed. 'When you work out what it is you want, Lexie, let me know.' And without another word, Ballantine backed away, disappearing into the darkness, leaving me with my overwrought thoughts.

I wrapped my arms around myself as if warding off a chill in the night, but it wasn't cold, far from it. My flushed cheeks were streaked with hot tears. A part of me thought I should have just shut my mouth and moved on to rebuild what we had, keeping the past in the past – how different things would have turned out. But now, in my bid to be honest and start with a clean slate, I stood alone in a grotty alleyway. I made my way up the back fire escape, stepping my way up the stairs like a zombie. I felt numb, mentally exhausted, as I yanked open the dodgy back door.

Standing in the middle of my room, in the dark, the only sound that was audible aside from the thumping of the music downstairs was my rapid breathing – the heavy rise and fall of my shuddery breath. The equilibrium I had so desperately tried to maintain was quickly falling apart. My breaths turned to sobs and I clasped my hands over my mouth as I totally collapsed – the tears streaming down my face as the image of attacking Lucy ran over in my head again and again. Any confidence, any progress I had made since returning had been completely obliterated in one single moment. The thought of what had happened in the pool room made me feel ill. I had let down Cassie, lied to Dean, and let Lucy get under my skin. I was flooded with shame. All I wanted was to be far away, back in Red Hill where I didn't have to see any of these people again. I had been right the last time I left. Paradise *was* a fucking lie. I had left with a broken heart and, as if that wasn't enough, I had come back and watched it shatter all over again.

I crumpled to the floor, my back pressed up against the edge of the bed, my forehead against my tucked-up knees.

I cried so deeply, until I was physically unable to anymore. I was completely and utterly spent of all thought, all feeling. My bloodshot eyes simply stared, stared until the tears welled again, blurring my vision and wetting my cheeks. I had never wanted to admit it before, but now I had to. Because as far as pain went, I couldn't feel any more than I did right now, in the dark, on the floor in my room.

Then my mind wandered to a very unsettling admission. Now that Ballantine was back and potentially mine, why was it that there was only one person that dominated my thoughts? All the things he had done for me, the way he pushed me and baited me, angered me, the way a simple curve of his infuriating mouth could be so bloody sexy.

Dean.

I was seriously fucked up.

Chapter Thirty-Eight

As I towel dried my long, damp tendrils I wiped the steam free from the mirror, revealing a very different reflection from last night. I had gone from a confident femme fatale with a twinkle in her eye, a girl full of hope and determination, to a washed-out, red-eyed mess. It was in that moment that I made up my mind. I was going to go back to my room, ring my parents and head back to Red Hill where I belonged, to hang with my parents and be entertained by Uncle Eddie at family gatherings and with the constant torture of seeing Amanda's MySpace updates as Ballantine and Lucy lived happily ever after. I wanted to vomit.

No-one answered on the first, second or third call home. I took this as a sign and wondered if I should really worry my parents with yet another Lexie meltdown? It had taken me so long to gain any semblance of independence. Maybe I could simply get the bus back to Red Hill, sneak out of Paradise and rock up back at home . . . surprise! That seemed far more plausible. Hopefully by then I would have calmed down a bit, although I seriously doubted it. I knew that once I saw my parents' questioning eyes, I would lose my shit. It's kind of what I did.

I methodically packed my bags, rolling up my clothes and placing them into my suitcase. I found the task quite therapeutic. Maybe I would dump them out again when I finished and start all over again. I needed the distraction.

I didn't want to leave with any fanfare, and I really didn't know how I was going to manage to escape this bloody building with my bag in tow and not raise any suspicions, until it dawned on me.

The fire escape.

Perfect.

Aside from my anti-climactic departure there was one thing I did aim to do, and it did involve doing a sort of right thing. Leaving my bag on the end of my bed, I made my way out of my room and down the hall, opening Dean's office door and stepping in, where the monitors were still alight from last night, after I'd run out without even thinking or caring to turn them off. I couldn't even bring myself to look in their direction. Knowing that Ballantine would be long gone by now I still couldn't bring myself to look. Besides, I had a very clear mission to achieve before I left. I sat down behind Dean's desk, which was far too clean to be practical when you wanted to leave a note. Luckily, he wasn't overly paranoid about people stealing stationery I thought as I picked a pen from his holder and, finding that the only available surface to write on was the back of a Wipe Out Bar coaster, I flipped it over to the blank side. I stared at it for a long moment, thinking about what I wanted to say, and then a disturbing truth came to mind.

Dean,
I'm sorry I can't do this.
Lexie

It was the truth, it was simple, it was all I needed to say, but then why did my pen still hover above the note?

And before I could question, my hand started to move of its own accord again.

Want to hear something scary?

Of all the people in Paradise you have been the most real. Thank you.

I slid the coaster into the middle of Dean's desk so there was no way he couldn't see it. I placed the pen back into the holder and pushed myself to stand, walking from behind the desk, only to be stopped dead in my tracks as my gaze lifted to the figure in the doorway, Ray Bans framing his face, his army green duffle bag slung over his shoulder, a wolfish grin spreading across Dean's handsome, stubbled face.

'Honey, I'm home.'

Fuck!

Of all the times he had to catch me out. There, standing in front of me, his smile fading slowly as he lifted his glasses onto his head to reveal those damn hypnotic eyes that seemed to change colour depending on the light in the room. But if there was something that was always clearly reflected in Dean's eyes, it's that they saw straight through me, every time. It didn't matter how well I thought I was faking it, he had an excellent built-in bullshit detector and . . . he was seriously onto me.

'What now?' he asked, looking at me warily. He probably assumed that I would have been settled in by now, left the dramatics behind . . . Ha! Far from it.

And on top of everything, I just really couldn't deal with Dean right now.

'Nothing,' I lied, trying to step in front of his desk so his attention didn't stray to my note. I really didn't want to have to explain myself, I just wanted to sneak out through the back and head to the bus terminal.

'Why is it that every time I come into my office, you're here looking like a rabbit caught in the headlights?' Dean asked, dumping his bag on the floor, sighing as he ran his hand through his thick brown hair. He looked tired, weary from travel, unshaven, wound up like he had the whole weight of the world on his shoulders, simply by just stepping back into his office. I guess one positive outcome was that I would finally be out of his hair and Sherry, his most prized bar possession, could come back and they could put Hank the Shark back up together and live happily ever after.

'Don't mind me, I was just going.' I broke eye contact with him. I didn't want him to see that when I said I was *going*, I actually meant I was *leaving*.

'Whoa, wait a sec,' he said, pulling me up to a stop just as I was right beside him. 'I want to ask you something,' he said. His voice sounded darker than I had remembered, and I thought maybe he had seen that the outside tables were different.

I swallowed, I didn't know why. I was leaving so what did it matter? Firing me would be doing us both a favour. Now I just really regretted the note, thinking there was no way of retrieving it without him noticing. I waited for him to say something snide about any of the changes, but then he asked, 'You think you're ready to start tomorrow night?'

'W– what?' I said, a wave of disbelief rolling over me.

'Cassie said you've studied the cocktail book. Do you want to try put it into practice, begin on a slow night?'

Practice, I thought? If only he knew that I had put in some serious practice last night, that I had totally smashed it when I had all my wits about me. As for when my world was turned upside down, I had gone from bartender extraordinaire to a hot mess within seconds. I wasn't ready, and being confronted with this question, I realised Dean deserved to know the truth. Inhaling, I went back to his desk, slid the coaster off it and brought it over, passing it to him without a word. I watched his brows knit together as he started to read. I brushed past him, quickly making my way out before he had the chance to respond. Hopefully it was enough and now I could just go.

I thought he might call after me, maybe even come after me, block my way and demand an explanation, true *Bold and the Beautiful*-type stuff; instead, the reality of my world was oh, so different, as I heard him call out.

'You are un-fucking-believable.'

I paused, feeling the hairs on the back of my neck rise at the tone of his voice. I slowly turned to glare at him leaning in the doorway of his office, his brows lowered in challenge.

'Excuse me?' I said.

'You heard me.' Dean crumpled up the coaster in his hand and threw it so it landed at my feet.

My mouth gaped as I watched it fall. To think I had actually complimented him. Did he not read that part?

Dean pushed off from the doorway, striding towards me, his anger rolling off him. 'Never in all my life have I met such a spoilt, ungrateful, whining, self-absorbed, infuriating princess like you,' he shouted.

I should have had tears welling in my eyes, I should have slapped him for insulting me, for yelling at me, I should have yelled back that of all the bossy, moody, smart-arsed bastards I had ever met, he was lord of the arseholes, but I didn't because aside from everything Dean had just said, there was one very important detail . . . Everything he had just said was the truth.

I defiantly looked in his stormy and feral eyes, unblinking. 'I know,' I said.

Dean's scowl deepened. He looked at me like I was insane. 'What?'

I shrugged. 'I'm all those things,' I admitted.

Dean's expression shifted to one of total amazement as his gaze flicked over my face, as if waiting for me to reveal the truth.

'And if I am all those things, then I think I'm doing you a favour by leaving.'

Dean's frown returned. 'I think I'll be the judge of that,' he said.

'It's too late, I quit.'

'Like hell you do.'

'Excuse me?'

'You're not going anywhere, there's work to do,' he deadpanned, turning to walk back to his office as if the issue was non-negotiable. 'Seven tomorrow night start,' he called back over his shoulder.

Now I was getting mad. 'You can't make me,' I shouted after him, sounding like a defiant teenager.

Dean laughed, turning to look back at me. 'Oh, yes, I can.'

'No, no, really, you can't.'

'Yes, I can, times infinity, no returns,' Dean said, crossing his arms and arching his brow at me in cocky challenge.

I scoffed. 'You're such a fucking child.'

Dean's smile spread across his infuriating face. 'Yeah, but you would miss me if I were gone. In fact, did you miss me? Is that what all this is about? Punishing me for going away while you pine away for me?'

'You are delusional,' I said.

'Or, am I the only real person in Paradise City?' he said, his voice mocking, as he referred back to my note.

Honestly, I could just shoot myself between the eyes sometimes.

I started forward. This time it was me who was stalking him. I came to stand right before him, breathing out a laugh. 'There is nothing real in Paradise, not you, not anyone, and if I could have my time over again I would have never, ever come to this city.' I said my words with such steeliness there was no way Dean could have ever questioned my meaning and as his eyes searched mine, something came over him, almost an air of acceptance, of knowing that nothing he could do or say could change my mind.

He shifted slightly, nodding his head. 'Okay, go then. If that's what you want, go.'

I lifted my chin, meeting him in challenge as I nodded in return. I stepped away from him, thinking there was nothing left to say as I made a long, silent, determined line towards my room. I reached in for my suitcase, trying not to grimace at the weight of it as I extended the telescopic handle and rolled it behind me down the hall. I didn't dare look back, but I could sense he was watching me go as I put all my energy into walking away. I turned the corner at the end of the hall, finally out of sight as I quickened my steps towards the exit door, almost at a run. I felt weightless and a new determination kicked into gear as I held my hand out, ready to push the heavy steel door open with all my strength. I could hear a voice singing in my mind . . . freeeedoooooom

BANG!

'Aaaahhh, what the . . . owwwww!'

I felt as though I'd run straight into a brick wall. No, make that a steel wall. The usually unlocked, dodgy back door was now not so open and not so dodgy. I had jarred every part of my body upon impact; my teeth had literally rattled. I probably had fractures. I winced and rubbed at my right shoulder. It was then I heard the laughter from behind me, the infuriating laughter as Dean was hunched over, trying to control his hysterics, although he was failing miserably.

Bastard.

'Oh, well, when I said what's stopping you, I kind of forgot to tell you that the back door probably might. Sorry, my bad, I got it fixed,' he said, wiping his eyes and trying to blink himself into gaining his composure. He walked over to me, reaching out. 'You okay?' he asked, still laughing.

I snatched my arm away from him. 'Don't touch me. Thanks for telling me,' I snapped, rubbing my wrist.

'I thought you knew?' he said, wiping away tears of mirth.

'How the hell was I supposed to know you'd had it fixed?'

A crooked smile lined the corner of Dean's face. 'Yeah, well, you can never be too careful of what deviants might be lurking on back fire escapes,' he teased, leaning against the wall next to me.

'Dean?'

'Yes, Lexie?'

'Open the fucking door.'

Chapter Thirty-Nine

Three hours I waited.

I waited until some random passer-by happened to tell me that there were no buses running today.

Just great!

A thunderous cloud settled over me. No, really, an actual, honest-to-God cloud came over the city, and the heavens opened up, drenching me in a heavy downpour. First the rain pummelled down heavily, then the sun pierced through the cloud and the rain stopped, causing steam to rise off the hot concrete, cranking up the humidity to at least ninety per cent. I threw caution to the wind and made a break for it, rolling my bag back to where I had come from, until, of course, the cloud closed in and the rain poured down again. I walked on, one of the sole figures walking in the storm as everyone around me scurried under cover to wait it out. Others ran with papers, jackets, bags, anything they could grab to shield them from the weather. But I didn't care, I was over caring, I simply walked on, my hair plastered to my drenched t-shirt, my suitcase rolling behind me as I veered back into Arcadia Lane, heading back to the Wipe Out Bar. I would rip off one of those bloody tablecloths and use it as a towel if I had to, but as I neared, I decided on another course of action.

'Dean Saville!' I screamed up to the balcony like some crazed lunatic, standing in the rain. Oh my God, I really was in a Jane Austen novel, minus the ladylike decorum.

I went to yell out once more but just before I did, a figure appeared at the edge of the balcony, his hands plunged deep into his pockets as he took in the tragic, and amusing, if his smirk was anything to go by, sight before him.

'You just can't stay away, can you?' he called down.

'You knew the buses weren't running today,' I accused.

Dean squinted up to the heavens as if deep in thought. 'Now that I think about it . . .' he said, tapping his chin.

Forever the smart-arse.

'You are such an arsehole,' I shouted.

Dean roared with laughter. 'For Christ's sake, woman, I gave you a job, shelter from the storm.' He swept his arm out to the streetscape. 'What more do you want from me?' he yelled.

My mouth gaped, ready to speak but unable to as I actually didn't know what to say. He was right, he was trying to help me, and all I was trying to do was run away, so eternally emotionally screwed up there really was no way of helping me. As much as Dean had given me there was only one thing I had been searching for this whole time. The only thing I'd wanted from anyone was Ballantine, and as my eyes blurred with the rawness of that emotion, I looked up at Ballantine's older brother, gripping the railing of the balcony, his arms corded with his toned, tattooed muscles as the tension coiled in his body, staring down at me. It was then I realised, as I shook my head, there were tears joining the streaks of rain on my face.

'I don't want anything from you,' I said as I backed away, turning and rolling my bag down the arcade. No more would

I put him out, no more crazy, selfish behaviour, this was done ... it had to be.

'Lexie, wait!'

I glanced back briefly, only to do a double-take. I stopped still, my eyes widening as Dean climbed over the balcony railing, the downpour of the overflowing guttering drenching him.

What the hell was he doing?

He slid along the edge of the lip, side-stepping slowly to the left, while hanging onto the railing. His shoe suddenly slipped and I slapped my hand over my mouth, muffling my scream. But he quickly regained his footing as he steadied himself and reached out to grab the downpipe, the dodgy downpipe.

'Dean, no!' I shouted, running forward, looking up in horror as he ignored me and took hold of the downpipe, edging his way slowly down. I could hear the pipe groan under his weight. Nothing about the old building was solid and everything was made even less reliable by the rain. I held my breath, thinking him mad, that anyone even attempting to climb down in such a way in the pouring rain must be insane. I held my breath until finally, a few metres from the ground, he jumped, splashing a puddle on the drenched cement. I breathed a sigh of relief that was very short-lived as I took in Dean's murderous expression. By this time I should have been used to these death stares but this was something else entirely, this darkness took on a whole new depth, and I knew if I ran it would be of no use, that he would simply chase me down. He stormed over to me, glaring, the rain drenching him now too as he blinked wildly, his chest heaving.

'Really? You want nothing from me?' he shouted.

I blinked against the rain. Scared, shocked, dumbfounded by his words and his death-defying actions, which were all for what? So he could shout at me? I shook my head, more determined than ever to no longer owe Dean Saville a thing. He had done so much for me and I had screwed him around enough. 'No,' I said, with the utmost certainty.

Instead of being pleased, my answer had the absolute opposite effect on him – he got mad, madder than I had ever seen him.

He reached past me, grabbing my suitcase and moving inside.

'Hey!' I yelled after him. 'Who said I was coming back?'

'Sleep on the street then,' he called over his shoulder as he stormed past an open-mouthed pedestrian sheltering under the eaves of the Wipe Out Bar verandah. She wasn't the only one watching. The people at a group of tables in the bistro area were taking in the turbulent scene, their heads turning back and forth as if they were at a tennis match. There was no time to care, I was too busy being furious. I stormed past them, trying my best not to slip over as I squelched my way inside, my eyes boring into the back of Dean's head as he took my suitcase upstairs.

Everyone in the bar, including Cassie, watched on silently as two waterlogged people with murderous dispositions left a slippery trail along the floor and up the stairs. I couldn't bring myself to look at them, I was too busy thinking of ways to murder Dean Saville as I stomped up the stairway after him. He opened my door, throwing my suitcase roughly inside.

'Hey!' I yelled, pushing past him after my bag, picking up the sodden suitcase to stand on its right side. 'Don't throw it.'

My attention snapped from fussing over my suitcase to hearing the door slam, realising that Dean was standing in front of it. I swallowed, standing slowly as we looked at each other: wet, dishevelled and angry. The tension was so thick you could cut it with a knife. Luckily there was no knife to speak of because the way we were looking at each other we probably would have tried to murder one another had there been one. I left my suitcase, caring little if it fell over on its side as I went to stand before Dean.

'Get out of my room.'

Dean scoffed. 'What, you want it back now, do you?'

'Only until the bus comes.'

Dean rolled his eyes. 'When are you going to grow up, Lexie? I mean, it's really good to see that turning eighteen has made you more responsible. Look at you.'

I glanced down at the puddle forming at my feet and my sodden attire. 'Look at me? Look at you!' I yelled, pulling at his sodden t-shirt. His hand caught my wrist with such lightning speed I was taken aback with how quick he was, and how my heart beat so fast feeling him touch me, feeling the strength behind his hold, but above all hating the traitorous thrill that surged inside me when my eyes flicked up from his hold to meet his gaze. I knew I was in trouble, I knew it the moment I saw his eyes dart briefly to my lips, I knew it when I didn't fight his hold – if anything, I leant into it – I knew it when I was aware of nothing other than my breathing, deep and heavy, and I knew exactly how much trouble that meant when I noticed that Dean's matched my own. And even though the anger we had still remained, it morphed into something more, and there was nothing I could do to stop it, and what was more disturbing was that I really didn't want to.

Chapter Forty

Pulling me forward Dean crushed his mouth against mine, cupping my face and kissing me so passionately I felt the violent thrill twist in the pit of my stomach as my hands grabbed the damp fabric of his t-shirt, pulling him into me with a desperation that surprised and excited me. His tongue delved, searching, teasing, tasting me in a way I had never experienced before. I felt like a goddess under his touch, the way his fingers expertly danced across my wet, sensitive skin that was speckled with goosebumps, my nipples hardened and exposed through my sodden clothing. I gasped as he pulled me around, pressing my back against the grooves of the wooden door. His hand skimmed down over my breast, trailing down, down. A shiver ran along my spine, the anticipation of where he might go, but when his hand instead moved away from me, I was all but ready to protest when I heard the delicate click of the lock on the door. Only when my eyes briefly followed where his hand actually was, clicking the button on the door handle, did I get it as my eyes lifted to meet his, sparkling with amusement as he once more lowered his mouth on mine, kissing me deeply, robbing me of breath and pressing me hard against the door. He pulled away, hovering against my mouth, taunting me by being so close yet not giving me what I wanted, the added torture of his thumb skimming across my bottom lip, his free hand hovering and flicking playfully at the top button of my skirt.

'You still want nothing from me?' he whispered against my mouth.

'No. Nothing.' I breathed out the lie. I felt his lips smile against mine, before he kissed me again, this time slower, softer. His touch skimmed across my body as if I were made of glass. I felt very much on the edge, as if I could shatter underneath him at any moment as his hot lips traced a line down my neck. Telling him I didn't want anything from him was an absolute lie, because as he playfully nipped at my earlobe and whispered dirty promises into my ear, all that ran through my mind was what I did want from him, or, more appropriately, what I wanted him to do to me.

He was completely in control and I could feel the desperation building inside me. There was an inner urge, one I didn't know existed, almost like another Lexie, the one that was working to peel the damp fabric from Dean's body. He quickly caught on, finishing the job for me as he removed his t-shirt for me, over his head, and threw it to the ground. My hands slid up over his chest, his skin damp, smooth but blisteringly hot to touch. His body was built in all the right places, curves and dips in his torso that made for a beautiful landscape, one I wanted to explore, until Dean flinched as my fingers traced up his rib cage. He grabbed my hands and kissed my fingers with a small smile.

I raised my brow. 'Ticklish?' I mused, loving this small vulnerability I had just discovered. He didn't answer. Instead, he distracted me with his lips, his body pressing against mine as he took my mouth as if he was dependent on it for survival, stealing my breaths, making me whimper as he slowly peeled my top up and over my head, only then breaking away from me to throw it aside, before lowering his head to kiss me through my wet bra, already see-through from the rain. My head thudded against the door as I closed my eyes, my hands sliding through the wet tendrils of his thick hair as he tasted me. I was lost in the throes of pleasure, feeling his hands holding me prisoner on either side of my waist until I felt his hand skim up to my shoulder to work on peeling the strap down, exposing me to him and his hot mouth.

My breath hitched as he took my nipple into his mouth. Oh God, it felt good, so good, so utterly wicked as my hands grabbed at his hair and pulled him into me. Dean moved to slide down my other bra strap, freeing myself completely to him as his mouth moved to my other breast, bringing me undone, running his tongue over and nipping at the sensitive peak, the incredible heat of his tongue compared to the cool of my rain-soaked skin. I could feel my legs turning into jelly as a pressure built between my thighs. I could have cried when he broke away from me, but it wasn't for long. His hands moved up my body, sliding up to edge the wet denim of my skirt over my hips. The wet fabric of my undies was now the only barrier between me and the hard bulge in his denim pressed against my thighs. I linked my hands around his neck. He lifted me as if I weighed nothing. I wrapped my legs around his waist as he kissed me, deep, hard and in rhythm to his hips grinding me against the door. I groaned as he continued to move his hips, creating the most delicious friction that was robbing me of all my thoughts. His hot whispers against my neck only built the intensity.

'You want this? You want me to fuck you against this door?'

All I could do was nod and pull him closer to me, stopping his dirty mouth by kissing him into silence, trying to draw out the intense pleasure mounting inside me. I didn't want it to stop, ever. How I had missed the feeling of desire, of the heat, the weight, the longing for more. Never would I have believed I had wanted it like this, but just like Dean it was raw, rough, intense with fleeting moments of tenderness. All I knew was I did want Dean to fuck me, I had never wanted anything more in my life and I didn't know if it was built on the edge of a deeper emotion. All I knew was that I wasn't afraid, and there wasn't any part of me that said I shouldn't be doing this, even though it was definitely something I shouldn't be. The devil on my shoulder wanted this, wanted me to open myself up entirely and that was exactly what I was going to do.

I took Dean's hand and slowly guided it to touch me in my most intimate part. I looked him straight in the eyes.

'I do want something from you,' I said, my breaths heavy.

Dean's hand delved into the damp fabric of my undies, feeling exactly what I needed, teasing so slowly. He swallowed deeply. 'What do you want, Lexie? Tell me what you want.'

And just as he was about to slide his finger inside, as a promise of what was to come, I whispered against his mouth, 'I want it all.'

He closed his eyes, letting my words roll over him as he placed his forehead against mine. He exhaled as if that was exactly what he'd wanted to hear, and as my reward he pushed his fingers inside me, catching my gasp and urging me to be quiet as his magic fingers worked me into a passionate frenzy. I was ready to scream, to explode under his touch when something else shattered the moment.

Knock-knock-knock.

'Lexie? Are you there?' Laura's voice sounded through the door.

Fuck!

Dean and I were frozen, looking at one another: my eyes reflecting a blind panic, no doubt, and his complete and utter annoyance. I clamped my hand across his mouth.

'Um, hang on a second,' I called out.

Dean let me go, and panic kicked in as I righted my bra and he picked up his shirt, then mine. We didn't need to voice what we were both thinking as we searched around for an alternative exit, one we knew didn't exist. The window wasn't an option, the single bed was too small to squeeze under and I had a blind, no curtain to hide behind. It was then our heads both snapped around to my oversized 1970s Art Deco wardrobe. Perfect!

Dean skidded across to it, opening it up and stepping inside; we were doing our best not to laugh, but as a last-ditch reminder I placed my finger over my lips for him to be quiet as I closed the wardrobe door behind me. I then frantically worked on grabbing a towel to wrap my wet hair in a turban-like twist on my head. I peeled off my bra, throwing it into the washing basket as I wrapped myself into another towel. I looked at my flushed complexion in the mirror, and with the light sheen across my face I very much looked like I had just stepped out of the shower . . . perfect! I only hoped Dean could remain quiet and that there was enough ventilation in there. I would have to make this quick.

'Coming!' I called out, hearing a small laugh from the wardrobe. I paused, rolling my eyes before whispering *shhhh*. What I really wanted to say was *get your mind out of the gutter*.

I opened the door to Laura. 'About time,' she said, pushing past me into my room.

'Sorry, I just got out of the shower,' I said.

Laura glanced around my room. 'I thought you didn't have a shower?'

'Oh, yeah, no, I don't, I have to use the one down the hall.'

Laura made herself at home by sitting on the edge of my bed, idly flipping through my *Cosmo* magazine.

'So, what brings you to these parts?' I tried to change the subject. My eyes shifted to where my suitcase sat on the opposite side of my room where Dean had thrown it. I hoped Laura would stay immersed in the glossed pages before her, but like all things with Laura, she chucked away the magazine, seemingly bored already, until she straightened, her eyes locking with mine, wild with excitement.

'Oh no you don't!' she said.

'What?'

Crap, had she noticed the suitcase, and how unusually tidy my room was?

'Don't act all coy and innocent with me, Lexie Atkinson. Tell me what the hell happened last night.'

Oh God.

I cringed, hoping they built soundproof wardrobes in the '70s.

'Um, look, how about I get dressed and we go grab some Wendy's?' I suggested.

'Nah-ah, you are going to tell me right now. I heard you got into a scrag fight with Lucy Fell in the pool room?'

Oh-no-no-no-no-no . . .

There was no way of stopping this, of doing any kind of damage control, short of bashing Laura unconscious right now.

'I think you're getting a little carried away with rumours.' I tried to laugh it off, make it sound crazy, and hearing it out loud it did sound crazy.

'Oh, yeah, and the rumours about you and Ballantine disappearing into the back alleyway aren't true either, huh?' Laura wiggled her eyebrows.

Oh God, please just shut up. I just wanted the ground to open up and swallow me whole.

'Honestly, Lexie, bar room brawling and hanging out with hot boys in alleyways. Why does all the exciting stuff happen when I'm not around?'

'Trust me, nothing exciting happened, and how many times do I have to tell you about listening to rumours?' I replied, grabbing her arm and yanking her to stand, as good as frogmarching her to the door. 'Now, I have to get dressed, I have training to do, I'll see you tomorrow.'

'Ahh, so is Darth Vader back from his trip then?' Laura asked.

I really wanted to end this conversation right now.

'Goodbye, Laura, I have to get ready,' I insisted. I didn't have to work too hard at putting on the panic, knowing Dean was listening to every word of this conversation was making me feel sick.

'Well, unless you tell me something remotely juicy, I won't go,' she said, crossing her arms.

'How old are you, five?' I accused her angrily.

Laura smiled, batting her eyelashes. 'Just a tiny bit of gossip, please.'

'Okay, but only once you're out the door.'

'I'll stand here,' she said, wedging herself in the open doorway, 'just so you don't trick me.' She waited expectantly.

I thought for a long moment. What hot goss could I tell her? What hot goss did I know?

I kissed Dean, I kissed Dean, I kissed Dean, I screamed inside my head.

I blocked it out, thinking of something more appropriate.

'Okay, here's the goss . . . Amanda and Boon are back together.' And before I could take in her shocked, open-mouthed look I nudged her out of the doorway and closed the door, locking it behind her.

'Oh. My. God! Wait until I get home and see Boon,' came the outraged, muffled reply through the door. I would have laughed but I knew I had a much more pressing issue at hand.

I turned to see Dean making his way out of the cupboard.

'Good ol' Laura . . . she's so –'

'Annoying,' he deadpanned.

'And funny . . . She is good value, if not something of a romancer.' I wanted to chuck that in for good measure, hoping that he wasn't like everyone else in Paradise and believed everything he heard.

'Yeah, well, I guess last night's video surveillance should sort a few rumours out,' he said darkly, looking at me with his knowing eyes.

Oh shit.

He was going to look at the tapes, see me working the bar when he'd explicitly told me not to, see me storming into the bar picking a fight with Ballantine, then my wrestle with Lucy, and oh God, was there alley footage of me and Ballantine? I felt sick, ashamed.

'Is that why you were leaving?'

'I thought I would save you the trouble of firing me.'

'I'll be the judge of that,' he said coldly, moving to the door.

'Dean?'

He paused beside me, looking down on me, his face like thunder. I desperately wanted to shy away. 'For what it's worth, Cassie had nothing to do with any of it. Everything she does is in the best interest of the bar. I simply bullied her into letting me do things around here.'

Dean straightened. 'Bullying, tampering, fighting, loitering: I don't remember any of those attributes on your résumé.'

I blushed, clutching my towel tighter around me. 'I'm not proud of myself.'

He shrugged. 'It is what it is.'

My eyes snapped up. Is that all? What did that even mean? Did he even care that I was in the back alley with Ballantine? His stony, emotionless gaze said he didn't and it finally dawned on me. He'd just wanted a quickie against the door: no strings attached, no emotional baggage. I could have kicked myself for confusing the emotion between lust and more. Holy shit, I nearly lost my virginity to Dean Saville. Thank God Laura had interrupted us. I felt like such an idiot, so utterly, utterly stupid.

'You're right, people make mistakes all the time,' I said coolly.

Dean nodded. 'Some bigger than most.'

OUCH!

I tried to let my expression remain neutral but no doubt something flashed in my eyes. 'Yeah, well, I have a few things to sort out, so –'

Dean didn't seem overly interested. He moved towards the door to leave.

His lack of a response was more unnerving than anything. Was I fired, out on the streets? I guessed only time would tell.

I stood there long enough to watch him walk down the hall without so much as a backwards glance before I slammed my door closed, my heart racing, my thoughts in a whirl.

What the hell had just happened?

Chapter Forty-One

The pool room incident gave me a certain amount of cringeworthy street cred at school, fuelled by the usual rumour mill that had by now completely sensationalised the reality of the actual story. By the week's end, the story had blown out to me having been sent to Paradise after a stint in juvie and that I enjoyed kinky sex and collecting knives in my spare time. I had gone from Lexie Atkinson, mousey new girl, to that chick who works at the pub and beats up chicks for kicks. I had been all about reinventing myself but this was ridiculous.

I had also gained another more worrying status, one that I should have been used to, but whenever I overheard whisperings or the none-too-subtle questions about me and Dean being more than just employer and employee, well, that just made me feel awkward.

With the week moving on at an agonisingly slow pace, Dean avoided me at every turn and if there was an exchange I was lucky to even get a grunt for a response. I suppose that was better than I'd expected, which was to be given my marching orders. I never knew if he saw the tape from Saturday night but it was never mentioned. As for any bar shifts midweek or otherwise, my name was never on the roster and I didn't dare ask. All I wanted to do was fly under the radar for a while, not draw attention to myself.

The moment in my room seemed like a lifetime ago, but it was something that was always on my mind every time I sat in my room, and that was a lot. It took a good while for Cassie to decide she'd speak to me again. Thankfully Dean didn't seem to blame her for any of my bad behaviour, and I'd sworn to myself that I would toe the line, lay low and keep my mouth shut. No wonder the week had gone on for so long. There was silence in all aspects of my life, Ballantine included. I knew it would probably come down to me having to make a decision about our future. Whether I wanted to rekindle what we'd had?

My mind kept flashing back to the scorching press of Dean's mouth against mine and I sunk down deeper into despair. If it wasn't for the unlikely duo of Laura and Amanda keeping me company, I think I may have wallowed in a bit of self-pity. Funnily enough, I think they equated my weirdness solely to my problems with Ballantine. Ha, if only they knew.

There were lots of things that I couldn't stop thinking about, but one of the more positive things was a particular craving for a white buttermilk cupcake, and what better way to feed your emotions, as I finally stumbled across the mint green shop front, with *Paradise Cakes* hanging from a sign. I walked up to the window, my mouth instantly salivating at the decadent display of sugary perfection. This was the best kind of comfort food and would surely give me a much-needed lift. Maybe I could buy a cake to share with the staff after hours, a nice coconut-cream layered cake. Would the staff think I was a suck? That's what someone would do in Red Hill.

I pressed against the glass door. The bell above chimed my arrival and a lady with a head scarf and a kind smile looked up from straightening one of the dinky little coloured cards. Each marked out exactly what the item was. My eyes skimmed through all the delicious options. Blueberry coffee cake with vanilla glaze, chocolate fudge brownies with butterscotch chips and pecans, peaches and cream pie with sugar cookie crust, Hummingbird cake, lemon layered cake: I wanted them all.

'Decisions, decisions,' joked the lady.

'Far too many,' I replied with a grin.

'Are you after anything in particular?'

I sighed. 'I really can't decide.'

'Do you prefer something sweet or savoury, something a bit glitzy or something with a bit of substance? The strawberry double-crust pie is a crowd pleaser, but the Hummingbird cake is a classic. We do that in cake and cupcake sizes.'

I smiled to myself. Who knew you could draw a parallel between life and baked goods? I was all ready to go with a New York cheesecake when the back door swung open from behind the counter.

'Mum, Mary said she wants twelve more of the poppy seed cupcakes.'

My eyes snapped up to hear the familiar voice. 'Sherry?'

Sherry placed down her bag and her tray. 'Oh, hey, I'm gathering the cupcake was a hit then?'

I blinked.

'Dean's cupcake, said something about a belated birthday or something. Mum, this is Lexie, she works at the Wipe Out Bar.'

'Lovely to meet you,' said Sherry's mum warmly. 'Any friend of Dean's is a friend of ours.'

Sherry rolled her eyes. 'Mum.'

'Shush, it's true, and I am honoured that you're coming back for seconds.'

'It was absolutely delicious. This is your business?'

Sherry's mum straightened with pride. 'It is: Sherry, her sister Alyssa and I do all the baking. It's a real family affair.'

For once Sherry wasn't dressed in her usual black. Instead, she had a frosted pink polo and light denim jeans on, her hair was pulled back in a messy bun, and she even smiled when she listened to her mum. She was unrecognisable as the intimidating Sherry of last year. I recalled Cassie telling me Sherry had left the Wipe Out Bar because her mum got sick and it all made sense now seeing them together.

'Well, you're lucky to have a daughter like Sherry. I've seen her work, she's an absolute gun behind the bar.'

Sherry frowned at me. Obviously receiving compliments wasn't exactly her thing. I cleared my throat. 'I can't decide; could you please put a sampler box together for me, whatever you think is best.'

'One sampler box coming up!'

It took everything in my willpower not to crack open the box and devour one of the sweet, not-so-little morsels inside. Instead, I remained steadfast and focused, crossing the main road across from the boardwalk and heading towards the Wipe Out Bar. It was part of my afternoon ritual to disappear after school, to just get away from the stifling atmosphere of the Wipe Out Bar. This had been my first venture to Paradise Cakes, and if it was going to be a common destination, I was desperately going to need to do a lot more walking.

Maybe it was the unmistakeable frosted pink box I was carrying, but Cassie seemed uncharacteristically happy to see me.

'You are not going to believe this,' she said, her arms folded, shaking her head in disbelief.

'Oh?' I sat the box on top of the counter, waiting for her to elaborate. 'Go check the roster,' she said, her attention flicking to the box. 'Are those for me?'

'One is, just one.' I held up my finger to accentuate the point as I walked around the bar to check the roster. Every week, Dean re-did the staff roster, working in any changes, or if people were on leave or if staff were needed for special events. It never changed too much, but as my eyes roamed over the colour-coded chart I took in the fact there was a change: a big change. My name was scheduled on for a Friday night shift, as in tomorrow.

'What?' I mouthed, a line creasing my brow as I looked on in confusion.

Cassie leant next to the wall where the clipboard was mounted. 'Talk, abowt a cart with nurhn lives,' she managed past a mouthful of cake. If that was the case then surely I was on my last.

My heart beat faster; maybe Dean was coming around? Surely he couldn't stay mad forever, right? It was a glimmer of hope, but I wasn't going to get too distracted, I had a maths quiz to study for, and with the aid of a sugar rush and the reality of working tomorrow night, I felt the spring in my step already.

I grabbed the cake box, essentially rescuing it from Cassie as I headed for the stairs. 'Thanks for the cake,' she said, licking the frosting from her fingers. 'Feel free to donate anytime,' she called out.

I laughed, taking the stairs two at a time. Coming up to the landing, walking past Dean's open office door, I crept closer, noticing he wasn't there before I walked in the opposite direction down the hall, making it halfway before I stilled. I flipped the lid of my cake box, smiling at the contents, when I had an idea. I doubled back down the hall, tentatively walked into his office, selected the Hummingbird cupcake and placed it on his desk. Something with substance, I thought, thinking if the shift was him offering an olive branch of sorts, well, here was mine.

Chapter Forty-Two

With so many bridges to rebuild I was determined I was going to smash my shift. It was of the utmost importance that when Dean watched on from his little black-and-white monitor from mission control, I looked like a natural. Fast, efficient and without a thirsty patron in sight, that was my aim. I played down my slutty pub attire of the previous weekend. Really, who did I have to impress? I just needed to focus. Mercifully even Dean was nowhere in sight. I had to try not to think about him watching, I couldn't afford to be distracted.

Cassie and I were the dream team, both working in unison to keep up, but also finding enough time for a joke and a laugh. After the onslaught of the dinner rush with family jugs of soft drinks for tables to the late-night rush of people on the last leg of their bar crawl, time simply flew by. I was taking a moment of down time to slice up some lemons when I heard an obnoxious banging on the bar top.

'Oi, barkeep, make it snappy, would ya?'

I turned slowly, the hairs on the back of my neck rising until my eyes locked onto Amanda, laughing at herself.

'Hey, what are you doing here? Weren't you traumatised enough last weekend?' I grimaced.

'Ha! Where else am I bound to find such drama in town?'

'Well, you're just going to have to find it elsewhere. Tonight I am a saint.'

'Booriiing.'

'Boring is severely underrated.'

'I don't know about that. A week staying at Boon's and I could do with some excitement.'

I cringed, thinking about how awkward it would have been for Amanda to have had to collect her stuff from Lucy's.

'I'm so sorry.'

'Ha! Don't be. Do you want to hear something hilarious?'

'Yeah, okay, tell me while I make you a drink,' I said, glancing up at the camera above the bar. 'What do you want?'

'Hmm, I'm feeling a bit dangerous tonight. How about a Fruit Tingle?'

'Wow, you rebel!'

Grabbing a highball glass with ice, adding two nips of vodka, Blue Curacao and lemonade, giving it a brisk stir before topping it with a dash of raspberry cordial, transforming it into the most divine bluish-purple cocktail, I placed it in front of Amanda.

'So what's so hilarious?' I asked, taking her money as I moved to the till. Not much amused me these days so it would have to be good.

'Are you ready for this? Mum and Dad are coming home.'

'What? Why?'

'I was all set to head up there, but apparently the house is a disaster, the family in our house won't stop whingeing to them, so they're forfeiting the contract and heading back next week.'

'Next week?'

'Yep! Which means you can come home, you don't have to stay in this dive anymore, you don't even have to work here if you don't want to. Because you won't have to pay board. Isn't that great?'

Go back to the 'burbs? Leave here? I didn't know how I felt about that, but I knew Mum and Dad would be relieved.

'And I promise you . . .' continued Amanda.

'That you're not going to be a bitch to me anymore?'

'Oh God, no, I can't promise that, that's just crazy. What I was going to say was I promise you, no more Lucy Fell coming over.'

'Thank God!'

'Hey, thanks for the Fruit Tingle, bar wench, I'll catch you round.' Amanda saluted me with her drink. 'Oh, we're heading down to the boardwalk later if you want to come?'

'Okay, cool, do you have my mobile number?'

Amanda scoffed. 'I keep forgetting you have a mobile number, it kind of freaks me out.'

'Why, 'cause I'm not "cool" enough?'

'Cool? You're the one slinging drinks behind a bar, living in your own place. Do you have my number?'

'I do.'

'Okay. Text me and we'll meet up later?'

'It's a deal.'

Amanda broke away from the bar with a smile. 'Laters, taters.'

Did Amanda and I actually just plan to hang out? Did she actually accuse me of being . . . cool? Surely not.

But as the clock ticked on to the end of my shift I actually regained some kind of nervous excitement about doing something normal like hanging out with friends and, above all, keeping myself out of trouble.

•

As we shut the doors to the Wipe Out Bar, I was relieved that I hadn't got into any brawls, and stayed way clear of the back alleyway. As far as shifts went, I'd have gone so far as to call this one a successful one.

I printed out the bar takings receipt and gathered up the till insert. 'Cass, you ready with that?'

'Almost,' she said, pulling at the long paper trail of receipts from the till at the other end of the bar. 'I'll bring it up in a tick.'

'Cool. Hey, I'm heading down to the boardwalk. You wanna come?'

Cassie looked up with a smile. 'Yeah, why not?'

I nodded, spinning around and climbing the steps to deliver Dean a portion of the night's takings so he could count it out and put it in the safe. With every step my anxiety grew. I hadn't seen him all night but was well aware that he was up here, sitting, watching like he did most busy nights. I knew this had been a major test for me, my second chance not to screw up. Cassie and I had done a great job tonight, we'd even shut up shop and did the clean-up in record time. We were undeniably a great team. Dean was in his usual position, looking moody and in deep thought behind his desk.

'Well, I'd say that was a resounding success – nobody died,' I offered, plonking the till on his desk.

'Hmmph,' he managed as he stared at his computer screen.

I waited, thinking he might mention something about the cupcake I left him, but he just ignored me.

Okaaaay . . .

'Well, here's the last of it!' Cassie entered the office, mercifully breaking the awkward silence.

'Hey, Dean, we're heading down to the boardwalk. You wanna come?'

My head spun around to Cassie, trying to give her my best telepathic message for: *Shut the hell up!*

This had his attention. He broke away from his screen and leaned back in his chair, a glint of amusement in his eyes. 'Ahhh, the kiddies are going to play in the park; I think I'll pass,' he said.

'Well, it's up to you,' shrugged Cassie. 'I'll meet you downstairs, Lexie.' Cassie looked at me with raised brows before leaving me alone with the big bad wolf.

'So, how did I do?' I asked, regretting it the moment the words came out of my mouth. I should have known better than to ask him while he was in one of his black moods.

Dean pinched the bridge of his nose as if warding off a migraine. He sat forward in his chair, flicking through the paperwork on his desk, before eventually locating a notebook.

He idly flicked through the notebook, bored with every flick. 'Right, here. You need to be faster; memory retention is good but your service is a bit sloppy and you lack focus; there were two occasions when you needed to sweep the floor for a glass run; based on the tip jar people were either tight tonight or they just weren't fussed on the service. I'll have a better idea when I check the till balance and providing there's no active complaints from anyone . . . there's more. Do you want me to go on, because I can write it up for you?'

I stood at his desk, my hands balled into fists as I could feel the steam coming out my ears. I leant forward, placing my palms on his desktop. 'I nailed it tonight.'

His eyes shifted from my hands to my face. 'Is that right?'

'Nailed. It.'

Dean also leant forward, placing his elbows on his desk. 'And I say you need work.'

'Why are you being like this?'

Dean sighed, pushing himself back in his chair. 'Look, if you can't take constructive criticism then maybe this isn't the job for you.'

'Are you firing me?' I asked, in disbelief.

Dean looked at me. Gone was the open, unguarded person from the boardwalk, the smirky, teasing smart-arse I had become accustomed to or the Dean who had pressed me up against my door and shown me a side of myself I never knew existed. Maybe I had pushed too far, asked too many questions.

'I'm not doing this now,' he said, standing from his desk and making his way out the door. 'Go play with your friends, and we'll talk about it later.'

My mouth gaped, watching him leave the room. 'Don't you dare walk away from me,' I said, storming after him and for once grabbing his arm and pulling him up short, getting into his face. 'Who the hell do you think you are, talking to me like that?'

'Oh, I don't know. Your boss?'

'Look, rake me over the coals if you want, I can take it, but I know I did good tonight, you can't say I didn't.'

'Okay, you can take it, can you? Tell me, how'd you go last Saturday night when you worked behind the bar, after I specifically told you not to? And how did you go when you abandoned your post with Cassie to go and make a scene in the pool room, which led to you attacking a patron? Did you know I had the police here and I had to provide a false statement to prevent me from losing my licence? And don't even get me started on how you let Cassie handle the aftermath of your shit storm while you went and fucked around with Ballantine. Yeah, you think I don't know about that?' Dean stepped right into my face. 'You think you nailed it? The only thing you drove a nail into was the coffin for your job.'

I swallowed, chanting over in my mind.

You can take it, you can take it, you can take it.

I remained calm, so eerily calm I even scared myself. 'Are you sure you don't want to come down to the boardwalk?'

Dean looked at me like I was crazy, like he wanted to throttle me.

When he didn't reply, I continued. 'I just wanted to catch up with everyone before I moved out. You're right, this isn't the job for me and my aunty and uncle are coming back early so I won't be needing the room or the job any longer.'

Don't cry, don't cry, don't cry.

'I will put everything as it was before I leave.' I took off my bar apron, folded it up and held it out to him. Dean took it. His hand brushed against mine and I tried not to think about how that made me feel, because at this moment I couldn't allow myself to feel anything.

'Lexie.'

My eyes lifted to meet his. He no longer seemed angry, he seemed defeated.

'You need to be with someone like Ballantine, he will be good for you . . . right for you.'

I could feel tears brimming in my eyes. I was so angry, so frustrated. Was that what this was about? Pushing me away so I could run off with Ballantine and live happily ever after?

'Don't tell me what I need,' I snapped.

I turned away and walked down the hall.

Chapter Forty-Three

'You're not coming?' said Cassie, watching me descend the stairs.

'Listen, I'm just going to have an early night,' I said. 'But you go.'

'Yeah, I might go check out the action, be a tourist,' she said, her head tilting to the side studying me. 'Don't take any shit from him, Lex, push back.'

'Ha! Push back anymore and he'd be sailing over the balcony.' I had to admit the thought did tempt me.

'Wow, he really gets under your skin, hey?'

I blinked from my violent thoughts, as I looked at Cassie. 'Like no-one else.'

Cassie laughed. 'Seriously, you sure you don't want to get away from the beast?'

I glanced up at the stairs, thinking I could stay here and stew or go out with friends and let my hair down. It took me all of two-point-five seconds to decide as a smile spread slowly across my face. 'Let's go!'

Turning the remaining lights out only served to highlight the glow from upstairs in Dean's office. I glanced at the shadow standing in his doorway and quickly averted my eyes as we walked through the front door, Cassie locking up behind us. Before we moved on, I grabbed Cassie's arm.

'Cass, I'm so sorry about last week, what I did was just... unforgivable.'

Cassie laughed. 'Lexie, you've apologised six times a day, every day, for the past week. Please get over it, because I sure have.'

It made me feel a little better, but not enough to make me forget everything else I had done as Dean's furious words rang in my ears.

'And just for the record,' she said, linking her arm through mine, 'if it means you apologising with cake, then you can offend me anytime.'

I laughed, grateful that Cassie was such a beacon of light in what otherwise would have been complete blackness.

•

We met the others at the boardwalk but my heart wasn't really in it. Well, not until we had made our way down to the beach and a stash of peach coolers had been unveiled.

Classy.

By the early hours of the morning I was circling the beach, dancing like Stevie Nicks and cursing Dean Saville to the entire group, who simply looked on in uncomfortable silence.

As much as Cassie had been entertained by my rants about The Devil Man Upstairs, she'd had to say her goodbyes early because of the babysitter.

Boon and Amanda sat on the beach, watching on as I stood before them, my arms flailing as I retold Wipe Out Bar stories with passion and gusto.

'And then, and then... get this, you're going to love this,' I said, taking a swig of my wine cooler. 'Dean kisses me into oblivion.'

'Oh shit, I'm not hearing this.' Boon shifted awkwardly, while Amanda watched on with wide eyes.

'You and Dean?' she asked.

'Yep, definitely not listening.' Boon plugged his ears.

'Yep! Into the middle of next week, and now he's all like, oooh, I'm broody and angry and blah, blah, blah . . . pffft . . . whatever.' Another long sip.

'Okaaay, time to head back, I think,' said Amanda, moving to stand, brushing the sand from her pants as she moved over to take me by the arm.

'Whaaaat? But the night is young,' I called to the sky.

'Ugh, Boon, help me,' Amanda gritted.

Boon snaked my other arm over his shoulders, so I lifted my legs, swinging them like a kid.

'Wheeeeeee . . .'

'Come on, Lexie, stop mucking around,' said Boon, who was struggling to find purchase in the sand.

I recalled lying on the back seat of Boon's car, and then seeing Amanda's blurry face blink into blackness.

I was awakened rather forcibly by three slaps to the face.

'Ugh, okay-okay-okay-okay,' I shouted, pushing the hands away from my stinging cheeks as I pulled myself into a seated position. I felt like I had been out for hours, but it had only been a power nap.

'What time is it?' I croaked, squinting through one eye.

'Two a.m. and time for bed,' said Boon, his no-nonsense eyes reflected in the rearview mirror of his car. I turned my bleary gaze from where he sat to the passenger seat where Amanda looked at me, worry etched across her face. She was looking at me like I was a stranger, like the Lexie of old was lost, and she was. Good ol' Lexie Atkinson of then, the one she knew, was long gone. I grinned, looking between Boon and Amanda, with a wiggle of my brows as if to say, 'I know what you're going to do.'

I slapped the back of Boon's seat. 'Thanks for the lift, Mum and Dad,' I said cheerfully, before wrestling with the door handle then sliding out rather inelegantly. I stood in the back alley, squinting up to see the moon's rays light the graffitied back wall of the Wipe Out Bar.

'Aaaah, home crap home,' I said through a hiccup.

Amanda leaned over Boon, looking at me through the opened window. 'I think I should come with you.'

I rolled my eyes. 'Please, I'm like a homing pigeon, I don't need your help.' I waved her away.

'Lexie.' Amanda's voice sounded stern.

'Shhh,' I motioned with a finger to my lips. 'Don't wake the beast.' I glanced back to the building.

Boon shook his head. 'Night, Lexie.'

Again my eyes shifted from Boon to Amanda, grinning like a fool. Boon quickly put the car into gear and pulled out of the car park before I said anything humiliating.

Okay, so I was a bit sloshed, but it was all good. I knew my limits. I knew that climbing the back fire escape was probably a bad idea. I knew it would be best to go in via the basement. That would be no sweat, except, like most back entrances would be at two a.m., it was locked, and I was sober enough to know I didn't have a key.

Using the wall to help me balance, I managed to zigzag my way around to the front of the building. Optimistically, I grabbed at the front door and gave it a jiggle.

Locked.

'Noooooo,' I groaned, banging my forehead lightly to the glass. Whether it was the knocks to my head, or the sudden realisation of my rather hopeless situation, I came up with a genius idea. Shucking off my annoying sand-filled shoes by the door, I padded my way out to the arcade, to stand right where I had the day I stood in the rain. There was a light shining up on the balcony, and if I knew Dean, he would have the balcony doors open.

I clasped my hands on either side of my mouth. 'Romeo, Romeo, let down your golden hair.' I squinted, mulling over what I had just said. 'Was that right?' I shrugged, ready to call out again when a figure appeared on the balcony above.

'I think you're a bit confused,' Dean deadpanned, leaning shirtless against a pole and sipping on a beer. He was backlit by the light of his apartment. I wasn't too drunk to notice that he looked like an angel.

Damn him.

'Let me in by the hairs of my chinny-chin-chin.'

'Almost,' he mused, taking another sip like he didn't have a care in the world.

'What is this, Aladdin's cave? Do I need a freakin' password?'

'What's with all the fairytale references?'

I pouted. 'I'm tired.'

'You're drunk.'

I rolled my eyes. 'Can you please let me in?'

Dean stared down at me, nursing his beer. 'Let me think about it,' he said, backing away from the balcony and disappearing.

'What?'

Oh, so he was going to be a smart-arse, was he? Well, fine, he asked for it. I will just roof rock his house. I turned around, looking desperately, only to find no rocks, just concrete. Right, okay.

'Dean, come on, I could be kidnapped or anything,' I pleaded, in all seriousness.

I heard laughter coming from up above, causing me to squint as Dean was nowhere to be seen. 'I don't think there is any danger of that, sweetheart.'

My eyebrows knitted. Now I was getting angry. It was amazing how quickly that sobered me up, and long enough to have a rather ingenious brainwave too. My eyes roamed to the downpipe and I smiled.

'Well, what do you know, Jack and the motherfucking beanstalk.' I laughed, thinking myself far too clever. I grabbed onto the pipe, hitching my foot into one of the stirrups. 'Fee, fie, fo, oh shit.' I slipped, having to re-grip and pull my way up. Miraculously, I seemed to be getting somewhere.

'Ah haaa, I smell the blood of a businessman,' I sang.

'Lexie, what the fuck?'

'Oh, yeah, now I've got your attention,' I panted, continuing my climb.

'Seriously, get down, it's not safe.' Dean sounded panicked. Dean never sounded panicked.

He made me pause and look down. Whoa! Bad idea. I was a lot higher than I thought. I would've been impressed if I wasn't so terrified.

Dean cursed under his breath. I could hear a creaking from above; oh shit, was he climbing over the railing?

'Here, take my hand.'

I glanced. He was a mile away, there was no way I could reach him.

'Keep moving, Lexie, that pipe won't hold your weight forever.'

I frowned, throwing him a filthy look. 'What is that supposed to mean? I share my cupcakes, thank you very much,' I snapped, 'Oh, and don't bother thanking me for the Hummingbird. Yeah, no worries, Lexie, anytime, Lex–'

'Lexie, if you don't shut up and start moving I will unbolt the drainpipe from my end. Now, MOVE IT!'

'Geeeez, okay, keep your shirt on.' I stepped up, once, twice. 'Not that you're wearing one,' I mumbled.

'That's it, keep moving, you're almost there.'

Dean kept on with the encouragement, as I climbed and climbed, not seeing his hand until it was literally touching me, grabbing my arm and pulling me up and guiding me to cling onto the railing.

'Now, come on, the railing isn't much safer.' The warmth of his breath blew across my face as I stood eye to eye with him. 'Come on, one leg at a time, I've got you.'

One leg at a time in a short black skirt was no easy feat, but it was that or death, so I chose the lack of modesty.

The dismount was a disaster as my second leg found no purchase and I fell straight into Dean's arms, knocking us over and landing with an oomph on the balcony floor, my fall broken by Dean's body. He was not so lucky as he winced in pain, grabbing the back of his head.

'Oh God, did I break you?' My eyes searched his face, trying to see if there was any evidence of damage.

I could feel the vibration of laughter through my palms as Dean laughed, and laughed some more. My brows rose in surprise, thinking the worst – he had gone mad, I had driven him to the point of breaking, not only physically, but mentally too.

Dean sobered, looking up into my eyes. If I wasn't a bit drunk already, I would have become drunk from this look, the way it felt like he was looking inside me, into the deepest, darkest corners, places I would gladly let him go.

'You are a danger to yourself and to everyone else around you, Lexie Atkinson.' Dean swept a piece of hair out of my eyes.

I breathed, 'I know.'

That answer only caused him to smile. 'Wow, the one thing we agree on, and it's a doozy.'

Chapter Forty-Four

I sat on the edge of Dean's bed, quiet as a church mouse, sipping a glass of water. Much to my disappointment I watched as Dean padded back into the room, peeling a shirt over his six pack and covering up the vast spread of his tattoos that always caused me to stare. Coming to stand before me he held out a black piece of material. 'Here, put this on.' My eyes narrowed to his outstretched hand.

Dean sighed, chucking it on the bed next to me. 'Where the hell did you go tonight? You look like you've been dragged through a hedge backwards.'

My eyes flicked up, the insult evident, which only amused him all the more. 'You've got sand everywhere.'

I glanced at my dirty clothes and the sand marks I had left on Dean's polished boards.

'Oh, shit, sorry.' I jumped off the bed, afraid to touch anything now. 'I better go and clean myself up.'

Dean looked at me, a small, crooked grin in the corner of his mouth, as he reached again for the material on the bed. 'You, my bathroom, clean yourself up and put this on.' He unflicked the material to reveal a black t-shirt. My brows knitted together, confused.

'I do have my clothes.'

'And right now you couldn't so much as navigate your way out of a paper bag. Clean up, sober up and go to bed.'

'Well, I did manage to navigate my way up a drainpipe.' I cocked my brow.

'Yeah, and that ended well,' he said, rubbing the back of his skull. 'There's a towel, face washer, and a spare toothbrush in the drawer: knock yourself out. Well, actually, try not to,' he added.

Oh, he was sooo hilarious. 'Lock on the door too, from memory,' I mused.

'There is. It prevents me from wanting to ravish house guests,' Dean deadpanned as he channel flicked his big-screen TV.

I closed the bathroom door behind me, clicking the door locked, more so out of habit from showering in a dodgy bathroom down the hall, that had a flamingo-pink sink and tiles, with a nice dash of mould. Here, in Dean's plush apartment, it was quite different. The bathroom was modern with brass fittings and polished stone surfaces. I worked on getting ready for the shower, not wanting to make a mess in here as well. Whoa, was I a mess! I looked in the mirror; my cheeks were flushed, no doubt from the daredevil excitement, and my hair was windswept and wild. I looked like a blonde scarecrow. My eyeliner was all smudged so I was rocking that racoon-eye look. Oh God, I was mortified. How Dean had not tossed me out of his room was anyone's guess. I was hideous. I must have looked quite the sight, climbing up his drainpipe. I was starting to definitely sober up enough to recognise the emotion of full-fledged embarrassment. I let the scalding hot water spray over my neck and shoulders using the industrial-strength water pressure. It was glorious, better than any massage. I could feel the heat seeping into my muscles, into my bones, and all of a sudden I could feel my eyes closing as I leant against the wall, almost drifting off to sleep, until I heard an almighty pounding on the bathroom door.

'You okay?' called Dean.

My eyes snapped open. 'Yes, YES!' I yelled. I stepped back into the stream, washing the rest of the suds from my hair, the fumes from the herbal shampoo waking me up a bit.

I brushed my teeth, feeling not exactly alive, but a cleaner version of my train-wrecked self. Dean's t-shirt swam on me, resting just above my knees, and a lucky thing too seeing as my knickers were folded up with my dirty clothes. My drainpipe climbing days were over. Taking the towel from my head, I combed my hair with my fingers, sweeping the long tendrils over my shoulder. I quietly opened the door, padding my way into the main room, before stopping. The flickering of the TV in the distance was the main source of light other than the lamps by the bed, the bed where Dean was lying, with his arm tucked behind his head, asleep.

I smiled, tiptoeing over to him, standing to the side, tilting my head to take in his sleeping form. The usual lines of worry and anger were melted away in his sleep. He looked so peaceful, so young, his wavy dark hair tousled with sleep. Dean usually carried the weight of the world on his shoulders, storming around, being a constant authority figure. It had me exhausted just thinking about it. No, wait, I actually was just exhausted.

Dean held the remote control to his chest, which rose and fell in that peaceful sleeping slumber. I bit my lower lip, working to gently move it from his grasp, slowly, slowly edging it away. I lifted it so as to point and turn the TV off, plunging the room into semi-darkness.

I gently placed the remote next to his bedside and looked down on him for a long moment, thinking I may never see him like this again, so vulnerable, so at ease in the world. I wanted to reach out and touch him, push the rogue curl away from his brow, and before I could catch my sanity, I slowly, gently reached down, and tucked the silken fold aside. I brought my hand away slowly, ready to creep away, but Dean's hand snaked around my wrist so fast I yelped, scaring him and myself as he woke, blinking and confused as he finally got his bearings and looked up at me.

'Lexie?' he croaked.

'I'm sorry, I was just leaving. I didn't mean to wake you.'

Dean held me still, cementing me in place as he rolled onto his side, glancing at his clock and blinking. 'Jesus, I didn't mean to fall asleep.'

I laughed. 'You were dead to the world.'

'Really?' He frowned, before realising he still held me, and then quickly let me go. 'Sorry, um, it's just, I don't sleep.'

'Like, ever?'

'Well, not much, put it that way.'

'So maybe putting up with me has exhausted you in ways you could never possibly understand,' I smirked, joking, but nevertheless thinking there might be a bit of truth to it.

Dean smiled, wider than I had ever seen him do so before. He nodded to the spare side of his bed. 'Do you want to exhaust me some more?'

'What?' I replied, my eyes widening.

Dean's brows lowered in confusion until it finally sunk in. 'Oh, Christ, no, what I meant was you can . . . oh, bloody hell, what I meant was you can sit down and talk to me and maybe I might fall asleep. I'm really not making this any better, am I?'

I couldn't help but laugh, hearing Dean stumble over his words. His embarrassment was something I had never been witness to. I liked it. I didn't know if it was because we were in his environment, the comfort of his apartment, but it just felt different. 'Wow,' I laughed. 'I don't know which way I should be offended? The fact my conversation could send you to sleep or that the idea of sleeping with me is so repulsive.'

Gone was all Dean's boyishness, embarrassment and lighthearted gibberish. Instead what replaced them was the Dean I recognised: the serious, no-nonsense man who made his way to sit on the edge of his bed, a wicked grin curving the corner of his mouth. He stood, towering over me, causing me to tilt my head back so as to look into his hypnotic eyes, eyes that were studying every line of my face, before landing on my mouth.

'Make no mistake, Lexie, I assure you neither one of those things is remotely true.'

I swallowed, aware of the rise and fall of my breathing as I was lost in his gaze. 'Really?'

He nodded once. 'Really.'

'What if you can't get back to sleep?'

Dean shrugged. 'Stay and find out.'

Considering I was usually being told to leave by Dean, or getting frogmarched in a particular direction, this bout of hospitality was a truly foreign concept.

'Okay, if you promise me one thing.'

'Oh, look out,' he said, curving his brow. 'What's that?'

I frowned, 'Try not to ravish me.'

Dean burst out laughing, a deep, genuine belly laugh as he nodded before finally managing the words, 'Okay, I'll try not to.'

Chapter Forty-Five

The TV was back on. I lifted my head, squinting at the time on the digital alarm clock: 4 a.m. I saw the blurry silhouette of Dean sitting on the couch in nothing but his boxers. He was watching one of those repetitive infomercials about what looked like some kind of magic blender. I shifted, realising I was underneath the warmth of a blanket. Dean, at some point, must have placed it over me. The fabric of the linen smelt like his aftershave, it kind of added to the cosy, comfy feel, and I was so tired it didn't take me a moment to roll over and fall back to sleep.

The next time I stirred, I felt a dip in the mattress. The TV was off and the room was in complete darkness. Dean settled in under the covers, his leg accidentally brushing against mine. He quickly flinched away, stilling and listening to see if he had woken me, but I was already awake, he just didn't know it. Dean eventually settled, melting into the soft mattress. I waited for his breaths to become even, and for sleep to eventually claim him before I shifted. Slowly peeling off the covers I padded quietly to the bathroom. Wincing against the delicate screech of the hinge, I gently closed the door behind me before I clicked on the light.

I rinsed my mouth out, brushing my teeth for a second time to get the remnants of stale alcohol from my tastebuds. I looked at my sleepy complexion, my hair dried in a mass of blonde kinky waves, no makeup, a big, black, baggy t-shirt. I breathed out a laugh.

What a sight.

I clicked off the light before creeping back to stand in the middle of the darkened room. Looking on at the sleeping bump in the bed, I turned my attention to the apartment door. Now was the time I should probably go. I was sober enough not to make a complete nuisance of myself anymore, I could just creep back to my room, go to sleep, and just like the kiss, pretend that none of this ever happened. And just as that smart, reasonable, respectable thought passed through my mind, I somehow found myself creeping my way back to Dean's bed, lifting the covers and sliding in underneath, careful not to wake him. I would simply wake up and opt for ignorance, as I confessed my embarrassment over having fallen asleep, using the whole 'how much had I had to drink?' spiel.

I smiled broadly in the dark, snuggling myself into the blankets as I marvelled at my cunning plan. That was, until Dean's voice pierced through the darkness.

'You just can't stay away from me, huh?'

I lifted my head, scowling at the darkened silhouette of his profile, which was a lost cause seeing as he couldn't see my expression.

But he could get my meaning when I shoved at his shoulder. 'Shut up!' It was like pushing granite, and having lashed out at him only made him laugh all the more.

'Go to bloody sleep,' I snapped, getting more annoyed with every second he kept laughing at me.

'Keep talking and I will.'

I sat up, using my pillow as a weapon to whack him hard: once, twice. He defended himself, grabbing the pillow and pulling it away from me. 'Geeez, did you wake up on the wrong side of the bed or what?'

'Fine. Sweet dreams,' I said, whipping the blankets aside and storming my way to the apartment door.

'Oh, come on, Lexie, don't be a diva.'

Dean leapt from the bed, his bare footsteps padding quickly from behind me as he came to slide to an abrupt halt before moving to stand between me and the exit. He was laughing still as he pressed his back to the door. 'Look, I'm sorry. I'm just messing around.'

I folded my arms like a true diva should.

Dean's breaths were uneven after having made the dive from the bed to the door with impressive speed. 'It's late, you don't have to go.'

'I don't know, I'm pretty offended,' I teased.

Even in the dark I could make out the brilliant line of his smile; there was enough light filtering in from the city for me to witness the sexiness of something he didn't do often enough.

'How can I make it up to you?'

His words were filled with meaning, spoken tauntingly, dangling the question in front of me as a way to make me speechless or blush even. But I wasn't feeling either of those things. My tummy flipped in excitement, and the heat I could feel from his skin was undeniable, he stood so close to me dressed in nothing but boxer shorts. We stood in silence, the longer I drew out my response the bigger the meaning the silence had.

How can I make it up to you? hung in the air like a promise, put out for me to do with as I wanted. To laugh at it, to be offended by it or to take advantage of it. I could, of course, do the one thing, the right thing and that was to say goodnight, push him aside and go to my room. That would be the decent, grown-up thing to do, but like I had proven tonight, getting drunk on a beach, scrambling up a drainpipe and climbing into a hot man's window, I was clearly none of those things. And just as I might say something to break the silence, Dean lifted his hand to the side of my face, causing my breath to catch in my throat as he gently swept his thumb over my bottom lip and repeated the question, almost in a whisper.

'How can I make it up to you?'

And then I realised, I didn't even have to tell him, I simply had to show him. I stepped closer into him, my breaths gusted across his bare skin as I stared up at him, a kaleidoscope of colours from the city lit the lines of his beautiful face, the smallest of flashes reflected in the dark set of his brooding stare. It was a far more breathtaking view than I had ever seen. It was all he needed to know before he slowly took hold of the fabric of my t-shirt and dragged me up to him, a devilish, cocky smirk lining his lips just before he met me part way, hungrily claiming my mouth.

There was something so intense about being shielded in the dark with a man like Dean, to feel the vulnerability of his breathing change whenever I did something right, when I gently slid my arms along his toned torso, splayed my hands across his back or tortuously pushed my fingers through to divide the thick folds of his hair. I opened myself up to him, tilting my head to the side to gain access to his beautiful mouth. I moved to link my arms around his neck, to anchor myself to him in some way, but he had other ideas as he grabbed my wrists, spinning me around so fast he pinned my arms on either side of my head, caging me in as he kissed me with wicked intent, pushing his leg between my thighs, creating the perfect friction. The feeling of Dean's shirt I was wearing rubbing against my nipples as he pressed against me was only a small part of the incredible torture he was inflicting on me as I rocked and groaned against his body. What was with us and doors, I mused, recalling the last time I had been lost in Dean's arms. I playfully bit his shoulder, causing him to push back and frown down on me with that cheeky smile.

'You don't play fair,' he said and before I could argue that I was actually the one pinned against the door, Dean scooped me up. Wrapping my legs around him, walking me to the bed, he moaned into my mouth, discovering I was wearing no panties. Sitting down on the edge of the bed as I straddled him, he made quick work to peel my t-shirt off, in one fluent swoop, causing my hair to tumble and fall over my shoulders and breasts. He gently brushed my hair from my shoulders and his eyes devoured the delicate view of my naked body. The way he looked at me made me feel like the most beautiful woman alive. His mouth was on mine again, his tongue delving and teasing my own as he placed his hands behind my knees and dragged me closer to him, grinding on his hardness. Dean's hands skimmed up my back. Grasping my shoulders he tilted me back so his mouth had access to the hardened, pebbled peaks. One at a time he feasted with his swirling hot tongue, eliciting a foreign sound from me I barely recognised as I rocked into him. It wasn't enough, none of it would be enough. I was close but not close enough. I could feel his hardness grind into me through the infuriating, thin barrier of his boxers.

'These,' I breathed against his mouth, as I flicked at the

elastic band of his boxer briefs, 'have to go.' Dean smiled against my kiss.

'I thought you would never ask.'

Dean shifted me from him. I rolled onto my back, trying to catch my breath as I watched him stand by the side of the bed, removing the final barrier; his naked silhouette made my heart beat faster. Oh God, this was happening, this was really happening. The bed dipped as Dean climbed up my body, kissing a blistering trail up to my mouth, before pausing. He leant over, tapping the side lamp into a low light.

'What are you doing?' I asked, panicked, covering my breasts.

Dean smiled, lowering his mouth and kissing me so softly, so sweetly, I almost forgot my question . . . almost.

'I want to see you.' Dean kissed my neck, moving back down my body, gently pulling my hands aside. I bit my lip and covered my eyes, ready to die of embarrassment feeling so exposed to him. My mind was reeling, panicking at the thought of him seeing me like . . . *Oh my God.*

Dean's head disappeared between my thighs, kissing me, licking me, devouring me in a maddening rhythm that caused my back to arch and all worries of dignity to flee my mind as his fingers dug into my thighs, pinning me to the mattress. I hitched myself onto my elbows, looking down at Dean doing the most wicked things to the most intimate part of me, and then he did something even more wicked: he looked up at me, locked me with his eyes, full of hunger as he relentlessly teased, and nipped and . . . thank God the light was on as I looked right into his eyes. He must have read me, read my sounds because he worked my body like a musical instrument, pressing and pulling in exactly the right places, until I collapsed back, arching and grabbing at the sheets, trying to move away from him, but he torturously held me in place until I was screaming, begging, falling, falling, falling... BANG!

I jolted awake, breathing heavily, blinking as I tried to claim back some semblance of what was happening. The bang was that of the apartment door that Dean had walked through with two take-away coffees.

'Shit, sorry.' He paused, taking in my panicked state. 'You okay?'

My hands flew up to my shoulders. I looked down to see I was dressed, in the black t-shirt, but not naked.

What the hell? Oh no-no-no... Go back to sleep, Lexie.

'Bad dream?' Dean asked, offering me a polystyrene cup of what smelt like coffee. I wanted it but my hands were trembling too much to take it. Dean's concern deepened as he placed the coffee on the side table and sat on the edge of the bed.

'Jesus, Lex, you're burning up.' Dean touched my forehead, which only caused me to flinch away out of his bed, the after effects of my hotter-than-hell dream still affecting me.

'I just, um, don't feel well.'

'The coffee will help the hangover.' He watched me.

Funnily enough, despite my alcohol consumption, it wasn't a hangover I was suffering from.

I swallowed. 'No, I'm okay, I just... had a dream.'

'Must have been some dream.' Dean blew on his coffee before taking a sip, his eyes lifting to me in a way that really didn't help settle my rampant hormones.

'It was very... real,' I managed, barely able to look at his face without the vision of him settled between my thighs. 'Um, so what happened last night, exactly?' I shifted awkwardly in my makeshift nightie.

Dean laughed. 'Well, if you don't remember, I'm not going to tell you.'

At the moment I was trying to decipher which was dream and which was reality.

'I was locked out, I climbed a drainpipe, had a shower and crashed in your bed?' I asked the question as if I was patchy on the particulars.

Dean stood, moving over to the kitchen. 'Yeah, so just your usual Friday night shenanigans then.' He chucked his cup in the bin and turned to me. 'This is beginning to be a bit of a habit of yours.'

I crossed my arms, aware that I wasn't wearing a bra underneath, and even with the t-shirt being longer than what my school dress was, in the light of day I did feel completely exposed. 'Yeah, well, it's not my usual behaviour,' I admitted.

'No?' Dean raised a sexy eyebrow as he leant against the kitchen bench.

'No, I mean, I usually climb through windows on Saturday nights.'

Dean smirked, rubbing his unshaven jawline. 'I see.'

'So, um, on that note, thanks for the coffee, and the loan of the shirt, and for not letting me fall to my death.' I gave him an awkward thumbs up as I moved to the door, a door that Dean met me at, grabbing the handle and opening it for me. It was a very different version from my dream.

'Thanks for the entertainment,' he said, leaning casually on the opened door. I paused in the doorway, biting my lip knowing I would instantly regret what I was about to say, but what the hell. I spun around. 'Nothing happened, like, last night, I mean with you . . . and . . . me?' I could feel my cheeks burn as I rather eloquently asked the question.

A devious sparkle in Dean's eyes matched that of the familiar cocky set to his crooked smile. 'Lexie, if anything had happened last night, believe me, you would remember.'

Oh God, why did he have to sound so bloody sexy. How was I supposed to respond to that? I broke away from his gaze, clearing my throat as I turned to walk down the hall. 'Very good.'

It was only a short distance to my room down the hall, but when you're leaving Dean Saville's apartment in the early hours of the morning wearing nothing but his t-shirt, well, it brought a whole new meaning to the term 'walk of shame'.

I could feel his eyes burning into the back of me, no doubt loving every minute of this. Never so glad to see my own bedroom door, I was ready to dive through it when Dean called out to me.

'Hey, Lexie.'

My heart stopped, turning to see him still standing in his opened doorway. It was like I was now looking at him for the first time – the jeans, the grey T, his hair still damp and tousled from his morning shower, a shower he probably took when I was busy having sordid, sexy dreams about him. I lifted my chin, trying not to think about how much my heart was pounding against my chest when he spoke my name.

'What?' I asked, thinking maybe he was going to say something meaningful. The way he was looking at me sure didn't help the heart palpitations as I swallowed deeply.

'Listen, do you think you could grab a bag of ice for the bar when you head down.'

What?

Okay, so I wasn't sure what I'd been expecting but that was certainly not it. I could feel my back straighten as an air of annoyance swept over me, disguised by my sickly sweet smile.

'Sure,' I said, thinking, well, if I was heading to the cool room at least I wouldn't need to take a cold shower. Sometimes you just had to look for the silver lining in every cloud, right?

Chapter Forty-Six

'What do you mean, you might stay here? Mum and Dad are going to be home Tuesday.' Amanda sat on the edge of my bed, looking around my room in horror.

'It's not that bad,' I said, folding up my clothes from the washing basket.

'Lexie, it's a tomb. I think people have died in here.'

I rolled my eyes; Amanda, forever the drama queen.

'Speaking of dying, thanks for chaperoning me safely to my door last night,' I smirked at her.

'Yeah, well, you didn't answer your phone. I thought I better check you were alive. I see you made it in okay.'

My mind flashed back to me climbing up the drainpipe. 'Yep,' I said, trying not to let the waves of embarrassment consume me. Seriously, that was it, no more drinking!

Amanda was still giving my room the once-over with her Judgey McJudgment eyes. 'I knew there wasn't any apartment. You just told your parents that so they'd let you stay,' she scoffed.

'Well, it's not entirely untrue. There's an apartment. It's just not mine,' I said with a laugh.

'Wow, who'd have thought you would go to such lengths.' Amanda scrunched her face up at the flaky ceiling. 'You would seriously give up a pool, Pay TV, 1000 thread count sheets, and a house near Ballantine, for Arcadia Lane.'

'I'm not giving up anything,' I snapped.

The mention of Ballantine hit a nerve. I hadn't heard from him since that night in the alley, and although that wasn't surprising, I feared all promises of together forever and happily ever after were completely out of reach, and with my head being in a constant state of confusion I didn't know if this was a good thing or a bad thing.

Amanda sighed, walking to stand beside me, grabbing a towel and folding it, in the first piece of manual labour I had seen from her in, well, ever.

'You need to choose, Lexie,' she said, placing the folded square on the pile with a friendly tap. 'You can have it all: live here, there, work, don't work . . . the world's your oyster.'

'What, wet and shrivelled?' I joked.

'He wants to be with you. You just have to decide.' Amanda looked at me pointedly before moving to the door.

'Decide?'

'Boy from the 'burbs, or boy from the city?'

'Wait, *who* wants to be with me?'

Amanda shrugged. 'Work it out.' She opened the door and stepped through it. 'See ya.'

'Oh, no, you don't,' I said, stepping after her. 'What are you talking about?'

Amanda laughed. 'Sorry luv, gotta go, I'm late for a very important date.' Amanda winked as she hit the staircase. I would have chased her all the way down Arcadia Lane demanding that she explain, but I was once again brought up short.

'Lexie.' I stilled, turning to the sound of Dean's voice coming from his office.

'Did you get that ice?' Dean asked, his tone non-negotiable.

I watched from the top of the landing as Amanda sashayed out of the Wipe Out Bar.

Damn it! I spun around, completely annoyed. 'Why can't Cassie –'

'Oh, for Christ's sake,' Dean sighed. 'Does everything have to be an argument with you?'

'I'm just saying –'

'GET THE ICE!'

'O. KAY!' I stormed down the stairs, mumbling under my breath each step of the way, and passed the bar, heading towards the kitchen, stomping my way through to the back alcove where the back freezers stocked the bags. I sighed, weary from a disrupted night's sleep and an overactive imagination, even more so with Amanda's cryptic words of advice.

Boy from the 'burbs: Ballantine, or boy from the city: Dean. Is that what she meant? If that's what she was playing at the decision was pretty much made for me. Ballantine, who was keeping radio silence until I ran away with him, or Dean, the bossy slavedriver who starred in my x-rated dreams and pushed my buttons in the best and worst ways.

'Get the ice,' I mimicked. Lifting the freezer lid and dragging out a bag, I swung around, stopping as I glanced through the open doorway to the back alley. I stood there for the longest moment, blinking, thinking that if I did that it might clear my vision because clearly my eyes were playing tricks on me. A coldness swept over me. Oh wait; no, that was the freezer door open. I moved to shut it, placing the bag on top of the freezer chest as I slowly made my way out the door to stand outside, where right there before me in all its shiny, undamaged glory was my Tiffany Blue vintage bike. It had been completely repaired, and was leaning on its kickstand. I edged forward to clasp the handlebars with a smile. It was like nothing had ever happened to it and I could have squealed through the sheer elation of the freedom it had brought me.

I couldn't help but laugh; did we even bloody need ice in the bar? A slow smile drifted across my face as I turned back to the bag of ice; it was then I had a cunning idea. Walking back inside, I grabbed the bag of ice, carrying it out to place into my cane basket, being overly careful not to topple over as I awkwardly mounted my shiny new ride. It took some shaky navigating to get into my stride as I slowly zigzagged my way out of the alley and around the corner.

Pedalling around to the main entrance I carefully stepped off, wheeling my bike through and past a curious line of men who were all perched up at the bar enjoying a pot and a counter meal. Cassie looked at me as if I were mad. Maybe I was, but I didn't care. I went to stand at the bottom of the staircase, where I rung my bike bell in a series of high-pitched trills.

'Hey, Romeo,' I called up the stairs.

Dean was so confusing: one minute he was threatening to fire me, the next he was doing things like this. Just as I was ready to ring my bell again, a tall, lean figure emerged from his office, coming to stand curiously by the bannister, all-knowing and smug as he leant his elbows on the railing and lifted his brows in question.

'Nice bike,' he said.

'It is now,' I smiled, looking over it and admiring its pristine condition before looking back up at Dean, making sure to look him straight in the eyes. 'Thanks.'

Something flashed in Dean's eyes. It was fleeting, but I saw it. His stoic stance broke the instant his mouth pulled to the right, in that cheeky way of his. 'I wouldn't get too excited; I fixed it so you can run errands for me,' he said, trying to keep a straight face.

'Well, the joke's on you because I will happily run errands, Mr Saville. In fact, if it takes me away from getting yelled at by you, then all the better.'

I lifted my chin, defiantly kicking out the stand to my bike and lifting the thawing ice out of my basket to take to the bar.

'Lexie?' Dean called out.

I spun around meeting his eyes. 'Yes?'

'Behave or I'll send you to pick up something from Red Hill.'

My lips pinched together. I bowed my head and continued to the bar.

Forever the smart-arse.

Chapter Forty-Seven

For so long I'd been adamant that I knew what I wanted, that I knew what made me happy. And my return to Paradise hadn't been perfect, far from it, but in the days that followed with Aunty Karen and Uncle Peter moving back, school rolling on and work getting better (as in, I still had a job), on paper it looked like I had found my feet, right? But if that were truly the case then why did I feel anything but grounded?

My thumb lingered over the send button, knowing that once it was gone, there would be no turning back. I would be sealing my fate in one way or another. I wasn't picking a boyfriend as it wasn't like that; it was about choosing a future, a future that involved a whole lot of leeway from my parents, and I just didn't know how much more they were willing to give. Despite my being of age, I still wanted their blessing in my choices. I guess I was a bit of an oddball like that. As tender as my heart was, I had known for the longest time what was right, what fit. And to imagine my life with that integral part of me gone was not a future I wanted. Sure, he wasn't perfect, and communication wasn't exactly his strong point, but there was something there, an undeniable link between us, one that didn't seem to dissolve no matter how bad things got.

Staring at the screen, my mind hovered between delete and send.

Delete – go on with my life. Send – and face the unknown. My teeth bit into my bottom lip and my leg jigged nervously as I ran each scenario through my mind, and then with a deep, calming breath I closed my eyes and pressed send.

Time to meet my destiny.

•

Here I was again, standing under a lamppost at the end of my cousin's street, waiting. Waiting for the boy who might not come.

Like last time, when a silhouette appeared in the distance, I dared not believe that it would be Ballantine, but as the figure neared, as I watched, shading my face from the sun, I smiled as he closed the distance.

'You got my text?'

It was a stupid thing to ask. Of course he had, why else would he be here? Nerves did strange things.

Ballantine slapped the side of the pole. 'Yep! Memories.'

'Good memories . . . and not so good.'

'A very poetic choice,' Ballantine said, leaning against the pole, plunging his hands deep in his pockets. He looked so gorgeous, the dimple puckering when he smiled. 'I think I felt my heart stop when I got your text.' He breathed out a laugh. 'But then I know that it really didn't, not really. Because it actually stopped the moment I saw the look on your face.' A sad smile spread across Ballantine's face.

'I'm leaving without you, aren't I.' He said it as a statement, not a question.

I nodded slowly. 'As much as I wanted it, I don't think you wanted it enough.'

'I always wanted you, Lexie.'

'You should have fought harder.'

Ballantine turned his head away, looking down the street, silence falling between us, until I broke it.

'My head says, what are we doing? Let's go. But then my heart tells me –'

Ballantine held up his hand to stop me. 'It's okay, I don't need to know what your heart says.'

'I'm sorry,' I whispered.

Ballantine, breathed in, gaining his composure. 'I'm not. I'll never be sorry, sorry about the girl from Red Hill who walked into that assembly like a dream.'

'And now you're going to chase your dream.'

Ballantine tried to look happy about it, and it made my heart hurt that our exchange was so wooden. He looked pained, but it wasn't the devastation I had felt when he'd effectively said no to us weeks earlier. That had been agony. *He never chased me. He never told me or even asked me to stay. He never wanted me enough.*

Ballantine stepped forward, kissing me on the head and pressing his forehead against mine. I wrapped my arms around him, breathing him in and remembering back to the first time I saw this boy, laughing in the dark. He was the sunshine in my summer and I would never forget . . . Never.

'Bye, Ballantine.'

He backed away. 'Bye, Lexie Atkinson.'

•

I checked my phone for the hundredth time.

There was no reply.

The text had read:
Meet me at the Ferris wheel at 1 pm.

It was now 1.30 and I had been shifting nervously for the past forty-five minutes, watching down the long strip of the pontoon leading into the amusement park, waiting to see him walk down.

But he didn't arrive.

By 2.15 p.m. I had my answer and all I could do was nod, nod my head and accept that my heart had been wrong, and that this was a mistake. I thought back to the last time we had shared a moment and it was no wonder he wasn't here. I was such an idiot for thinking it was anything more than what it was. I started to walk away from the Ferris wheel, down the long stretch, leaving the happy screams and fun fair behind, willing my feet forward and feeling the hot tears of humiliation rise within me. Just like the laughter on the wind, I thought I heard my name. Shaking it off, I walked faster, thinking if I just got away from here it would be like it never happened, but then I heard my name again, louder, and coming from behind me. I stopped, then turned around, confused, until I saw the tall figure standing beside the Ferris wheel, dressed in black, flicking his shades up on his head as he strode towards me.

You know that moment when a girl gets swept off her feet and taken away while some kind of romantic anthem plays in the background? Well, this was that kind of moment as Dean closed the distance, meeting me in the middle, coming to stand in front of me, shaking his head.

'Where have you been?' he asked, looking at his watch, annoyed.

'Where have I been? Where have you been?' I snapped.

'I've been waiting on the other side of the Ferris wheel for the past hour.'

'Why that side? I meant this side.'

'Well, you should have said what side. How was I supposed to know?'

'Everybody knows that's the side.'

Dean scoffed. 'Oh, is that right?'

This man infuriated me. Would we ever get through a conversation without arguing? He was staring down at me. His expression wasn't really one of anger, despite our tone. I wouldn't call it soft, but it was soft*er*.

'Why didn't you text me?' I asked.

'Well, I had romantic visions of you running up the boardwalk, and me lifting you above my head in an impromptu Swayze moment, but the mood has been completely killed.'

I smirked. 'You're an idiot.'

'And you're here.'

'I am.'

Dean's eyes were ever watchful, waiting for me to be the first to say it. I stepped forward, lifting my eyes up to his.

'I have a question for you.'

Dean smirked. 'Shock horror. What if I don't answer it?'

'You have to answer it, only you can answer it.'

'Okay, intrigued. Go on.'

'It's not a hard one.'

'I'll be the judge of that.'

Oh boy, I thought, it was a simple question, it seemed simple in my head, but when Dean looked down at me like he was now, his eyes a pale green in the sun, I suddenly lost all train of thought, and what's worse, he knew it.

His smile grew broader as I shifted under his ever-intense gaze. I took a steadying breath, one that was strangely enough found in the familiarity of his eyes as I looked up at him.

'It's a simple question,' I repeated.

Dean cocked his brow.

'Do you want me to stay?'

Something changed in Dean's expression. The humour fell away, a hardness in his eyes setting as he looked down at me. Maybe it wasn't a simple question at all. It was certainly one he was thinking over.

I shifted anxiously, taking his silence as a sign for what was to come, and I suddenly wanted to hide from those eyes, readying myself to walk away until, as always, Dean did the unexpected. He lifted his hand to trace a gentle line from the corner of my brow, down my cheek to my chin, lifting my face to him.

'Yes.'

A smile spread across my face, a reaction I had no control over at such a beautiful word to my ears.

'Really?'

Dean cupped my cheek, his hand holding the fabric at the back of my shirt as he drew me closer, his lips hovering against mine, a wicked glint in his eyes, his look almost incredulous as he smiled.

'What do you think?'

And without giving me a chance to answer, Dean kissed me, kissed me so passionately there was no doubt I was home, that I belonged in these arms. As much as he infuriated me, there was never any question he would fight for me. I felt it in his kiss, in his touch, and in the way he was looking at me now.

Chapter Forty-Eight

Humming a joyful little ditty, I made my way down the stairs, fixing my blonde hair up into a high ponytail. I rounded the corner of the bar, fussing and straightening my apron, all ready to start my Friday night shift until I saw the uncertain look on Cassie's face.

'What?'

'What are you doing?'

'Umm, what does it look like I'm doing?'

'Well, this is awkward,' laughed Cassie.

'What is? What are you talking about?' My head spun around, watching on as Cassie disappeared out back, only to return with the staff clipboard, chucking it on the bar top.

'Hate to break it to you, luv, but you're not on tonight.'

'What?' I replied, snatching up the clipboard, my eyes searching over the pages I flicked. 'That can't be right, I checked this morning; I'm on all weekend.'

'Well, not anymore,' Cassie mused as she folded her arms and cocked her hip against the bar.

I flipped: Friday, Saturday, Sunday . . . nothing. What the hell?

'Maybe you're a kept woman now?' Cassie nudged me. 'The boss's ol' lady,' she said, wiggling her brows.

'Oh, shut up,' I snapped, pushing the clipboard back at her as I stormed past her, taking the steps two at a time, letting my anger drive me upwards.

Who the hell did he think he was?

I burst through his office door into darkness, flicking the light to reveal an empty room. I backed out, slamming the door and made a determined line down the hall to the door at the very end, twisting the handle and pushing it open, breaking the number one rule of knocking, but I was far too mad for that.

'Look, Dean, just because –' I stopped in the middle of a once-again dark room, except this time I squinted, as my eyes adjusted to that of a darkened silhouette by the opened balcony doors. Dean was trying to flick a lighter into life.

Flick-flick-flick

'Dirty, rotten piece of shit,' he gritted, shaking the lighter.

Flick-flick-flick.

'What are you doing?' I edged closer to him.

'Bloody hell, Cassie was meant to give me the heads-up when you were coming.'

'What? Why?'

Dean sighed, chucking the empty lighter across the table. 'Because I am attempting to be fucking romantic.' He said the word as if it left a bad taste in his mouth.

'Oh . . .' My brows rose and I was suddenly glad that we were in the dark so he couldn't see my attempt not to smile.

'I have enough tea candles in here to torch the place.'

'Candles?'

'Yeah, well, don't get too excited.'

I grinned. 'Wow, you've got it bad.'

Dean's head snapped around to me. 'What?'

I stepped closer to him, so close I could sense the rise and fall of his chest. 'Cupcakes, now candles. You must be crazy about me,' I teased.

Dean stayed quiet for a long, drawn-out moment. I really wished that I could see his face, read his eyes – they always told me so much.

'Maybe,' he said, his voice low and rich. 'But at least I don't talk in my sleep.'

My smile fell away, as the colour drained from my face. 'W– what?'

Dean moved closer, leaning into me so his lips ghosted against my earlobe. 'Do you dream of me often?'

I could feel my cheeks flame, mortified by the outing of my dirty little secret. So I did what I had to do, what I was able to do with the cover of darkness. I laughed. 'I don't know what you're talking about,' I lied.

Dean pulled back a little. 'Oh, I think you do.' I felt his hand slide across my collar bone, touching me so gently as if I might break, which was probably a good thing, seeing how just listening to the way he spoke, so low and sexy, I could feel my resolve ready to shatter at any moment.

I swallowed. 'Well, I am not telling you about my dream,' I said, laughing a little nervously. There were just some things that were too mortifying to voice, and my inner deviant was one of them. No. Way.

Standing before the open door of the balcony, the summer breeze that rolled in off the ocean did little to cool the burn of my cheeks. The wind pushed my hair back, the salty air caused my eyes to water. I stood before Dean, waiting for him to answer, to say something smart because I knew he just wouldn't be able to help himself, so when he raised his hand and gently pushed the hair from my forehead away and said, 'I don't want you to tell me,' I instantly felt my shoulders melt in relief, until Dean lifted my hand to his mouth and kissed it. 'I want you to show me.'

'What?' It came out almost as a yelp, a yelp of terror. I could feel my breaths become heavy and my heart race so fast I swear he could hear it. I tried to think, to come up with something to say, something witty, lighthearted, or pick a fight: I wasn't fussy. Instead, there were no words, just Dean lacing his fingers with mine as he led me carefully through the dark and to the bed.

Oh God, oh God, oh God.

Why was I so nervous? I could feel myself trembling, my mind reeling. We stood near the bed, and just like in my dream Dean moved to tap the light on low, casting a light glow over the room. My breath caught when I looked into Dean's eyes; gone were the harsh, angry stares and wicked, cheeky glints I was used to. Instead, a rich warmth was there, looking at me like I was some goddess, when I felt anything but. Dean hooked his finger in my shirt and with a sexy smile he pulled me towards him, taking my hot mouth with a deep hunger. My hands wrapped around his neck, urging him into me so greedily I couldn't believe it myself. My hands then clumsily grabbed at Dean's shirt; in no uncertain terms I wanted it gone and he read me instantly, pulling the black t-shirt over his head and throwing it aside. I thought this might have helped but it didn't. Touching his chiselled torso made me swallow. This was definitely not a dream. This was very, very real. Real in the way Dean was unbuttoning my shirt in a long, confident line down to my belly button, peeling it aside to reveal my bra. My chest heaved up and down so rapidly Dean faltered, taking a moment to read my face.

'You okay?' he asked, kissing my forehead and gently peeling my straps from my shoulders. I nodded, perhaps a little too quickly. 'Yes; I mean, I am, but, I just . . . I think, maybe . . . I don't know.'

Dean stilled. I looked straight ahead, afraid to look up until he gently touched my chin and tilted my head up to look him in the eyes: his serious, questioning eyes.

'Lexie, you have done this . . .'

I turned my face away, my eyes blurring. 'I'm sorry, I just –' I shook my head. Clasping my shirt together, I ran to the door. What was I thinking? How could I ever be expected to make someone like Dean happy, to be able to give him what he needed when I was just this stupid little girl from the country who knew nothing about anything? I grabbed the handle, flinging it open before Dean had a chance to get in my way as I ran down the hall.

'Lexie, wait!' I heard Dean's footsteps behind me and I had nowhere to go as I reached for the safety of my room but my attempt to close the door was in vain as Dean wedged himself between the door and the frame. It was useless to fight him on this as he forced his way inside, shutting the door behind him.

I sat on the edge of my bed, feeling the tears rise and fall from despair, but most of all, mortification.

'Lex.' Dean came to kneel in front of me, leaning to look up into my eyes, now red and teary.

His hands gripped my calves gently. Resting them there was strangely comforting.

I sniffed. 'Pretty tragic, huh, the last living virgin in Paradise City.'

Dean scoffed, actually scoffed, morphing me from self-pity to anger.

'Well, I'm glad you think it's so funny.'

'You're right, it's tragic, you should have lost it years ago with some pimply faced wanker at the back of a footy club who would never speak to you again and tell all his mates about how many times you screamed his name. Yep.' Dean stood. 'You really missed out on the Paradise experience.'

I looked up at him, a small smile lining my face. 'What? No candles?'

Dean shook his head. 'No candles.'

I looked at Dean for a long moment. His face was like stone, serious and strong, not an ounce of self-pity, or crooning words of how I wasn't like anyone he'd ever met, or we can wait, wait as long as it took, it didn't matter. No, Dean was the most real person I had ever met, honest to a fault, but as far as faults went, his was certainly the one I wanted to have in my life.

I stood before him, not nervous, not afraid, not anything other than lost in the moment with Dean, who never spoke, never asked me any questions one way or another; instead, he left it up to me.

'I want the candles.'

Only then did Dean's face change, softening into confusion, his eyes ticking over my face in a silent question, a question I beat him to.

As I whispered ... 'Now.'

Chapter Forty-Nine

The room was aglow with a golden twinkling mass of flames placed on every surface of the apartment. I could feel Dean's eyes on me, waiting for my reaction, other than the beaming smile I was giving.

'I told you, it's a giant death trap,' he said, looking around the apartment.

I laughed, shaking my head. 'It's beautiful.'

Perfect.

I didn't know how to go about this, now that I had gathered myself. It was almost as if the roles were reversed, that Dean was the nervous one now, as I watched him slide and fidget with the tea candles, moving them away from objects of danger. I smiled. He wasn't the cocksure Dean; this was the uncertain, open Dean I had had glimpses of. I made my way over to the bed, sitting on the edge of it, bouncing up and down, testing the spring action.

'Yep, this will work,' I announced, taking great pleasure in Dean doing a double-take my way. 'So, where do you want me?' I slapped my thighs, looking at him expectantly.

Dean shook his head, smirking at me. 'Such a smart-arse.'

I shrugged. 'You are who you hang with.'

Dean moved the last candle aside, making his way over to me, without breaking eye contact, not once as he came to stand before me. Long gone were my nerves, my self-doubt, replaced by an absolute certainty, a new need that filled me, that had me sliding my hands up Dean's jean-clad thighs, skimming over the strain of his jeans to flick the top button, and work his zip slowly down, all the while watching his reaction, seeing his Adam's apple swallow as I edged down the denim, and his briefs, revealing what I wanted, but unlike the dream this time I aimed to torture him, please him, taste him. I took Dean into my mouth, his hands flying into my hair. 'Lexie,' he breathed, part groan, part shock as I drew him into the back of my throat, working my hands to build on the extra tension I needed to work him into a blinding pleasure. His fingers hooked into the elastic band holding my hair up, gently tugging it away, dividing the folds of my hair with a loving caress. I could feel the tingly sensation move up my spine as the tension ebbed, building into a new sensation as Dean buried his fists in my hair and guided my rhythm.

'You better stop, Lex.' Dean's voice was hoarse, gravelly and it only encouraged me, to think he was coming undone by something I was doing to him. I took him deeper, hollowing my cheeks and revelling in his laboured breathing. I was ready to take whatever he needed me to, but Dean pulled away, pushing me back onto the bed, peeling off his jeans. I began unbuttoning my top, but not near fast enough as Dean took over and tore apart the fabric, sending buttons flying and rolling across the floor. I giggled at the unexpectedness of it, as Dean worked on unclasping my bra with one flick. 'I hope those buttons aren't flammable,' he said, giving me a wry smile, before lowering his mouth onto my exposed breast, drawing my nipple into his mouth, puckering it into an aching peak before moving to the other. Watching him worship my body, exploring it with his hands and mouth was better than any dream imaginable. Lit by the warm glow of the candlelight, Dean was perfect. How could I have ever been afraid of this, with him?

Dean kissed me, deep, robbing me of my thoughts, stealing all of my breath before tauntingly edging my denim skirt up over my hips and hooking his thumbs into the elastic of my knickers, sliding them down my thighs. He flashed me a wicked smile. 'Now this is better than any Friday night shift,' he said, climbing back up my body. I giggled, wrapping my legs around him, drawing him closer, feeling the press of him against my thigh, gasping as he pressed against the most intimate part of me. That's when I sobered.

There's no way. He won't fit.

I blinked. Dean read me better than anyone I'd ever met and thank God he was reading me now, I could tell just by looking into his eyes. He knew I was scared, he could feel my body stiffen, my breaths growing more rapid. He never took his eyes from me. Instead, he watched. Watched me as his hand slid over my breast, over my ribs, ghosting along the softness of my belly and lower, sliding between my thighs and then slowly inside me. He caught my gasp with his mouth, my whimpers muffled as I rocked into his hand, desperately urging him on, until he slid a second finger inside and I spread wider for him, muffling my cries into his shoulder. I didn't think I could take any more of what he could give, but there was more. He gave me what I needed and he whispered encouraging, brilliantly filthy-sweet words into my neck, lifting me to the brink of madness, a quivering madness where I was begging for him, all of him.

He broke away from me, eliciting a cry of another kind, one of despair as he leant across and grabbed a foil square from his top drawer, tearing it open with his teeth, sheathing himself and climbing back over my body. He was shaking, his heated, excited breaths blowing down on me and without a word, he looked into my eyes, and he knew. Gently, easing at first, he rocked into me, his attention flicked from me to where we met. It was the most erotic thing I had ever seen and with his slow, tender patience he kissed me so passionately, a sweet, beautiful moment, before he thrust one long stroke into me. I gasped, blinking past the pain and the shock of feeling so completely filled. I couldn't take it, he was going to break me. I bit my lip, steadying myself, but Dean kept calm, even if his eyes said otherwise.

'You okay?' he asked with his forehead pressed against mine. I nodded, rocking my hips into him, encouraging him, urging him on. Dean slowly pulled out, and then pushed in gently, over and over, sliding his hand between my legs, urging me on to the point that beyond the pain, I craved the pleasure, demanded it in a series of pleas and whimpers, voicing the words that were even shocking to my own ears. 'Harder, faster. Please, don't stop.'

I dug my heels into the mattress, rocking my hips up, losing myself to this new world. My nails were grasping at his back, feeling the corded muscles flex with every thrust. My eyes stung with tears as I felt something grow inside me, felt the edge of something that belonged to both of us.

'Do you feel me?' Dean breathed, pushing deeper than before.

'Don't stop, please don't stop,' I sobbed, feeling rapid fire flickering through me, just like the flickering flames around us. The pleasure mounted and I cried, struggling to hang on as Dean took me to a place beyond any dream, a dream he followed, breathing and kissing me, sweeping the damp tendrils of my hair aside. Our breaths heaving, our skin flushed, our bodies sated.

Dean swallowed. 'You okay?'

I breathed out a laugh, earning a sceptical brow curve from Dean.

'What?'

'Can we do it again?'

Dean laughed, shaking his head. 'You'll be the death of me, Lexie Atkinson,' he said, looking at me with eyes that said so much without the need for words.

I smiled, big and goofy.

Dean's brows pinched together. 'What?'

'I may have taken the long way around, Dean Saville, but I think I have finally found my Paradise.'

Epilogue

Binning the last of our morning coffees, we walked down Arcadia Lane, hand in hand. Dean was silent as he listened intently to my nervous banter about Amanda and Boon and how they had finally got their act together, and how Aunty Karen and Uncle Peter were back home and back to normal. I barely drew breath as he led me around the back of the Wipe Out Bar, afraid that if I stopped talking, the reality would sink in. The only time my words fell away was when I realised Dean had led me into the alleyway, past the skip bins where countless sordid acts had taken place. A nervousness swept over me as I took in where we were. Dean followed my eyeline and laughed.

'Relax, it's not my style.'

I blushed, horrified that he knew what I was thinking. He guided me up the back fire escape, allowing me to lead the way all the way to the top, where he delved into his pocket and unlocked the steel door.

'Why this way?' I asked.

'I want to show you something.'

I crossed my arms across my chest, curving my brow. 'Really?'

Dean laughed, unlocking the door and holding it open for me. 'Get your mind out of the gutter, Atkinson.'

I grinned, stifling a laugh as I darted inside.

Dean opened the door to his apartment, dropping his keys on a table near the door. He grabbed my hand, leading me to the bed, motioning for me to sit. My eyes lifted to where he stood before me, my heart pounding so fast it was the only thing I was really aware of, that and Dean's penetrating stare.

'Close your eyes,' he said, his voice low and gravelly. I closed them immediately, feeling my stomach twist with excitement, hearing his footsteps move around the room, echoing in the large space. I was aware of my breaths now – in-out, in-out – my hands clasped over my knees with a white-knuckled intensity.

His steps moved again, closing in on me, standing so close in front of me I could almost feel the heat of his body. I blanched, thinking about what I had done in this very same spot the night before.

'Hold out your hands,' he said, his voice so damn sexy I bit my lower lip to try and rein in control of my wandering thoughts.

I held them out mid-air, eagerly; they hovered for what felt like an eternity, or long enough for me to speculate. Was it my pay cheque? Another pink box from Paradise Cakes? My hands dipped, mostly from the feel of Dean placing something in my palms. It was light, smooth and not overly cool. I gripped my fingers around it as I tried to guess what it might be.

'Open your eyes.'

My eyes blinked open, glancing down at what sat in my hands. I met Dean's amused stare as he finally sat next to me on the edge of the bed.

'They're blueprints.'

I unravelled them on my lap, taking in the drawn-up plans for –

My head snapped up. 'Is this what I think it is?'

'The new improved Wipe Out Bar.'

'Oh my God.'

'I'm going to bring it into the twenty-first century. You see those lines there?' Dean pointed to the map. 'Reinforced downpipes.'

I laughed, laughed so hard, Dean had to stop the map from sliding off my lap.

'Excellent!'

'There'll be a lounge area, the bistro will have a complete revamp, as will the pool room and the bar.'

I shook my head, looking over the plans. 'This is amazing, Dean, it's going to be a game changer to Arcadia Lane.'

'The jewel in the crown,' Dean said, with a sparkle of excitement I hadn't seen before.

'Exactly! So what else do I need to know?' I straightened my spine, looking at the blueprints expectantly.

'Well, I think you need to know it started with a shark named Hank.'

I cringed, thinking back to how mad he'd been.

Dean shook his head. 'You've brought something into this place, Lexie. You've forced me to look at things differently.'

'I didn't do much.'

'You did enough.'

I blushed, knowing that Dean wasn't a man of many words, so this admission was meaningful to me.

'So, if you want, I'd really like your help.'

I looked Dean in the eyes, because I wanted him to know that I meant what I said. 'Anything.'

Dean smirked. 'Wow, you've got it bad.'

I rolled my eyes.

Dean held up his hands. 'Hey, look, you're only human.'

I stood, then turned, walking away as he laughed. 'Goodbye, Dean.'

'Waaaait a minute,' he said, reaching out and pulling me towards him. 'You're not going anywhere.' He encircled his arms around me.

'Maybe I've come to my senses,' I said, lifting my chin.

Dean's eyes bore into mine, serious and intense. 'Maybe you should. I mean, I'm moody, bossy, not very charming, not very nice . . . but . . .' He paused.

'But?'

'There will be lots and lots of sex.'

Lots of sex with Dean Saville. Yes, I was so on board with that.

'Well, that's something that wasn't mentioned in my job interview.' I giggled as Dean edged me to the bed and we both tumbled onto it, my laughter filling the apartment until Dean kissed me into a sweet, sweet silence.

C.J. Duggan is the internationally bestselling author of the Summer series who lives with her husband in a rural border town of New South Wales. When she isn't writing books about swoony boys and '90s pop culture you'll find her renovating her hundred-year-old Victorian homestead or annoying her local travel agent for a quote to escape the chaos. *Paradise Road*, the sequel to *Paradise City*, is C.J.'s ninth book, and the second in her new series of New Adult romance.

CJDugganbooks.com
twitter.com/CJ_Duggan
facebook.com/CJDugganAuthor

Go back to where it all began . . .

If you would like to find out more about Hachette Australia,
our authors, upcoming events and new releases you can visit
our website, Facebook or follow us on Twitter:

hachette.com.au
facebook.com/HachetteAustralia
twitter.com/HachetteAus

www.ingramcontent.com/pod-product-compliance
Ingram Content Group UK Ltd.
Pitfield, Milton Keynes, MK11 3LW, UK
UKHW041300180426
11947UKWH00009B/583